Thief's War

A Knight AND Rogue NOVEL

HILARI BELL

courtney literary

Thief's War
Copyright © 2014 by Hilari Bell
ISBN-10: 0985564393
ISBN-13: 978-0-9855643-9-1

Cover art & design © Anna-Maria Crum
Book design by © 2014 DeAnna Knippling
Euternia Ornaments courtesy BoltCutterDesign.com

Courtney Literary, LLC, Colorado Springs
www.CourtneyLiterary.com

DEDICATION

To Charles Bell, Wilson Bell and Joyce Griffen, a.k.a. Aunt Kelly, Uncle Bill and Uncle Chuck. You are missed.

Thief's War

CHAPTER 1

Michael

The sounds of injustice reached our ears as we rode into the town square: shouted taunts, the mushy thump of soft fruit smashing against wood, and the low angry mutter of the crowd. It was a large crowd, for a smallish town—it looked like every adult in Casfell was out in the streets and our hound, True, moved in closer to the horses' heels. There were so many people that at first I couldn't see the object of their ire.

Fisk spotted it before I did. "There's someone in the stocks."

"No. Surely no one would..."

I followed his gaze and saw the flat wall of boards, two hands and a balding, gray-haired head emerging from it as if some obscene sportsman had mounted a kill there.

Fisk and I had seen these contraptions in several of the towns and villages we'd passed through lately. Except for the stocks, the towns appeared quite pleasant. The buildings were mostly made of plastered mud-brick in these treeless plains, roofed with thatch that glowed golden on days less overcast than this one. The stocks had been the only off note—and I'd not really believed that anyone would put them to use.

The law of the High Liege, which runs throughout the United Realm, is that crimes against property are paid in coin. If a man can't pay another can redeem him, and he then works off the debt. Crimes of blood and pain are paid with the lash, or in extreme cases, maiming. And if life is taken, the noose.

These stocks, we were told, were an innovation out of the great city of Tallowsport, and that a man who owed coin and couldn't raise it could pay back his victims and the law with this lesser pain. A "middle ground" of sorts. Though from what I could see, it might hurt as much as a flogging.

"He's not a young man. After a few hours in that position his back will begin to cramp. A few more hours, and he'll be in agony."

'Twas too late now, for anyone to pay this man's fine, but in any other part of the realm he'd have been allowed to work off his debt. A surge of anger, of the need to make this right swept over me. The Liege's law shouldn't have permitted this, but the Liege wasn't here.

I was.

"Maybe they'll let him out at sundown," Fisk said hopefully. He knew what I was thinking. "That's just a few hours off."

Indeed, the gathering clouds, which we'd been hurrying to beat into town, made it seem almost dusk already. The low buildings, none more than two stories tall, did little to cut the cold wind that swept before the storm.

"And if no one was willing to put up coin to redeem him," Fisk continued, "maybe he did something rotten enough to deserve this. Have you considered that?"

"Doubtful." I gestured to the sullen townsfolk. "'Tis the guardsmen who are throwing fruit and insults. These people are angry with *them*."

Indeed they were, an anger so bleak and dark that, True, who usually frolicked up to strangers for a pat, slunk behind us with his ears and tail drooping.

Fisk sized up the crowd with a gaze more expert than mine would ever be.

"There's no way I can talk you out of this, I know. But we'll have to wait till everyone's gone to bed. You do realize that?"

I did. I also knew that 'twould gall Fisk to leave the poor man to suffer till nightfall as much as it did me. However...

"I'm not that foolish. He needs a crafty rescue, not a noble failure."

"Then we might as well go to the inn, and get a room and a meal," Fisk said practically. "And more information as well."

I sometimes wonder if Fisk has quite forgiven me for rescuing Lady Ceciel—which I must admit, we shouldn't have.

Almost a score of guardsmen, in the blue and brown tunics of the Tallowsport City Guard, were standing around the stocks. A daring daylight rescue would only bring Fisk and me to join their victim.

And remembering Lady Ceciel, a bit more information might not come amiss.

Still, a deep and helpless pity dragged at my heart as I turned my horse, Chanticleer, toward the inn at the far side of the square. Righting things like this was my chosen profession, and I was loath to let it wait.

"So," FISK SAID as a waitress in a clean cap and apron set plates down before us. "What's all that about?"

Lanterns had been lit against the darkness of the oncoming storm, giving the large room a cozy air, and 'twas warm enough to hang my cape and Fisk's coat on the pegs near the door. The taproom was redolent with the scent of roast pork, and the hefty helping of turnips, carrots and potatoes that accompanied it looked delicious. Despite my anxiety for the old man in the stocks, appetite stirred. We'd been riding all day.

"That's a local problem." The man who spoke sat on Fisk's other side. He wore a blue cloth coat with brass buttons. A clerk, mayhap, or a well-to-do craftsman. "Bad business. But no matter for a stranger."

"'Taint a local problem!" a stout man across the board from us said. This inn seated most of its customers in the old way, at a single long table with benches, though there were smaller, more private tables along the walls. For our needs, this common board was perfect.

"Judicar Makey may have been born in Casfell," the stout man went on. "But he learned his law in Tallowsport. Those guardsmen are out of Tallowsport. Even those stocks are a Tallowsport perversion. Only thing local is the man in 'em! It's a curst shame, and if our mayor was here it wouldn't have happened!"

A number of voices chimed in to agree with that, and we soon had the story without having to ask more than a few questions.

The man in the stocks was a farmer named Ruffo. When the food train came through, Ruffo tried to sell them short measure, using crooked scales...or so the judicar who heard the case had claimed when he passed sentence.

Fisk and I had seen the long lines of freight wagons that hauled goods and coin out of the city and went back laden with food. Although in this early spring season, the only produce available was grain and a variety of hardy root vegetables, like those that vanished from our plates as we listened to the townsmen argue. The food trains were always accompanied by a large contingent of guards, which made sense, considering the coin they carried.

So what were those guards doing here, when the train had moved on?

Most of the townsmen said that Ruffo was an honest fellow who would never cheat on his scales, no matter how much he'd objected to the food train looting local larders. A smaller portion of the men around us thought that Ruffo hated the trains so much he might have cheated—but they seemed more admiring than disdainful.

Trust in the integrity of this Judicar Makey was notably lacking. Several men commented on how very well the judicar was doing these days, but no one uttered the word "bribery" aloud.

The argument was still rumbling on, and getting louder, when Fisk and I left the table and made our way up to our own room—a private room, which Fisk complained cost more than we could spare. But staging a daring rescue out of a room occupied by six other men was beyond even Fisk's notion of economy.

"What do you think?" I asked him.

"I think so many of the men downstairs are making suspicious statements, the sheriff won't even think to put a couple of strangers on his suspect list."

"You know that's not what I meant. Injustice is being done here. Do we need to bring this Judicar Makey down, after we've freed his victim?"

Fisk sighed. "I suppose it's no use trying to convince you that tackling every injustice in the world isn't our job. We're certainly not getting paid for it!"

"You agreed with me about leaving a bit of money for that widow and her children," I pointed out.

"It was more than a bit! And that has nothing to do with this."

That was Fisk, squirming out of admitting that he'd been the one who thought of setting the woman up in a business so she could maintain her new family. I must admit, the loom cost more than I'd expected.

"Besides, prying him out of the stocks might get that man into worse trouble," Fisk went on. "He's got a farm. It's not like he can take to his heels."

That was a fair point.

"Once we've taken out the guards, we can ask him if he wishes to be freed or not," I said. "Whatever the obstacles, we can't leave him to suffer. If need be, we'll find some way to return him to his farm."

"I love the way you say, 'Once we've taken out the guards,'" Fisk said. "There's a score of city toughs around those stocks."

"There won't be a score," I assured him. "Once the street clears, they'll only leave a couple of guards. Maybe none, if it rains."

"We couldn't be so lucky," Fisk said.

A brilliant flash outside the shutters and a grumble of thunder answered him.

THE COLD RAIN cleared the street, and with the clouds obscuring both moons 'twas dark long before folk went to bed. It was just after nine when Fisk and I locked True, who Fisk refuses to call by his rightful name, into our room and let ourselves out of the inn's back door.

The laundry maid must have doubted the storm as well, for a line of clothing dripped as we crossed the yard. We opened the back gate, and after we'd passed through I propped it nearly closed with a handy cobblestone. I didn't want anyone to see it swinging wide and latch it behind us.

The night was so dark we had to grope our way along the alley wall, back to the square. I heard the splash ahead of me, more than I saw Fisk stumble. His curse was almost inaudible in the pattering rain.

"You may be right," he said. "No one sane would stay out in this. They've probably already made their point. When we get there the stocks will be empty, and we'll be soaked and freezing for nothing at all."

"Mayhap." But neither of us turned back. And on reaching the mouth of the alley, I saw that for once Fisk was wrong.

The old man still hunched in his bonds. Rain poured down on his back, which must be aching like fire by now.

I could see this clearly because four lanterns had been set around the stocks, spread far enough apart to bathe a forty foot circle in the clear white light shed by magica phosphor moss—the only light source that gets brighter when it's wet.

One guardsman remained. He'd removed his tunic and thrown it over his head for shelter, but he hadn't had the decency to throw even a blanket over his prisoner.

"They're well equipped," said Fisk quietly. "If they can afford magica lanterns."

"It's a safe light source for moving carts down the road after dark."

I wondered why they'd left those expensive lanterns and a guard behind, for Fisk was right. They'd made their point—whatever it was—after Master Ruffo's first hour in the stocks. But it seemed they didn't agree with us, which meant *I* had a point to make.

"We won't be able to get there before he spots us," Fisk said. "Not even close."

"Yet we must approach to take out the guard."

I expected some smart comment about seeing the obvious, but Fisk stiffened.

"Wait here."

He turned and hurried back down the alley. I heard a splash, and a muttered "poxy potholes" as he tripped again.

I turned back to observe our target. The lanterns that surrounded the stocks had their downside. I had sat by enough campfires to know that the guard would be able to see nothing beyond that circle of brilliance. But the opposite side of that coin was that we would have to go into the light to disable him.

Only a few minutes passed before Fisk returned, carrying a patched cloak from the laundry line and an empty grain sack... "Because unless you're willing to kill him, it would be good if he never sees our faces."

I wasn't willing to kill, and Fisk's plan was better than anything I'd come up with. I emerged from the alley and set out across the square, walking easily, like an ordinary citizen returning from the inn.

It appeared I'd been right about the guard's night vision; he didn't even glance in my direction. So instead of going back behind the houses, I turned and made my way quietly up the square, simply keeping low enough that I wouldn't pass between him and the light that glowed behind the shuttered windows.

The fact that he clearly didn't see me did nothing to quell the mix of terror and elation that always set my stomach quaking before a fight. It's somewhat like the feeling I got looking down from the top of a precipice—part of my imagination playing with the feeling of taking flight, while the rest of it pictured the carnage at the end of the fall. That feeling, multiplied by twelve.

I reached the best position I could attain without coming into the light, and waited for Fisk.

Looking out of the shadowed alley, Fisk's night vision was better than the guard's. He set off across the square immediately. And if the guard couldn't see him at the first, he was still aware of his presence because Fisk kept up a high-pitched muttering monologue. As he drew nearer, I'd have sworn I heard him say something about "goat brains."

The guard had dropped his tunic down to his shoulders, staring narrow-eyed into the darkness with a hand on the hilt of his sword. Then Fisk tottered into the light.

The cloak's hood covered his face, but that might not have mattered, so perfect was the rest of his performance. His back bent into an old woman's hunch. His feet moved in an old woman's tiny, rapid steps—he even wobbled from side to side, as the ancient sometimes do.

His voice was an alto croak that certainly sounded like an elderly woman to me, as he trotted determinedly forward.

"Goat brains," he mumbled. "Gad rabbit, goat brains."

"What?" said the guard. "Mistress, you shouldn't be out here. There's nothing you can do."

"Whip snapper, goat brains, ressa frizzlitz," said Fisk. Or words to that effect. He had almost reached the stocks now, but suddenly he listed and then staggered to the side. Away from me.

The guard took his hand from his sword, and leapt to steady "her."

"I'm sorry, Mistress, I don't understand what you're—"

"Goat brains!"

Fisk exploded from under the cloak like a crossbow bolt, his fist smacking squarely into the guard's jaw.

The man dropped to his knees, then reached out his hands to catch himself as he fell forward.

'Twas the work of a moment to dash out of the shadows and pull the grain bag over his head. I pushed the guard flat, put my knee on his back, and bound his hands behind him.

Fisk hopped around shaking his fist and exclaiming, "Curse it, that hurts! How come I never remember how much that hurts?"

"Because you don't do it often enough?"

The guard began to stir and struggle. I rolled him over, and located his mouth by the way the sack sank in as he drew breath to shout. His first cry was muffled by my hand clamped over it. The second by the handkerchief I stuffed in, taking quite a lot of the sack with it. I didn't entirely manage to avoid his snapping teeth, but the heavy fabric blunted their sharpness. Fisk's handkerchief, tied over the mess to keep it all in place, ended any threat from the guard. I bound his ankles and left him to roll about emitting muffled shouts, which we both ignored.

Fisk had gone to the old man in the stocks, who'd been staring at us in shock. "Master Ruffo, do you know if this guardsman has the key?" He jiggled the padlock that fastened down the top board.

"No. That is, I don't know. He wasn't the one who locked it. My back..." Even in the rain, I could see that he wept with pain. "I don't think I can move."

"Then we shall move you," I told him. "Fi— uh, can you pick the lock?"

Fisk, who would never have forgotten that a man bound and gagged still has his ears, was already searching the guard's pockets. "Nothing. If I had the proper tools, warm hands, and all the time in the world, maybe I could. As it is? No. But there's another way. Hang on."

He threw his cloak over Master Ruffo's thin, drenched coat before he raced off. I was beginning to shiver myself; the poor farmer had tremors running all through his body.

I put my hand under the cloak and began to rub his back, briskly for warmth, but gently too. His muscles felt like wood they were so cramped, and I feared we'd have to carry him.

"Master Ruffo, what will happen if you vanish tonight? It occurred to us that an escape might leave you in even worse trouble."

"Get me out of this." The man's teeth chattered so much he could hardly speak. "I'll worry about the rest later."

My sensing Gift, which sometimes tells me when I'm followed or that someone is about to approach, must have been taking a nap. I wasn't aware of the woman's presence till an astonished voice demanded, "Who under two moons are you?"

Gifts are talents that anyone might possess, enhanced to an unnatural degree. Some of them are as reliable as breath. And some, like the sensing Gift, aren't.

She stood at the edge of the light, old, though not as ancient as Fisk had feigned to be. A basket hung over her arm.

"Madge!" Master Ruffo's voice shook. "Get out of here. You'll get—"

"We'll get both of you out of here," I promised, somewhat rashly. "Mistress, remember that guard is probably listening."

Indeed, he'd fallen silent to hear better.

"Have you any way to open the lock?" I nodded toward her basket.

"No. I thought he'd have the key." She rolled aside a loaf of bread and pulled out a short club, which she'd evidently intended to use on the guard to obtain it. It should have been comical, but something in her expression... That guard had gotten lucky with Fisk and me.

The basket also held a full bottle of liniment. Though I knew at a glance 'twas not magica, I still applauded her forethought. We were rubbing it into Master Ruffo's back when Fisk came trotting back, carrying a long crowbar.

He cast Mistress Ruffo an appraising glance. If he didn't immediately realize the whole story, he clearly understood that she was on our side.

We fitted the narrow end of the bar into the padlock's closed hasp, and pried. It took both Fisk's and my strength, and in the end it was the smaller loops attached to the stock that gave way, tearing free of the wood with a shriek like a dying rabbit.

I looked around, but all the shutters that faced the square stayed firmly closed. Given the amount of noise we'd made this night, that told me a great deal about how the townsfolk regarded Master Ruffo.

He couldn't move after we lifted the heavy plank off his neck and wrists. He could barely lower his hands to his lap, wincing with pain as he did. But Mistress Ruffo continued rubbing liniment into his stiff shoulders, and Fisk and I helped the man stumble to his feet and half-carried him away.

I thought about leaving the guard to his deserts, but lying all night in the cold spring rain... I went back and cut the rope that bound his ankles.

"You can stand up," I told him, not trying to disguise my voice, since he'd been listening to it for some time. "The inn's gate, on the far side of the square, is still open. You'll find it eventually."

He kicked at me, and started shouting through his gag again. I shrugged and returned to Fisk and Mistress Ruffo, who where hurrying the rescued man along at a fair pace now.

"Are we going somewhere?" Fisk asked politely.

"Willy!" Master Ruffo exclaimed. "Where's Will? Did you get him back?"

"I've been too busy getting you back," his wife snapped. "We've some friends in town, sir. They're at the inn, grumbling about the storm and not wanting to go home just yet, so they'll have an alibi. But their back door's unlocked."

It was, and a fire crackled in the kitchen hearth, with towels and blankets warming beside it. A kettle of hot soup hung near the blaze.

Our clothing steamed as we helped Master Ruffo strip off his wet garments, and warmth finished what the liniment had begun. He still hadn't straightened, but he was moving more easily as we seated him at the table and clamped his hands around a mug of soup and a spoon.

He didn't eat. There were tears in his eyes again, and this time the pain wasn't physical.

"Willy. Gone. And it's all my fault. My curst, stubborn, self-righteous—"

"Who's Willy?" I asked.

"Our grandson," Mistress Ruffo said. "Just turned thirteen. Not old enough to know better."

Her voice implied that someone else was old enough to know better, and I wasn't surprised when her husband snapped, "I already said it was my fault. What more do you—"

"What happened to young Will?" I broke in. This was clearly a quarrel that would go on for some time. Years, mayhap.

"The food train..." Master Ruffo pushed his soup away. "I think you're strangers to these parts, yes?"

"We've seen the trains," Fisk said. He is wary about answering personal questions, even from friends, while committing illegal acts. "You can hardly miss them."

"Then you'll know that they take laborers into the city, as well," Ruffo said. "Draining the countryside of both food and hands. Indeed, it's the lack of food that costs us the hands!"

"What do you mean?" I asked. We had seen laborers traveling to the city with the food trains, but I'd given it little thought. My father describes the slow migration of country men and women into cities and towns as an unstaunched wound, bleeding the countryside dry. At least, that's how he describes it when young men and women leave his estate, to look for jobs with better pay and more chance of advancement. The craft guilds in the towns describe it as man's natural desire to better his lot, and 'twas happening all over the Realm. And no matter how much the landed gentry grumble, no one ends up flogged, or in these new-fangled stocks.

"The markets in Tallowsport pay more for our crops than the local market can," Mistress Ruffo said. "Particularly now, when there's no new growth and winter stocks are running low. That means food here becomes expensive. When folks can't afford to feed themselves and their families, they've no choice but to go with the cart trains, to get jobs in the city workshops."

"It's getting so bad, we'll be short of men to plant and harvest soon," Master Ruffo continued. Clearly this was one thing he and his wife agreed on.

"So why don't you farmers, who are getting paid so much more, just pay your laborers more?" Fisk asked. "Or hold back part of your crop to sell to the local market, cheaper?"

"This ground may look muddy," I told him, "but down a few inches 'tis just beginning to thaw. From Oakan to Crocusa, there's nothing for a farm laborer to do."

"As for refusing to sell to them, that's what landed me in the stocks," Ruffo said bitterly. "I've been talking to my neighbors, townsfolk, anyone who'll listen, pointing out that if we can't keep local prices down, soon we won't be able to run our farms. When the train came through, well, it seemed like the time to put my money where my mouth was. I told 'em that our market needed my stores, and I wasn't going to sell no matter how much they offered. They offered a lot," he added. "Can't say I blame most for taking it. They went away. But next day Judicar Makey and a dozen guards, Tallowsport Guards, rode up to the farm and said I'd been accused of mis-weighting my scales."

"I said how could I do that, since I hadn't sold 'em anything, and brought out my scales to show him they were true. He said the fact that I had them so ready to hand proved I'd been using them recently, and that if I'd cheated, of course I'd have re-set them. It was a farce."

His soup was getting cold, but even his wife didn't press him to eat.

"So that's what these new stocks are for," I murmured. "To punish those who owe no debt in blood or coin."

"How does your grandson come into this?" Fisk asked.

"When I was arrested, and sentenced almost in the same breath, Willy came running out. And you were the one supposed to keep him in the house," Ruffo told his wife. "He said he'd make my debt good. That the train could take him to the city if they'd let me go."

"It could have worked." Mistress Ruffo looked almost as distressed as her husband. "I was trying to pull him back, but...but not that hard. The trains want labor even more than they want food. A lot of people settle with them that way. I thought that after the planting we could go to the city and find him, buy him out of whatever contract he might have signed."

"How could you think I'd sell our grandson, to get out of—"

"But it didn't work," Fisk interrupted. "They took your grandson and then arrested you anyway, right?"

"How did you know?" Mistress Ruffo asked. "They put Willy in chains on the cart. When they made the arrest he started screaming that he'd been cheated. That if they took him, they had to let his grandpa go. But how could you know that?"

"Because 'tis what such bullies would do," I said. "To increase their power over you and your neighbors."

Fisk closed his eyes, like a man facing some terrible accident he can't prevent. "I see it coming. It's not as if I can't see it coming."

"See what?" Mistress Ruffo looked around, alarmed.

"Don't worry, Mistress. He's just grousing from habit, because he knows we're going to get your grandson back for you."

Even Master Ruffo straightened his stiff neck to stare.

"You're...what? But why? You've done enough for me this night. Why are you doing this?"

"Because I'm a knight errant," I told him, "in search of adventure and good deeds. Fisk is my squire."

Most laugh when I tell them this, for it has been over two centuries since knights errant have roamed the Realm. Indeed, in these modern times I'm probably the only one alive so mad as to take it for my life's work.

But the Ruffos didn't laugh.

Fisk sighed, but he didn't deny it, and a flame of hope wiped the bitter despair from their faces.

"You mean that?" Master Ruffo demanded. "If it wasn't for what you've already done, I'd know you were having us on, but... Do you truly mean that?"

"He does," said Fisk glumly. "Every word of it."

The Ruffos were still staring in bewilderment, and time was passing.

"First, we must find some place to leave you, safely out of Judicar Makey's reach," I said. "Have you kin or friends in another fief?"

"No need for that." Mistress Ruffo's voice was rough with gratitude. "Our friends here will hide us till the Mayor comes back. He went to complain to Baron Benrick about how much of our stock the food trains have been taking, and when he returns... Well, Makey better have gotten a big bribe, because he'll not be a judicar much longer. Not in Casfell."

"Are you sure?"

They both nodded.

"Then Fisk and I had better return to the inn. Tomorrow we'll set out after the train that took your grandson, and add ourselves to it."

"As laborers?" Fisk asked. "What do you intend to do with the horses? Not to mention the dog. And won't that bring us closer to Tallowsport?"

The name of Jack Bannister hung unspoken between us, as it so often had when our erratic path took us a step or two closer to the city where Jack and his murderous employer laired. But even Fisk couldn't blame this turn of events on me.

"We have no choice," I pointed out. "Not if we're going to rescue young Will. And not as laborers. Even leaving the livestock aside, we'd not be allowed near a prisoner. We need to get hired on as guards. We shall have to pass ourselves off as ruffians, Fisk."

For a moment I thought he was going to protest, but then he sighed. "Well, at least we won't need disguises."

CHAPTER 2

Fisk

All Michael needed to do to look like a ruffian, was to pull his sword out of his pack and fasten it to his belt. He did it soon after we left town the next morning.

I decided to wait till we neared our mark to assume my disguise—which would pretty much consist of a few days accumulated grime.

But we could have left Casfell armed to the teeth, and I'm not sure anyone would have noticed. The taproom brimmed with townsfolk, who'd come to hear how the city guardsman had stumbled in last night with a sack over his head and his prisoner gone—and claiming that a little old lady had knocked him out! I saw several surreptitious toasts, but I kept my bruised hand in my pocket, anyway.

Michael, being outside the law already and mad as a hatter to boot, doesn't pay much attention to this kind of thing. Having spent most of my life breaking it, *I* have a great respect for the power of the law. And no desire to attract its attention.

"Keep an eye out for a tree," I told Michael as the town disappeared behind us. "If we're going to be ruffians, I want to cut myself a cudgel."

"That may not be easy. Finding a tree, I mean."

We'd been traveling for almost a month through the flat plains that drained into the Erran River, and it was the most boring countryside I'd ever seen. Not only were there few trees, there were also no real hills, no mountains, and no valleys. Nothing but flat, fallow fields, mile after mile. Muddy fields, as the snows and slush of Crocusa gave way to the rains of Grassan. And muddy roads.

But having listened to the Ruffos, I now saw those fields in a different light.

"This land is incredibly fertile, isn't it?"

Michael nodded. "When the High Liege—the first High Liege, that is—when he conquered all the other lords and barons, and united the Realm under his rule, most of the battles were fought here, on the river plains. Once he had the heartland under his control, he got fealty from the rest of them more through economic leverage than the sword."

"I know that. What was it…? 'The Erran Plains may not be the only land that matters, but 'tis the land that matters most.'"

My father was a scholar, and I've read a bit of history. Besides, the first High Liege was an illiterate barbarian—that was the only quotable thing he ever said.

"He built Crown City at the highest navigable point on the Erran, just so he could hold these plains," Michael went on. "He could boat troops downstream swiftly, but anyone coming against him would have to row upstream or go by land. Which meant he'd get warning they were coming and they'd be tired out, while his troops—"

"I'm sorry I asked. But if it's so fertile," I gestured to the sea of rutted mud, "then why is Tallowsport stripping the larder bare? Shouldn't there be plenty?"

"I don't know," Michael admitted. "But labor, food and other raw goods are flowing from the countryside into the towns all over the Realm. Tallowsport is the Realm's largest city. It makes sense that they'd need more food, more of everything, than other towns."

"Maybe." Though I still didn't see why they were willing to pay such high prices for the crops they bought. Or to put down the money to bribe a judicar. Educated men don't come cheap.

By the time we'd reached the small village that a groom had told us was the train's next stop, it had already left. When we reached the town where the villagers told us it went next, we found that another food train had come though two weeks ago, and they hadn't seen the train we were looking for.

We spent the night there, listening to rain beating on the roof, and cursing whatever clerk had cleverly reorganized the cart routes, then set out the next morning to find where our train had gone. It took us two more days, riding through the mud from village to village, before we found one where our train had stopped, and another two days to catch up with it. Our horses were muddy up to their bellies, and Trouble was coated from the tip of his ropy tail to his flopping ears. He didn't seem to mind.

By that time I didn't need my cudgel, or the knife I strapped to my belt, to look as ruffianly as Michael. Or at least, as dirty.

We tied the horses to the post in front of the tavern where the train boss had set up his office, and Michael told the dog to guard them. Trouble, trying to bark at a flock of pigeons circling overhead, paid no attention. I say "trying to bark" because Trouble is mute. Born that way, according to Michael, who persisted in the fantasy that he was a guard dog. A role Trouble never even attempted, as far as I could see.

Leaving the menagerie behind, we climbed two stone steps, knocked as much mud as we could off our boots, and went in.

The train boss's "office" was a large table covered with invoices, lading bills, ledgers and receipts. But all the piles of paper were tidily arranged, and as we drew near I noticed that a tea sieve sat on a dish beside his mug, which held a liquid darker than beer.

He might look like a bandit captain, but despite the knife scars on his arms he was a businessman, not a thug. Which would probably make this harder.

Michael stepped up to the table. "Excuse me, good sir. My friend and I were wondering if you could use more guards."

He leaned back in his chair and regarded Michael thoughtfully, taking in the light brown hair, now somewhere between a nobleman's shoulder length and a peasant crop. The old scars on cheek and chin, the calloused hands, the well-worn sword sheath...and those curst, honest eyes.

"Judging by your boots, you have your own horses?"

"Yes, and both sound. Well, Chant's leg comes up lame sometimes," Michael added. His eyes reflect the truth of him—he never thinks to lie, even when he should. "But he'll do fine with light work."

"You sound like a noble," the train boss said. "Younger son?"

"The fourth. Michael Sevenson. My father fancied me as a clerk for my older brother, but I...well, father doesn't always get his way."

Talking about his father made Michael's expression harden so much that his face almost matched the ruffian clothes. The boss looked past him, his gaze running from my brown curls to my muddy boots. Faces having nothing to do with a man's true nature; I look even less like a thug than Michael.

"Your friend, does he have a name?"

"Fisk," I said, since there was no reason to give a false one.

"He looks more like a clerk than a guardsman," the boss went on. "In truth, I could use a man. We lost one idiot back in Casfell."

"Not dead I hope," Michael said with genuine concern.

"No, he's in bed with a sore jaw and a bad cold. He'll meet us back at the Port. But I don't need two."

"We come together, or not at all." Now Michael sounded almost tough, but the boss shook his head.

"No. I need real guards, not a runaway nobleman and his valet."

Michael's lips tightened. We'd known this might be necessary, but he'd dreaded it so much that for a time I'd hoped we could call the whole thing off, and write to the Ruffos to pick up their grandson in Tallowsport.

But Michael has more spine than that. He pushed up his sleeves, coat and shirt together, revealing leather guards laced around his wrists. He had to use his teeth as well as his other hand to untie the knot, but the laces loosened easily, and he slid the leather cuff up...revealing the two broken circles tattooed there.

Master Makejoy had insisted on the wrist guards, claiming that theater troupes had enough trouble convincing folk they were honest without traveling with a man who might be revealed as unredeemed whenever his sleeves slipped. And even after Michael got over Rosamund, and we left the troupe, he kept the leather guards. They'd spared us a lot of aggravation. Unlike Rosamund, who was Michael's first love. Rosa was a sweet, beautiful ninny...and aggravation was a pale description of the disaster she dumped us into. If you asked me, Michael was *lucky* she'd chosen someone else. But no one ever asked me.

Even in winter, the skin beneath the guard was far paler than the rest of Michael's arm, throwing the black circles into high relief.

The boss's brows shot up. He looked at Michael again, speculating, and then at my unmarked wrists.

"And here I thought I could judge a man. That's not how I'd have placed you."

"I didn't get bribed out of it," Michael said stiffly. "At least, I don't think I did."

The Realm's law is based on criminals making things right with their victims. But in cases where reparation can't be made with coin, and someone is rich and powerful enough to buy their child, spouse or sibling off the gallows, the law uses this tattoo to mark the criminal's debt to the law and their fellows forever unredeemed. Which in turn means that the law owes them nothing. If someone harms them, the law won't intervene. If someone cheats them, they have no legal recourse...which is curst inconvenient when you make a living doing odd jobs in strange towns, let me tell you.

Honest people usually won't hire us, once they've seen Michael's wrists. And those who will hire us frequently don't bother to pay. I wondered into which category this man would fall.

"And I'm a clerk," I told him. "I could check those ledgers. Catch your mistakes before your boss ever sees them."

I half-hoped the subtle insult would tip the scales against us, but a gleam of interest dawned in his eyes.

"So if I sent you out to collect a farm load, you could keep proper tally of the weight? And make sure the price adds up to what we offered, instead of whatever the farmer claims?"

"Of course." Win some, lose some.

Michael pushed the guard back down, and held out his hand for me to retie it—not something a man can do, one-handed.

"You I could use," the boss told me. "Master Sevenson here..."

"We come together," I affirmed. "Or not at all."

The man looked at Michael again. "How long have you carried those marks? You're a bit young to be a hardened criminal, aren't you?"

"I'm twenty-one. As for the marks..." He had to think about it. "I've borne them for two and a half years now."

The train boss's lips pursed in a silent whistle. "Then you must be pretty tough, after all. I've heard that men starve, once they're marked unredeemed."

"'Tis not so bad as that," Michael said. "I do get cheated out of my pay from time to time."

"I won't cheat you," the train boss said. "Not if you don't cheat me. Or cause trouble in my train. You do that, you'll be out in a minute, and with nothing to show for whatever work you've done. Understand?"

"We do."

Michael held out his hand. After a moment's hesitation the train boss shook it.

If we weren't already plotting to cause trouble on his train, I'd have been hoping we might get paid.

THE FOOD TRAIN took to the road next morning. Our job as guards was simply to ride around it, and keep an eye out for trouble. In truth, we were mostly there to convince potential bandits that they wanted to stay "potential."

However, simple doesn't always mean easy. My horse Tipple was named for an unfortunate taste for beer. She's spotted like a jester, and her previous owner made a habit of getting her drunk for the amusement of his friends. Michael considered this iniquitous, and bought her from him...but judging by the determination with which she heads for the nearest keg, I don't think Tipple objected to it. Several of the carts carried beer, and their drivers scoffed at my warning—until Tipple managed to pull one bung out with her teeth. After that they took care not to park near the place she was tethered.

I'd thought Trouble would present worse difficulties, but after half a day of oxen rolling their eyes as he frisked past, he formed a passionate attachment to the cooks' wagon. For some strange reason the cooks liked him as well, and he spent most of the trip lolling among the pots—when he wasn't leaping off the cart to chase a rabbit across the field.

After a few more days the roads began to dry out. Bushes, which were becoming more frequent along the verges of the road, put out leaves and blossoms. New grass sprouted, lush and green, spotted with flowers.

It was still no light task to patrol a train of over two hundred enormous freight wagons, four hundred oxen, and their attendant ox-drivers, farriers and clerks...not to mention several hundred laborers, who rode perched on the loads of squash, potatoes or grain.

I talked to quite a few of them, as time went on. For the most part they were young, and eager to start a new life in the city. The contract they'd signed only required them to work for the train's owners for two months to pay their transport debt. Then they'd be free to find their own employment, in a town where laborers were needed more than anywhere else in the Realm. So they must be well paid, right?

I told them I'd never been to Tallowsport, so I couldn't say. But I noticed that their contract said nothing about helping them find that next, well-paying job.

These people had volunteered to go with the train, and they almost never ran off. But when someone had been sold to the train's owners for coin, or to pay some debt, their labor might be indentured for years. These ingrates sometimes tried to run, so they were regarded as prisoners.

There was only one prisoner at the moment, a thirteen-year-old boy. Willy was chained to a bench in a wagon about two-thirds down the line, but he wasn't treated too badly. The chain, cuffed to his ankle, was long enough to give him the freedom of the big cart bed—as much of it as held no other cargo. He had a tarp to wrap up in if it rained during the day. He had a pillow and blanket, and he could climb down and sleep under the wagon if it rained at night—and if he got cold, he could ask one of the four guards who watched his wagon at night for another blanket. He ate the same food as the ox-drivers, and was released from the shackle to go off into the fields and relieve himself—also under guard.

It took two more days of circling the train before Michael or I managed to be the guard in his vicinity when he told the driver he needed to go. In fact, I was the one who got lucky.

The breeze was still chilly, but the sun was warm enough that he'd shed his blanket. The driver pulled the cart off the road, set the brake, and climbed over his seat to unlock the shackle while I tied Tipple to the cart.

I hoped someone else had a key, because picking the pocket of a man driving a cart can't be done.

The driver, a muscular man, picked the boy up and handed him down to me. Will had barely started his growth spurt, still light-boned. I kept my hand on his shoulder as we marched across the grassy verge and into some farmer's rutted field. He said nothing. His expression was sullen—which I liked better than despair.

"That's far enough," I told him, and he stopped obediently and started to open his britches. "Far enough that no one can hear us. Your grandparents sent my friend and me to get you out of this."

Wide dark eyes flashed up, and a flare of excitement wiped the angry misery from his face. "You...you mean—"

"Yes, I mean it, but it's not going to be fast or easy. The first problem is that shackle. Does anyone else have a key?"

"The train boss does. He locked me in, gave the driver one key and put the other in a pocket on the inside of his vest." A small cold hand clutched mine. Are you... And your friends, you said? There's more of you?"

"Just one friend. He has longish hair..." Michael wasn't that remarkable. "He's riding a big gray gelding that looks like a tourney horse."

"I've seen him. But I'm out of my shackle. Can't we just run? Now?"

The young are cute, but impractical.

"And then what?" I gestured to the open fields around us. "The only cover is beside the road. If you go darting off, how long do you think it will take the train guards to ride you down?"

Some of the hope faded from his face. "Then how can I get away?"

"Mostly, you leave it to us. We'll find some way to stop the cart—hopefully when there are thick bushes nearby. You need to start pissing, by the way."

"Oh." He fumbled his britches open, and did so. "But won't the driver, and everyone else, see me climb down? What about the shackle? And even if I hide in the bushes, they'd find me."

"Not if it looks like you're still in the cart," I told him. "That's your job for the next few days; find a sack of something, about your size. And it has to be light enough that you could lift it quietly, wrap your blanket around it, and prop it up on the bench. You need to start traveling with the blanket wrapped around you all the time, too, so that's what people are used to seeing. If anyone asks, tell them you're getting sunburned, and that's why you've got it over your head. Is there a sack like that in the cart now?"

If there wasn't, we'd have to make up a reason to add one—though off hand, I couldn't think of any.

"Several," the good lad said. "A potato sack, maybe."

"Excellent." He was refastening his britches. We hadn't much more time. "As I said, this may take a few days. You'll

know when it's time because I'll pass you the key. Your job is
to free yourself and get the sack ready. When I give the signal
you go out of the cart and into the nearest bush, and hide
there till the train's moved on. Michael and I... Can you make
your way home on your own?"

"Of course," he said, with a thirteen-year-old's unjustified
confidence. But he should be able to make it. "I'd need some
money. Though I suppose I could work—"

"I'll toss a purse into the bushes for you." I turned him to
walk back to the wagon. "Michael and I will stay with the train
as long as we can. If they suspect we had anything to do with
letting you go—and they may—they'd follow us, so you'll be
on your own once the train is gone. Pass at least two towns
before you ask for help, right? And stop looking like that, or
even that dull-witted driver will know something's up. Keep
your eyes down and look angry, like you did when we came
out here."

"He's not really stupid." Neither was young Will. I couldn't
see much of his face, but his gaze was on the ground once
more, and his mouth had turned down. "He gave me the
pillow, and extra food sometimes."

"Well, he's going to be stupid," I said firmly. "At just the
right moment. Here we are. Back in with you kid."

I hoisted him up to the driver, who locked the shackle again
as I rode on. They'd get back into the line as soon as someone
fell behind enough to create a space. We'd already observed
that the wagons didn't travel in any set order.

We had considered the possibility of a night escape, but not
only was the prison wagon too well guarded, the whole camp
was too well-patrolled. The boss divided the night into three
shifts, and every guard had to take one of them. Being the
newest members of the troop, Michael and I got the second
patrol shift, right in the middle of the night.

This plan was too complex. But considering that we had to get the kid out of a shackle, out of a guarded wagon, and away from the train in the middle of open countryside, it was the best idea we'd been able to come up with. In fact, it was the only idea we'd been able to come up with. I gave it a fifty-fifty chance. If Michael had been willing and able to produce some magic for us, those odds would go up significantly. Unfortunately, he wasn't.

"THREE MONTHS AGO, in Rickerston, you calmed that drunk right down," I told him. We huddled in our bedrolls, out under the stars since sleeping under a wagon was no warmer. "One minute he was going to beat the crap out of you, the next he was calm as...as a cow being milked."

"I see you've never milked a cow," Michael murmured. Nobleman's son or not, he was raised on a country estate. "I don't control this, Fisk. I can't turn it on and off like a tap!"

"You might, if you'd practice."

It was an old argument between us. Whether magic comes from nature or from the two gods' grace is a question scholars have written tomes about. The undisputed fact is that some plants and animals, and even some humans who are so simple as to be close to the gods or nature, have the ability to make real magic. Magic usually enhances a trait that is normal for that species, not just beyond the ordinary, but beyond the possible. When a normal rabbit freezes, its mottled brown coat blends so well with the surroundings that it's hard to see. When a magica rabbit freezes, it becomes invisible. As in, you can put your hand behind it and still see how many fingers you're holding up. Magica wood is almost as strong as iron, but still light and flexible. Magica herbs will heal you more quickly than anything else can. A magica horse can jump over an oxcart—not from the side, but lengthwise, from the tail of the cart to the nose of the startled ox.

Yet it's hard for humans to use magica creatures and plants. If they're harvested without the proper rites and sacrifice, ill luck will dog, or sometimes destroy, anyone who tries to use the magica item until the sacrifice is paid. A truth that generally weighs on the "gods" side of the argument.

But due to the schemes and potions of one Lady Ceciel—who felt free to use an unredeemed man in her quest to give humans magic, whether that man wanted it or not—Michael, alone of all normal humans, has not just Gifts but the ability to work magic.

And I think that he could learn to use it at will—instead of having it well up out of nowhere and do completely unexpected things—if he wasn't so scared by its freakishness that he refused to study his strange ability.

"It only worked because the man was drunk," Michael insisted. "It was...it felt like the magic came forth, and poured itself into my animal handling Gift. And that never works on people unless they're drunk, or their wits are otherwise disabled. It couldn't calm someone who was alert and suspicious."

"He isn't supposed to be suspicious," I said. "The whole point is to keep them from associating us with the boy's escape. You don't need to convince him to walk off a cliff, just make him sleepy or distracted, so he won't notice when Will climbs out of the cart."

It was too dark to see Michael's expression, but I could feel him resisting.

"Just practice it for a few days, while I practice picking pockets," I said. "I'm rusty at that, too. And you can't say this cause is less worthy than the last time you did it."

There was a long silence, then he sighed.

"I'll try. But don't count on it, Fisk."

"We won't," I promised. Though in truth I was, for without that we were going to need a spectacular diversion. I could just imagine what Jack would have said about that... Come to think of it, when we first met he'd been using *me* for a diversion.

I'D MADE MY EXIT from the spicer's shop I'd just robbed, and been surprised by a guard dog that I swear wasn't there when I'd scouted the place last night. Unfortunately, the board I'd pried out of the fence let the baying dog out the back, even as I exited, hastily, out the front. At least the dog was following my trail by scent rather than sight, and the spicer and his two apprentices were following the dog. But the bag of spices I carried left plenty of scent for the dog to follow, and they seemed to be gaining.

I had to slow to a rapid walk as I came up on the garbage collector's cart—the driver would notice someone out and about at this hour, particularly if he was running. But I could hear the distant voices of my pursuers, and they seemed to be drawing near. I was about to start running again, despite the danger of being recognized, when a door opened right beside me and a man stepped out and seized my collar.

"Hey!" I said, as loudly as I dared. "What do you...?"

His free hand rose to his lips, gesturing for silence. He took two long strides forward, dragged the spice bag off my shoulder, and slung it on the back corner of the garbage cart.

"Hey! That's mi—"

His free hand clamped over my mouth and he hauled me back to the door, though he let go of my collar as he went through, leaving me standing on the stoop.

"You can come in, or you can stay here and be caught. It's all one to me."

The dog and his attendants rounded a corner onto the street. They were about four blocks back, but their presence made the decision for me and I darted in after him.

He closed the door, latched it quietly, and then moved back into the shadows where he could see out the window without being seen. We appeared to be in the entry of a lodging house, with a long hallway, and a staircase climbing into the darkness.

"That was mine," I said. He might have just saved me a long spell of indebted labor…or he might have cost me several night's work. I preferred the later theory.

"It's only yours if you can keep it," he said. "You wouldn't have, even if I hadn't intervened."

He was probably twice my age, which put him in his late twenties. Medium hair, medium height, a bit slimmer than I was, but every bit as unremarkable. This didn't necessarily make him a criminal—it was simply convenient, if he happened to be one.

"I might have," I said.

"You wouldn't."

"You don't know that."

"Actually, I do. The spicer's hound is famous for never losing a trail and never giving up."

They passed the window then and we both fell silent. The dog wasn't moving fast…but neither was the garbage cart. They'd catch up with it in about five minutes, and I'd lose days of…

"Wait a minute. How do you know about the spicer's dog?"

"Because I did a better job of scouting his shop than you did. I spotted you doing it, too. You're curst clumsy, lad."

"I am not."

He looked at me, and enough of the tan moon's light came through the window to let me see his eyebrows rise.

If he'd seen me, and guessed enough about my plan to be waiting here, then maybe I had been clumsy.

"So you decided to use me as a diversion? Isn't that shop a pretty small target, for a big-time type like you?"

"A box of saffron was delivered to that shop today—it's priced at a silver roundel per quarter cup. And thanks to you, the dog, the spicer, and all his apprentices are gone." He cast me a flashing grin and stepped back into the night. "So long, lad. It's been…profitable to know you."

"Wait a minute." I scrambled after him. "I cleared the way for you! And lost my whole night's haul. The least you can do is cut me in. You can trust me."

"Can I? Then you're a fool. I never trust anyone."

He was walking swiftly back toward the shop. Which would now be wide open…except for him.

"Cut me in on that saffron," I said. "It's the least you can do, since I pulled them away for you."

"I got you out of it. That debt's more than paid."

"All right, maybe you don't owe me. But I can help you clear out the shop. In fact, I could have been *more* useful if you'd let me in on the plan from the start."

He didn't stop walking, but he glanced aside at me for the first time since we'd left the lodging house.

"You know, you might be right about that. But don't expect me to apologize."

"I won't," I said, half-jogging to keep up. "I'm Fisk."

The man winced. "That's your real name, isn't it?"

"Um. Yeah."

"Figures. Well, my name *isn't* Jack Bannister. You can call me Jack."

Over the next three years, Jack had taught me not to give my real name. And some of the other skills he'd taught me might just make our mad plan work.

OVER THE NEXT FEW DAYS Will kept his blanket wrapped around him, so the rest of the train became accustomed to seeing a blanket-wrapped lump on that bench instead of a sulky boy.

We pulled into a small village, and the boss sent me out to one of the farms along with a cart, to keep an accounting of the purchase—though the price the train paid was so high I'm surprised anyone bothered to cheat. I brought back a neatly written inventory, and the boss was so pleased he sent me out to every farm I could reach.

That evening, among the villagers, I had a chance to practice dipping on people who weren't part of the train—though in most cases I added a few brass fracts to their pockets, instead of subtracting. People are less likely to make a fuss when money mysteriously appears, and a lot of the people in that village looked purse-pinched, their clothing patched and mended. The price of food in that market was as high as I've ever seen it, anywhere.

Before we set out next morning, the boss had me help him sort and file receipts, and check his ledger. I was leaning over his shoulder when a waitress on the other side of the room dropped her tray—the perfect moment, and I seized it. It's no harder to pick an inside pocket than an outside one, if the vest is unbuttoned.

But that meant Will's rescue had to happen today, before the boss checked his pocket—the sooner the better.

I briefed Michael, who was going to create the distraction.

"Everyone's eyes have to be on you. Particularly Will's driver. Can you manage that?"

"Yes." He sounded unnervingly certain.

"Are you sure? The cart may rock when Will goes over the side, and he's got to get that bag up right behind the driver. That's something a man will notice unless he's *really* distracted. Or in a magica haze."

"I can't promise the last," Michael said. "Though I'll try. But Chant and I can manage the first."

His eyes were bright, and the corners of his mouth kept turning up. Michael, being a mad knight errant, actually enjoys this kind of thing.

It gives me nightmares.

I let Michael pick the place, since the first move was his. Jack, who was a master of distraction, had once told me that it was like a dance. You had to trust your partner to be in the right place at the right time, or the whole pattern would fall apart. But when he's there, when the pattern runs, then it's a work of art.

And for all his craziness, Michael delivered.

We'd encountered Jack last summer, when we got entangled with a troupe of players and a gang of wreckers—not connected with each other. Well, only one of the players had been part of the plot. It had been a terrible mess, but some might say we'd won. Not those who'd died at the wrecker's hands, but some.

Jack hadn't done any of the killing, but Michael was still determined to track him back to his employer and bring them both to justice. He'd been nudging us in the direction of Tallowsport ever since we left the troupe, and I'd been trying to nudge us away. Whatever else had passed between us, I didn't want to see Jack punished. Taking down his employer, that I'd have been fine with…except that doing it would probably get us killed.

Will's cart was toward the front of the line today, which was bad because most of the train would be perfectly positioned to see him climb out. And then they'd have another chance to spot him hiding in the bushes as they drove by.

Michael chose a place where the brush on the near side of the road was thick, and the far side more open. When I saw him draw Chant up beside the driver, I took a slow loop around the front of the train to give him time, and then headed back down the line on the opposite side from him.

Riding up to Will's cart, I could see at a glance that his magic had failed. Michael looked harassed and the driver looked puzzled—no doubt wondering why Michael had been talking to him all this time.

It had to be now. A sort of bright terror flooded my veins, and everything intensified. The bird song from the bushes sounded sharper; the cool air cut into my lungs.

As I rode past the driver I cast a small brown purse into the bushes beside the road, then tossed the key into Will's lap. Michael's odd behavior had warned him, and he caught it.

Seeing me approach, Michael had finished his conversation and ridden on. He was now two carts ahead, exactly where we wanted everyone to be looking when the show started.

Then the show started.

Chant snorted, then shied sideways into an ox team, which I hadn't expected.

The oxen were too heavy to shy, but they moved aside rapidly and the driver, shouting, brought them to a stop.

"Stop the train," I shouted, riding between Will's cart and the one behind it, blocking that driver's view.

This precaution may have been unnecessary. I just had time to see Will bend to the shackle, when Chant followed his sideways leap with a lunging kick that drew cries of alarm and excitement from everyone in sight. The ox-drivers brought their teams to a halt, watching as Chant crow-hopped across the verge, followed by another of those incredible airborne kicks.

I knew that Chant was tourney trained. In fact, I'd seen Michael ride him in tourneys. I'd never seen anything like this. He planted his front feet and hurled his heels skyward again, and I realized that this wasn't for tourney; this was the training of a war horse.

Michael's father was a man of the old school, in more than disowning disobedient sons.

By the time I dragged my gaze from this amazing equine display, Will had a potato sack up on the seat and was wrapping his blanket around it.

He could afford to take a moment to get it right. His driver, like all the others, was standing up and yelling, completely unaware of what was happening behind him.

Will finished the job and rolled off the cart into the bushes, neat as could be. I'd have liked to tweak that blanket a bit, but there was no way I could touch it unobserved.

Michael chose that moment to let Chant's antics unseat him...or maybe he really was bucked off. It certainly looked like it; he went flying through the air, and hit the ground with a bruising splat.

I'd asked for a spectacular diversion, and he'd provided it. It's nice, having a partner you can rely on.

Chant, good-natured fellow that he is, stopped bucking and went to sniff at his master. Michael grabbed the reins, as if he believed that his horse might go dashing off. He clambered to his feet as I rode forward, shouting in realistic-looking alarm.

The train boss galloped past me.

"What's going on here! Why's the train stopped?"

"Sorry." Michael's voice was perfect: breathless, exasperated, rueful. "I think a wasp got him."

He moved to Chant's other side and ran a hand down his rump. "Yes, here's the stinger."

A pinching movement, something cast away. Chant twitched.

"He got stung badly as a colt. He's never gotten over it. This one got him deep, too."

Chant turned on command, a trace of blood bright on his pale hide.

"Are you all right?" I asked. Since no one else had.

"Fine." Michael bent to check Chant's weak leg, though even I could see that he was putting weight on it.

The train boss turned to his drivers. Stopped, waiting drivers.

"Show's over," he said. "Get moving."

Once they had, he turned back to Michael. "Your horse all right? Then you get moving too."

So we did.

It was more than three hours later when the potato bag tipped over and they realized their prisoner had escaped. Michael and I only heard about it that evening, and it wasn't luck that we were both near the back of the train when the discovery was made—we'd been finding excuses to lurk there all day.

No one seemed to connect us with the escape, but as we sat near the campfire eating dinner the train boss came over and gestured for us to follow him.

Michael cast me a wary look and I shrugged—both perfectly natural reactions for men called aside by the boss.

"Our prisoner escaped today," he announced.

"We heard," I said. He'd started this dance, let him lead. But he stared at us, unspeaking, for a long moment.

"We picked him up in Casfell. I checked the books to be sure. Where'd you two sign on?"

"Ludder," said Michael.

He stared some more, but we managed to hold up under it. Then he drew in a breath and sighed.

"I decided not to send anyone after him. No way to know, for certain, where he left the train. And he didn't owe us a real debt, after all. Nothing on the books."

"Then why were you hold—"

"That sounds sensible." I interrupted before Michael, could give the game away.

The boss snorted. "All right. But I expect the two of you to work all the way to the Port. And I don't expect any more trouble, either. Right?"

"Of course," said Michael.

The train boss walked away.

"He knows it was us," Michael said.

"He suspects it. If he knew, he might not be so generous. If he could prove it, it would probably be us in the next town's stocks. He's not a nice man."

"Mayhap not, but he's been generous to us. The least we can do is to go on to the city as he asks. Besides, I think he's going to pay us. You don't want to waste this last week's work, do you?"

So we came to it.

"You just want to get to the city," I said. "You've been pushing us in this direction for six months. You're going after Jack."

"Not Master Bannister, so much," Michael said, "but his employer. That man was responsible for three deaths that we know of, Fisk. Not to mention all those whom the wreckers killed."

"You can't blame Jack, or even his employer, for the wreckers' murders," I said. "He was just fencing their goods."

"I still lay those deaths on them, at least in part. But even leaving the past aside, how many more will Jack's employer kill if he isn't stopped?"

I had no answer, except that it wasn't our business—which has never stopped Michael for a minute.

"If we meddle with his affairs, Jack's employer is going to kill the two of us. I know you don't care about that, but I do. And it's not our business! Crime on this scale is the Liege Guard's job, not ours."

"They don't seem to be doing it." Michael was wearing his I'm-a-knight-errant-expression, which meant he was no longer susceptible to rational argument. But I still had to try.

"I don't want to go after Jack," I said. "I *won't* go after him."

Michael's face sobered, but his accursed, stubborn, noble determination never wavered.

"I can't force you to come with me. You paid your debt, years ago. You're free to do as you like."

But he was going after Jack, and his powerful, deadly boss, no matter what I said. And I wanted to see Michael die at their hands even less than I wanted to see Jack on the justice scaffold. Which meant that I'd have to find some way to help Michael, and pull Jack out of it—while keeping all three of us alive. There are limits to what's possible, even for me. But...

"You know I can't let you go alone. You'd get killed in a heartbeat, without someone sensible to restrain you."

"Then we go together, as always. My squire."

Michael clapped me on the shoulder, and his smile was like the rising sun. He knew perfectly well that I couldn't let him go into danger alone... and he'd used that knowledge against me.

On the other hand, if he was going to lay down ultimatums, then he could hardly blame me for getting...creative.

Chapter 3

Michael

To my surprise, Fisk made no further argument about going on to the city. I know that in his heart he wanted to bring down Jack Bannister's wicked employer as much as I did. 'Twas only this Jack he wished to...avoid, I think. At times Fisk seemed to hate the man, and I've gathered some great betrayal lay between them. But for betrayal to leave the scars that this one had, there must once have been great trust, and even love.

To me, Jack hadn't seemed at all loveable. But I wasn't a teenage boy, learning the skills to survive as a thief and con artist.

If Master Bannister was innocent, of murder at least, I might be willing to spare him. But if the blood his master shed had splashed onto his hands...

TALLOWSPORT WAS LARGER than I'd been able to imagine, and not nearly as...I think "grand" was what I had expected. A shining, bustling richness that nothing else in the Realm could rival.

Traveling at the food train's slow pace, we reached Tallow-sport's outskirts early in the morning. All towns have craft yards on their outskirts, so at first I assumed that the grandeur I expected would eventually appear. The craft yards were indeed bigger than any I'd seen, noisy and bustling—and even I wasn't naive enough to expect shine and richness from such places. They ran for mile after mile. Most towns have just one central market, some larger towns have two or three, in different neighborhoods. We passed through five markets, on this road alone during the full day it took us to ride through the town. And the prices...

"A bushel of potatoes sells here for *less* than we paid the farmers for it," Fisk told me. "And that doesn't take transport, warehousing, and the merchant's profit into account."

"I know nothing of how food is handled in a place this size," I said. "Mayhap they stockpile food that doesn't spoil, to keep the price the same year-round."

Fisk knows no more of a great city's food markets than I, but his scowl deepened, and I was reminded that he hadn't wanted to come to Tallowsport at all.

"Mayhap we'll be here long enough for you to get a letter from Kathy," I said, hoping to cheer him. My sister was forbidden to write to me, so she wrote to Fisk instead. And since she'd been sent to court, her letters had become even more amusing. "She never did tell you her scheme to get out of the Heir hunt."

"Maybe," said Fisk. But his expression brightened a bit as we rode on.

The laborers that supported all this industry were housed in tall, unadorned rooming houses, some of them four or five stories high! The folk we saw in streets and yards appeared well-fed, busy, and as happy as folk anywhere. Looking down the lanes I saw laundry lines, strung like bunting between the rooming houses. And if the clothing on those lines wasn't brightly dyed, 'twas plentiful and not too often patched.

Dusk was falling when the carts finally rolled into a great warehouse, which they said was somewhere near the Old Market. The laborers were taken off to temporary quarters, having been told that some of them could start repaying their travel debt tomorrow by unloading the freight wagons they'd traveled with. I went to fetch True from the cooks, and Fisk went to get our pay.

I'd taken the train boss's measure well enough that I wasn't surprised when Fisk returned with two reasonably fat purses. I was surprised by the difficulty of finding a rooming house that had stabling for two horses and would admit a dog. And in a port city, I shouldn't have been. But eventually, Chant, Tipple and True found a home in a garden shed, and pasture in the rooming house's fallow garden. The landlady had once been a countrywoman, and had no problem taking care of our horses for a reasonable fee. And her son was enchanted with the idea of having a dog, even if 'twas only for a time.

True was equally enchanted with the idea of having a boy, so I left them to each other. Fisk and I settled into our two meager rooms, with a plan to seek out employment in the morning—as an excuse for seeking the information we had really come for.

The landlady served breakfast, for yet another modest sum, to any tenants who didn't cook for themselves. Given the size of her house and the good quality of the meal, I was surprised how few showed up for it.

"It's a bit expensive for most, day to day," a thin, middle-aged clerk told me, stirring butter and honey into his porridge. "Not that they can't afford it now and then. Just not every day."

Several other men, seated around the long table, gave the self-satisfied nods of those who could afford it. They willingly held forth on our prospects for employment, until they learned that Fisk and I weren't interested in joining a guild.

"You've got t' be in a guild," a red-faced butcher said. "No one'll take you on, not for any decent job, if you're not."

Fisk asked how much the guild fees were in Tallowsport, and the answer made him choke on his porridge. Then he asked how we could get an indecent job, which sparked a roar of laughter. Though I'm not sure he was joking.

We decided to seek work at a tavern. I've hired on as a bouncer in such places often enough that Fisk has learned to make himself useful behind a bar, and there's no better way to learn what's happening in a town. And those jobs don't require guild membership, though brewing does.

However, we soon found that in Tallowsport you had to be guild certified to get almost any job. Or, some told us, you had to be "approved." When we asked who had to approve us they changed the subject, usually by telling us about some less respectable establishment that we might try.

It was from other tenants in our rooming house that we got some of the answers. The landlady's son wasn't the only child who liked playing with a dog, and within a few days I was meeting their parents, and talking to them about our failure to find work.

They told me that the guilds ran the town, which was common enough. But there was another power in the town as well. If "they" approved, you were in. And if "they" disapproved, best leave town quickly! Sometimes this mysterious "they" became "he," and once, "the boss."

"Do you think they're talking about your Jack's employer?"

Fisk and I were settling into bed, after our third day of failing to find work.

"I'd give it better than even odds," Fisk said. "But where under two moons is the rest of the town government? Nobody talks about the mayor, the council, the town guard—or the Liege Guard, and they've got to have post in a town this size. I've been wondering if I shouldn't try to find employment on my own."

"Not with this boss," I said. "We don't know enough. 'Tis too risky."

Fisk said nothing.

"Do you really think your friend would look out for you?" Jack Bannister had, after all, tried to recruit Fisk for his employer the last time they'd met. 'Twas the fact that Jack had been willing to let the wreckers kill me that had gotten in the way.

"I know he wouldn't," Fisk said. "But I might be able to learn something from him."

"'Tis too dangerous," I insisted. "You'd be on your own, in a nest of vipers." For there was no way they'd also hire me.

"It would be safer than burgling the man's offices," said Fisk. "I warn you now, I'm not going to do that. I hate burglary. I gave up burglary!"

"I've never asked you to commit a burglary," I said. Fisk keeps accusing me of this, though I swear 'tis always his idea. And at this point, we didn't even know what to burgle. "Let's continue as we are for a time, and see what chance occurs."

So we went on seeking employment, which we didn't need, and learning our way about the city—at least, the area by the great port. We also discovered more about how things worked here.

Many of our neighbors had come in from the countryside, some of them on food trains like the one we'd accompanied. They were content enough, with jobs that let them feed and house their families. But those who'd been here longer complained that while you could live on the wages paid, 'twas never enough to put aside savings. And once your status as a lowly worker was established, you couldn't rise to any higher position unless you paid a guild for extra training.

This was not common, for the guilds promote from within, and they assist the talented to rise in rank and pay as their skills improve—for the sake of their craft, as well as their members. Having to pay for training with anything but the work of your hands was yet another Tallowsport innovation... and one that might, in the long term, prove more cruel than the stocks.

We soon heard that a goldsmith had received "approval" to open a shop in the expensive streets west of the Old Market. Such folk need extra guards (myself) and clerks who are familiar with the price and quality of valuables (Fisk) so we determined to try our luck there.

But as we passed among the haberdashers, glass sellers, glovers, and fine boot makers, I heard the sound of smashing wood from the open door of a chandler's shop.

I first thought 'twas some accident, and if no cry for help came I'd have gone on. But then a rough looking man, carrying a short cudgel in one hand, dragged a plump man in a wax-splotched apron out of the shop and shoved him into the wall so hard the windows rattled.

"Don't, don't," the plump man whimpered. "You don't have to hurt me! I'll get the money."

"You should've thought of that before," the thug told him.

I would have expected the man's neighbors to come to his aid, but the street around us emptied with remarkable speed. From the nearby shops I heard the clack of falling latches and the rattle of closing shutters.

Clearly, 'twas up to Fisk and me.

"Don't hurt anyone else then," the chandler begged. "Don't hurt my family. Or the boys. Don't—" The cudgel's tip thudded into his stomach and he doubled over.

A second thug came out of the shop, carrying a handful of long white candles.

"The town guard?" Fisk murmured.

"If they'll come, the neighbors are already running to get them. But if the guard would come, I don't think this would be happening in the open street."

After we reached the city, I'd returned my sword to its usual place in my pack—it was curst inconvenient to carry, and in these peaceful times there's seldom any need. This was the exception to that rule…so of course now my sword was back in our room. I looked around for a weapon.

No loose cobbles, in this neighborhood. Almost nothing in the street that wasn't fastened down. Except two doors up, beside an herb seller's shop…

I unbuckled my cape and passed it to Fisk, freeing my arms to fight. The terrified joy of righteous battle sang in my blood.

"Pull your hat down over your face," Fisk said, "so they won't be able to come after us."

"I can't fight that way."

I cast my hat aside and Fisk promptly donned it, and turned his collar up into the bargain.

"We don't have t' hurt your family." The first thug's voice was conversational, as if he did this all the time. Another cudgel blow to the chandler's stomach, and one to the face that straightened him back up.

"First we're going t' break all your candles," the thug went on.

The other thug made the words true as his comrade spoke, snapping one of the expensive candles in several places.

"Then," said the first thug, "we're going t' break your fingers, just like the candles."

The lengths of wax dangling from their wick did look like a horribly mangled hand. The chandler made a choked sound of terror.

"Then we're going t' break your windows," said the thug. "And next time our collectors come you'd better have the payment. Or we'll stop fiddling around, pour wax all over this place, and burn it like—"

The clay pot I'd taken from a rack outside the herb seller's door cracked over his head, scattering dirt and bright shoots. Basil from the scent of it. The thug kept his grip on the chandler's apron, but it looked to be more for support now, as he sagged to his knees.

The second thug had been watching his colleague work, and failed to notice my approach. Now he dropped the candles, and his cudgel left his belt and whistled toward me... and passed over my head, as I dove to retrieve the first thug's club, which was rolling across the cobbles.

I brought it up just in time to keep his second swing from cracking my skull, scrambling backward and to my feet, opening distance between us.

My opponent shouted for aid. Fisk, who'd been about to throw my cape over his head, turned toward the shop door as yet another thug appeared.

The newcomer went for Fisk, but I had no chance to see more as my opponent closed on me.

There are tricks to fighting with short clubs, instead of swords. One of them is that there's no guard protecting the fingers holding the club. This means that much of a cudgel fight is spent in circling your opponent, protecting your hands, and hoping that something will distract him long enough for you to get a blow in.

A cape flying over his head would have been perfect, but a stream of breathless curses told me that Fisk had his own troubles—possibly because he had my hat pulled so far down he could barely see.

I feinted a quick stroke at the thug's right arm, and when his cudgel blocked it, I reached up and grabbed his club with my other hand—yet another thing you can't do in a sword fight. It took him only a moment to wrest it free, but while he did my cudgel flashed down, rapping him smartly across the shin.

'Tis a blow that hurts enough to disable an opponent, even when the bone doesn't break. The man screamed and staggered back, and I looked around for Fisk...just in time to see three more thugs run out of the chandler's shop.

The man with mud and basil clinging to his hair wobbled back to his feet. The chandler was crouching against the wall, his arms over his head. Fisk's opponent clawed my cape off his face, and turned toward me as well.

Fisk, as is his habit when we are seriously overmatched, had vanished.

Which left me free to pursue the only possible tactic when the odds are six to one.

I threw my cudgel at the nearest uninjured thug, and ran.

My first burst of speed let me build a good distance between me and my pursuers, for they stayed to bring all their comrades together, and the man who limped slowed them down.

I'd hoped they might do that; such men are accustomed to hunting in packs, and rely on outnumbering their opponents. Though five of them would have been more than enough to do the job, in my opinion.

I could probably have outrun them then, but my job was to keep them from returning to the chandler's shop, to give Fisk as much time as I could. I actually slowed my pace a bit as I headed for the market square.

My thinking was that dodging through the crowd would slow them down. But when we reached the square I heard them shout behind me, and the crowd I dodged through thinned like magic as folk scuttled out of their way.

My breath was beginning to come hard, and I had to pick up my pace crossing the square. A wheel-barrow of beets, on sale today, sat beside the entrance to a narrow lane. I grabbed a handle in passing and tipped them over the cobbles.

I heard a shouted curse, and looked back to see my pursuers dancing and hopping amid the rolling garnet balls—and despite my breathlessness, I summoned a laughing cheer.

It lured them on, as I'd hoped. I ran for the next street, turned right, and jogged onward. Slower now, less because I needed them to see me than to ease the stitch in my side.

When I heard a gasping shout, "There he is!" I darted left and jogged down an even narrower lane. This was an alley between rooming houses, but the laundry flapping overhead was too high for me to pull it down to slow them, or to hide behind.

Fortunately they were in no better case than I, and I led them left, and left again, into the twisting maze of streets near the oldest part of the port. Fisk and I had applied for work in several low taverns there, and I was confident of my ability to lose them in that warren. Right, left and left again, clutching my aching side. By now I was so winded I could barely jog. But even the man whose shin I'd bruised was still clinging doggedly to my heels—which I took as a bad sign, if they ever caught up with me.

I turned into another narrow alley and put on a staggering burst of speed, gaining as much distance as I could. I planned to go left or right at the next street, before they could see which way I'd turned, and then lose them. The alley I'd chosen even curved, the better to hide me. I was thinking I'd made my escape, till I rounded the curve and found my road blocked by a wall of tall stakes, sharpened at the top like a crude palisade. Mayhap in the distant past this had been some fortresses wall. But now, decrepit warehouses ran right up against it, their tall wooden walls trapping me like a mouse in a box.

A handful of broken crates were tumbled about, and mounds of refuse, including a tall carved chair with its stuffing leaking out—nothing tall enough to help me over a twelve foot fence, even if I wasn't wheezing like a bellows.

The only plan I could think of seemed a scant chance, but 'twas the only chance. I dragged the chair over to the fence and stood on the seat, looking for a protruding nail or spike. When I found one I pulled off my coat and hooked its hem on the nail, as if it had been caught as I climbed over.

Then I ran for the nearest shelter, a big, overturned bin and threw myself down in the narrow space between it and the warehouse. I tried to soften my breathing as the thugs drew near, but if they hadn't been gasping themselves they must have heard me.

I couldn't see them from my hiding place, and I wasn't crazy enough to try. There was no need. A string of panting curses greeted my ruse, and for a moment hope leapt in my heart. Then:

"I don't believe it. No one could get over that fence."

"I don't know. He was pretty cursed spry."

"Besides," another voice chimed in. "If he didn't climb the wall, how come his coat's hanging there? And that chair has fresh mud on it."

Footsteps, as they all moved forward to look. My breathing was under control now, but my heart pounded so hard I was afraid they might hear that.

"No," said the first voice. "Even with the chair, it's too high. And how could he slip out of his coat, hanging onto...what? The top of the fence is five feet from that nail."

Could I dart out of my hiding place and down the alley before they could catch me? I'd have almost no lead, and weary as I was 'twas a daunting thought.

It might be my only choice.

"Then where is he? We saw him run in. Did we pass any doors?"

"I don't remember. There's a lot of stuff around here. Maybe he's hiding."

I rose to my knees. I'd wait till they scattered to search and—

A hand gripped my ankle.

So taut were my nerves, I almost yelped aloud with the shock of it. I looked back, and saw that one of the planks that made up the warehouse wall had swung inward, leaving a gap near my feet.

The hand, small and grubby, tugged on my boot, clearly inviting me in.

I knew not what awaited me in that warehouse, but it had to be better than facing six men with cudgels—and at this point, a considerable grudge.

Moving quietly, I backed through the opening. I had to twist my body to get through the narrow gap, but a number of hands were tugging on me now. The quarreling thugs never heard the soft scraping sounds of my passage.

My rescuers were children. The warehouse roof was less sound than the walls, emitting shafts of sunlight through a score of holes. It held tall stacks of crates and barrels, and three children who crouched beside me.

A boy, with one eyelid sunken over an empty socket, lowered the plank back down. The oldest, a girl, held a finger to her lips—unnecessary, since I had no intention of giving the game away. She was about fourteen, her dark hair pulled into an untidy braid.

The other boy, whose fair hair looked as if he'd cut it himself, eyed me warily. One hand rested on the hilt of a knife that was too large for him to handle—but he wore it with a more accustomed air than I wore my sword.

All of them, including the girl, had knives on their belts. And though only three had joined me, I heard rustlings in the dim corners that told me there were more of them. A lot more.

Children or not, I'd best go carefully. I sat back, my hands in plain sight, and waited for some time before the one-eyed boy, who'd pressed his ear against the wall, announced, "They's gone."

"Good enough." The girl rose to her feet. "We can let you out the door. It opens onto Sailmaker Lane."

"I thank you," I said. "For saving my life."

They stepped back as I stood, opening distance, and the blond lad wasn't the only one with his hand on his knife. I resolved to make no sudden moves.

"We didn't do it for you," the girl said. "Door's this way." She gestured for me to precede them, instead of turning their backs on me. I've seen trained guards less skilled at handling a prisoner.

The warehouse was long, with a clear central corridor lined with towering piles of crated merchandise, dusty and stained by leaks from the rotting roof. But 'twas the sounds of stealthy movement behind those stacks, and the odd glimpse of movement in the shadowy gaps between them, that held my attention. How many children lived here? It might be unwise, but I had to ask.

"Who are you? What are you doing here? Where are...?"

A sudden suspicion of the answer stopped my tongue, but they knew what I'd been about to say.

"Yah," said One-eye. "We're orfinks, mostly. Those as ain't, they's better off here than home."

I'd heard bits of the Tallowsport accent this week, but never so thick and pure.

"Surely you have kin in this town who'd take you in."

There was a long silence, but then the girl shrugged. "They were chasing him," she told the others. And it's not like he can tell them anything about us they don't already know. No harm in talking I can see."

The blond boy growled under his breath, and a murmured echo came from the shadows—a feral sound that lifted the hair on the back of my neck.

"That's how come we's here," One-eye said. "It's the Rose. He says anyone takes us in, they get the same as our famblies got. We're supposed to be dead, see?"

He said it with a casual acceptance that chilled my blood, even as it broke my heart.

"Who is this Rose?" I demanded.

All of them stopped, staring as if I'd asked why the night was dark.

"The Rose," said the girl. "Tony Rose. Atherton Roseman. The man who runs this town. The man who owns the six thugs who were about t' beat the crap out of you!"

"Ah," I said. "I've spent the last week trying to find out who 'he' was. So now, I'm doubly indebted to you."

"How can you not know about the Rose?" The blond boy's voice was rough with suspicion.

"I'm a stranger to Tallowsport," I told him.

"Then why were they after you?"

All the children eyed me suspiciously, now.

"I came to the aid of a shop-keeper they were threatening. I take it Atherton Roseman demands extortion from all the shops?"

"He calls it a city tax," the girl said. "But people have to pay the regular taxes too, t' the city and the High Liege. And this 'tax' goes straight into Tony Rose's pockets, according to my..."

She pursed her lips, turning away. But when she turned back there were no tears in those bleak eyes.

That much hate precludes tears.

"I take it your parents, all your parents," I gestured to the shadows, "stood up to Master Roseman?"

"That's how you get t' be an orfink," One-eye said. "'Least, here in the city."

"But... Did the town guard never intervene? The High Liege's guard?"

Never had I heard of a place where the law of the land had vanished so completely. Lords and barons pay the Liege directly, but he sends tax collectors to the towns. They act as his eyes and ears throughout the Realm, and the guards who accompany them are both well-trained and loyal. As you'd expect, in men who guard the crown's money.

"Nobody stops the Rose, Master Stranger-in-town," the girl said. "I don't know where you come from, but if you interfered with his enforcers you'd better get back home before he finds you."

"They have no way to find me," I assured her. "My friend and I were just passing by. And from what you say, I'm fairly sure that the reason we came to Tallowsport was to bring Atherton Roseman to justice."

This man had to be Jack Bannister's employer. Not only did logic tell me that, but Jack had spoken of him with the same resigned fear that sounded in the children's voices. They didn't give my announcement any more credence than Jack would have.

"Bring him t' justice?" The blond boy was too young to be able to sneer so cynically. "I'd give odds against you even getting out of town alive."

"Well, I mean to try."

"Then it's been nice knowing you," One-eye said. "Anything partic'lar you want on your headstone?"

I laughed. They all jumped, as if such a sound was never heard in these gloomy shadows.

But the girl's eyes had widened. "You mean it? You're going to take on the Rose?"

"I am."

They were all staring now, and the girl's next words took me completely by surprise.

"Let us help. We know this town. We've been spying on him."

She was completely, heartbreakingly, terrifyingly serious.

"I'm sorry. But you're only children."

"We're tougher than you think."

Her jaw set in a way that almost made me believe it.

"And you owe us, stranger. We saved your life back there. 'Least you can do is let us help take him down. Or at least hurt him. We'd do anything. Anything you need."

"I'm sorry, my partner and I work alone. But be assured, if there's anything you can do to help I shall call on you."

They knew I didn't mean it and their faces fell, like children denied some promised treat.

I wanted to take every one of them home with me—or at least to some place where they'd be safe, and learn to laugh once more. If I could bring this Rose down, someday I might be able to. And to worry about leaving them here alone— though I couldn't help but do so—was more presumption on my part than anything else.

They had, after all, rescued me.

Chapter 4

Fisk

Six thugs took off after Michael, like dogs after a cat. But these dogs were nursing several injuries, and the cat had already gained considerable distance.

On the other hand, he wouldn't be able to lead them on forever—and when they lost him, they might return. I'd better get things moving.

By "things" I meant terrified, probably stubborn, people.

I crossed the street to the chandler, who still leaned against the wall.

"Can you stand up?"

He flinched when I knelt beside him, but I clearly wasn't one of the thugs, and the arms that had risen reflexively fell again.

He had a darkening bruise on one cheekbone, but his eyes were clear so it probably wasn't broken.

"What? I mean, what are you doing?"

"I'm trying to get you to stand up," I repeated. "Because my friend won't be able to draw them away for long. And it'd be wise for you and your family to be packed and gone when they come back."

"Packed? Gone where? I have a business here!"

"Not anymore, you don't." I kept my tone brisk, but I felt some sympathy. He'd no doubt put considerable work into this place.

However, Jack had taught me that holding onto a failing plan gets you nothing at best, and dead at worst. The sooner this man figured that out, the better.

He jumped again as the shop door banged open, and a plump woman in a starched cap and apron rushed out. She carried a long, wax-coated paddle and she glared wildly around the street before she flung it aside and knelt beside her...husband, no doubt. Two girls in their late and early teens followed her, and then a boy. His narrow face and lanky form bore no resemblance to the chandler or his family, and his clothes were rougher and shabbier—apprentice.

"How badly are you hurt?" The wife lifted a hand, and tilted the chandler's face gently toward the light. For a moment I thought she'd weep, but then her soft lips firmed and she turned to me.

"Will you help me get him into the shop?"

"I told you t' keep them upstairs!" the chandler said to his apprentice.

"Like he could," said the youngest girl. Her older sister was weeping.

The apprentice shrugged.

"How much damage is there?" the chandler asked.

"That doesn't matter." I made my voice sharp enough to cut through the rising hubbub. "You all have to be gone when those men come back, or they'll take up where they left off. Unless you've got enough money to talk them out of it."

"We could have paid the tax," the wife said. "But no one bribes the Rose's enforcers. And he's decided to make us an object lesson. You're right, sir. We've got t' leave."

The Rose. After all these days of digging, pay dirt.

"We can't just abandon—"

"It's up to you," I said. "Though I'd think it would be hard to run your business with crippled hands."

"But where could we go?" the older girl asked.

"To your uncle Lionel, in Hinksville," the wife said. "That's out of even Roseman's reach."

"We've put ten years into this shop!" The chandler looked as if he was about to cry too. "All our savings."

"There won't be any shop, after Roseman's through with it," his wife said. "Do you have a better idea? Then we're going to Hinksville."

Between us, we got the chandler to his feet. He leaned on me as we followed the rest of his family into the shop's front room—well lit, and no doubt usually a pleasant place, with the smell of fresh wax and sunlight gleaming on the long counter. Now glass from fancy candle lamps crunched underfoot. The candles had been broken or stamped on.

The mistress was already giving her daughters brisk instructions about what to take. Since they wouldn't be around to tell anyone what I looked like, I removed Michael's hat and folded my collar back down. If Roseman's thugs offered a reward for information about someone matching his description, Michael would have to stay off the street. Which would have made any sane man give up and leave town…but I knew better than to expect that of Michael.

"Take nothing a horse can't carry," I told the chandler's wife. "And you'll need to buy the horses. If you rent, whoever brings them back could tell Roseman where you've gone."

"But where…"

We passed through another door into the workroom, and the chandler's voice failed him. They'd smashed most of the hanging racks—that's probably what made the noise we'd heard—and spilled the big copper kettles of melted wax, which had run over the floor in thick congealing sheets.

The apprentice made a sound of distress, and went to lift one of the spilled tubs off the fire. The small amount of wax that remained in it was beginning to smoke.

The chandler looked at the ruins of his workplace, and the tears finally came.

"I should have paid. I should have shut up and paid, like everyone else."

"Could you stay?" I asked. "If you agreed to pay...oh, double for a year, or something?"

The woman had already chivvied her daughters up the stairs. Brisk footsteps sounded overhead. She seemed a sensible woman, willing to salvage what she could, and leave the rest without looking back.

Michael could run for a long time. I hoped the thugs were in good shape too. Still...

"You keep watch out the front window," I told the apprentice. "Yell if you see those men. I'll take the back door."

It opened onto an alley, with a clear line of sight for several blocks in either direction.

The chandler sat on a keg, staring around in despair.

"So, you could stay if you paid extra?" I asked it more to keep him talking than because the answer mattered. Rumors of Tallowsport's corruption and wickedness abounded throughout the Realm, but I'd been skeptical. It seemed I was wrong.

"No. If I'd paid up like I should've...well, I can't say those payments weren't a problem, but I could have managed. But I had t' get brave... I started talking t' my neighbors, see. I had plans t' raise a delegation, go t' the Liege Guard in Gollford. There's a post there, though it's not as large as the one here. Witnesses, signed statements. I'd already begun t' gather them. So many people said they agreed with me, that we had t' stand up... I guess I got too cocky. I decided not t' pay. And look. Look!"

I did, and under the wreckage I could see a tidy business. It would cost to clean it up and repair the damage, but spilled wax could be scraped up and melted down again. Broken candles could be recast.

"Do you have money on hand, for the payment you skipped and one other?"

It was almost as crazy as one of Michael's schemes. On the other hand, we'd been looking for work and there was plenty of that here. And eventually, some of the chandler's rebellious neighbors might be willing to talk to us.

If we could gather sufficient evidence to convince the Liege Guard to pay Tallowsport a visit, I might be able to talk Michael out of trying to deal with Roseman himself.

"Yah, I've enough set by for three payments. But it won't be enough to start a new business, in a new town, with no shop, no supplies, no—"

"Sound hands, our health, and each other." His wife was coming down the stairs, carrying two canvas bags and a travel case. "That's enough t' be starting with. And I was with you all the way, doing something about the Rose, so don't go blaming yourself. We all agreed."

The apprentice had left the door to the front room open behind him, and I saw his head turn sharply. Judging by his expression he hadn't agreed, but no one had listened.

"You can't stay here," I said. "Even if Roseman didn't know your plans, now that they've fallen apart one of your neighbors is bound to say something to someone, and it will all come out. But suppose you had someone you could leave behind, to run the shop for you?" I went on. "Someone new in town, who could convince Roseman's men he'd be happy to pay whatever it takes to make reparation and regain their trust. And eventually, find a buyer for this place, and send you the money from the sale. Minus a reasonable broker's fee, of course. That should give you enough to set up shop in Hinksville, or wherever you choose."

"No one would dare take the place," the chandler said bitterly. "All my friends live here. And they've their own businesses to run."

"Your wife's nephew from Huckstable might be able to do it. And his best friend. Since they came to give the chandelling trade a try, to see if it suited them."

The chandler stared at me blankly.

"Me, you nitwit!"

His face came alive under the spreading bruise, suspicion warring with hope. "Why would you be willing to do that? And why should I trust a stranger t' pay me?"

"As if we've a better choice?" his wife asked tartly. "No one we know would dare take the place. Indeed, sir, you don't understand what you'd be risking."

"Then I'll charge a larger fee," I said. "And you might not be able to trust me, but you can trust my friend." I expected Michael to return soon. Him, or the enforcers. "He's too crazy to care about the risk, anyway."

I did care, but if we paid up promptly, with interest and plenty of groveling, Roseman should consider a cowed shop owner who paid him regularly more profitable than a burned-out building and couple of corpses.

Chasing the chandler and his family out of town was enough to make his point.

"But you've got to leave now," I added, as the daughters came down, laden with bundles. "Can you buy horses and still leave me enough for the payments? The horses don't have to be good ones."

I preferred not to tax Michael's and my purse more than was necessary.

"Yes," said the wife. "I'll show you where. We're trusting you, sir."

"What about me?" The apprentice spoke up for the first time.

"Why...why, I suppose you'll come with us." But the chandler, perhaps thinking of the price of even a not-so-good horse, sounded dubious.

"It's the least we can do, to reward you for not running off like the rest," the wife added. "We'll be able to use you, I'm sure. Or Lionel will."

So this boy would go from apprentice chandler to servant. And no one had spoken of pay, either. I saw the boy's expression change as he realized this.

"Or you can stay here," I said. "And teach my friend and me what we're supposed to be doing. You'd be the lead apprentice, and paid...well, more than the other apprentices. When we have other apprentices."

THE CHANDLER AND HIS FAMILY departed, promising to send me an address where I could send the money from the sale of their business, and I had a chance to talk with our new employee.

We began picking up and tallying the damages—him doing the tallying, and me tossing broken racks into the alley and scraping wax off the floor.

I was beginning to wonder what had happened to Michael, who should have been back by now. Him or the thugs.

The boy's name was Hannibas, and he'd been apprenticed first to another master who, he said succinctly, was a right bastard. The chandler had been a better one—but he'd probably have run off with the others, if he'd had anywhere to go.

Michael showed up almost half an hour later, just before I had to go looking for him. He didn't even appear ruffled, much less in the dire straits I'd begun to imagine. He was also surprised that the thugs hadn't returned to finish the job.

"If they're not back by now, they probably won't come till tomorrow," he said.

I was too busy restraining my irritation about how long Michael had been gone to worry what he'd been doing all this time. And I should have.

But Hannibas told us that the other apprentices' contracts had been with the chandler, and they were scared enough of this Roseman that they probably wouldn't return at all. And when Michael said, "Don't worry. I think I can find us some workers," I didn't think twice about it.

CHAPTER 5

Michael

The the thugs returned next morning. Hannibas and I crouched upstairs, listening while Fisk "handled them."

I had great faith in Fisk's ability. But I'd also gone back to our lodging house last night to pick up a few things we might need—including my sword. My hand rested on the hilt, as I listened to Fisk ply his trade. If things went awry, I'd not hesitate to use it.

The thugs introduced themselves by throwing the shop door so wide it crashed into the wall. All the doors between the front room and the staircase had been left open, so we could hear.

"Can I help you...ah...gentlemen?" I'd never heard Fisk sound so nervous, so timorous. Not even when we faced death. Come to think of it, facing death makes Fisk brisk, bossy and snappish. I'd add sarcastic, but he's sarcastic most of the time.

"Where's the chandler?"

The last time I'd heard that voice, I'd been lying behind a crate preparing to run for my life. Now, safe, and probably facing nothing alarming, prickles of rage and fear ran over my skin and my palms began to sweat.

"Uncle Martin? He...ah! You're the...um... You're here to collect a payment, aren't you? I'll get it right—"

Fisk's words ended in a squeak and a thump, as if someone had grabbed his vest and banged him into the wall.

"We don't want the money." The thug's voice was so threatening, 'twas almost a growl. "We want that cheating cur of a chandler. And then we want that interfering bastard who led us a chase yesterday."

"He's gone!" Fisk squealed. "My aunt and him, they got scared. I mean, my cousins are girls, and that guy said he was leaving town that afternoon anyway, and why didn't— Hey!"

"You're lying," the thug said. "We left word at the livery stables; anyone tried to rent a carriage or horses, they were to notify us."

"Didn't rent." Fisk's voice rasped now, as if his collar was being twisted around his neck. "That guy, he said you'd be looking. Said he had three pack horses, and if the younger girl rode double with his groom they could get to the next town. But Uncle was sorry, very sorry, for any inconvenience you were caused. He left the money for me to pay you, and to...ah, reimburse you for your trouble, and please I...I can't...."

A thud as his feet hit the floor, and an extravagant gasp. If they'd really been strangling him, he couldn't have been so verbose. But my hand still tightened on my sword hilt.

"You've got the money?" The thug sounded thoughtful. Reluctant to give up his vengeance, but if his victims weren't here...

"Money, yes. For you and your...ah, for the city tax. Yes, of course."

A wooden clack as Fisk opened the hidden compartment behind the counter, revealing its location in his eager haste.

"Here, here's ten silver roundels for the payment, and an extra six! One for each of you, to apologize for that little misunderstanding. Because we're all very, very sorry."

"There's some silver left in there," another voice said. "Almost another ten, I think."

"Yes, yes. I've already started saving for the next payment," Fisk babbled. "Wouldn't want to fall short again. I won't fall short. I really, really won't."

"Take another five," the first voice said. "Call it Master Roseman's interest."

"Interest?" I swear, Fisk's voice shot up a full octave. "But that's half a— No, wait!"

A crash, as one of the remaining glass candle lamps dropped to the floor.

"No, that's fine, interest is fine! I'm happy to pay it. Delighted. Delirious. Just don't break anything else. Please?"

"Week after next, Master Roseman wants twelve silver roundels from this shop. And every week after that, till he's satisfied."

"Twelve? But that's... That will be fine. I'll get it. Somehow. But I'll have the money. Promise."

The door closed.

Silence, for a long moment, then a derisive snort from Fisk. A cupboard door opened and a brush swept glass into a dust pan, then 'twas emptied into a bin.

I came down the stairs quietly, Hannibas thumping at my heels. Fisk greeted us with the lazy grin of a well-fed cougar.

"Told you. Nobody bothers to intimidate someone who's already cowering. And the 'tax' only went up twenty percent. Master Roseman must be feeling generous."

I glimpsed bruises beginning to darken under his loose collar, but I wouldn't sully his victory by saying so.

"That was brilliant. What next?"

"Next, we need to get this place running again," Fisk said. "You mentioned something about workers?"

ON THE WAY to acquire our new apprentices, I took a detour to pick up the rest of our gear and make a deal with the landlady. The shop had beds for the family and a number of workers on the second floor, but there was no stabling. Chant and Tipple seemed content in the landlady's care, even putting up with the gaggle of girls who'd taken to braiding flowers and ribbons into their manes, so we'd decided to leave the horses there.

As for True, it seemed to me that there were other children who might like a dog.

I PUT TRUE on collar and leash, to take him to the abandoned warehouse where the orphans had rescued me—only yesterday, though so much had happened I felt as if a longer time had passed.

To use the door on the street might attract unwanted attention, so I led my child-bait into the alley where I'd so nearly been trapped. It seemed rude, and possibly dangerous, to enter uninvited. I pulled the heavy bin a bit farther from the wall, and knocked on the loose board to announce myself.

Then I stepped back into the open to wait. I could feel their eyes, behind the knotholes in those weathered boards, but several long minutes passed before One-eye came from behind the crate to confront me.

"Did you figure out a way for us t' get the Rose?"

"Already? That will take weeks. Months, mayhap."

I had, of course, no intention of involving them—but I knew better than to say so.

"Then what're you doing here, wasting our time?"

In the daylight he looked to be about ten, but his young voice held an adult's terse challenge. His gaze strayed to the brindled hound who sat beside me. True wagged his tail and grinned invitingly.

"I'm still thinking about how to bring down Master Roseman, but I do have another need you and your friends might fulfill. One that may fill a need of yours, as well. I don't think you have much money?"

The word "money" drew his gaze away from the dog, which told me I was right.

"What do you need, and what's the pay? We got a couple can steal, but we won't put no one down. Not 'less they deserves it."

It sounded as if they'd been offered such jobs before, which probably shouldn't have shocked me, but it did. Fisk calls me naive, and mayhap he's right.

"Nothing like that," I said. "My friend and I have acquired a chandlery, but we've no workers beyond one senior apprentice. He says we need at least six men."

Actually, Hannibas had said three. But these workers were half-size, so I thought I could persuade Fisk to take that many.

One-eye was patting True by the time I finished listing my requirements. And if I'd had any doubt that the whole orphan clan was listening on the other side of that wall, it vanished as my new employees began trickling out.

First came two burly lads, about thirteen, one with straight brown hair and the other with black curls.

"What are your names?"

As their employer I had both right and need to know, but they froze, turning to One-eye. The younger boy hesitated a moment, then shrugged.

"They's Bran and Talts. I'm Timasus."

Next came a boy, mayhap fourteen, who introduced himself as Jig and made a bee-line for the dog. After him was a girl, about eleven, with fine, flyaway hair. She said nothing when I asked her name, but she gave me a shy smile and offered True a hand to sniff before she started petting him.

Timasus, who had somehow gotten the leash out of my hand without my noticing, told me Alessa didn't talk much, but she had deft hands for fine work.

I had known Fisk long enough to guess this meant she was good at picking locks.

The last boy barely fit through the gap in the planks. He must have been at least sixteen, with a scraggly beard. His britches were too small and his shirt too large. But his open, eager smile was that of a much younger boy. When I asked his name, he said he was Jer. Timasus added, a bit defiantly, that he was strong, willing, and a hard worker.

"Then he'll be perfect," I assured them. "In fact, I think all of you will do just fine."

We set off for the shop, which I hoped these waifs would soon be calling "home." They were more interested in True than me, and Timasus had to settle a quarrel about who got to hold his leash. He also ordered Jer to carry my packs, and I began to see that while Hannibas might be the master craftsmen, Timasus was clearly the shop foreman.

Noting that True had stopped to scratch, I made another stop at a herbalist's shop and picked up a large batch of fleabane.

I knew better than to try to keep True from sharing the children's beds. And I probably wasn't the first employer to insist that his workers start their job with a bath.

I DIDN'T REALLY THINK the neighbors were reporting to Roseman's thugs, but I took my workers in though the back of the shop anyway.

Fisk had been going through the chandler's accounts, but he looked up when we came in. His eyes widened, then narrowed, and his expression became very bland as child after child trooped through the door.

Hannibas' dubious expression was more open. "Bit young, ain't they? For a whole shop, at least."

"You'll have Fisk and me and Jer here—" I slapped his shoulder, and after a blink of surprise he beamed at me. "—for any task that needs a man's strength. And how many such tasks are there, making candles?"

"A standard slab of wax," Fisk glanced at the ledger to confirm it, "weighs thirty pounds."

His voice was as neutral as his face, and I opened my mouth to reply. But Timasus stepped forward, glaring from him to Hannibas and back.

"We can do anything a man can do, 'tween us. 'Cause we work *together.*"

All the children nodded firmly, and I realized that this creed was how they'd survived on their own.

"Well then," said Fisk. "I'd better figure out how to feed you. Unless Michael is prepared to handle that?"

I'm a fair camp cook, for one or two, and might manage a simple breakfast for nine—but anything more was beyond my skills, and Fisk knew it.

"You wanted a labor force," I told him. "I brought them. It's your turn to figure something out. But baths before food."

Several young faces fell.

Despite his initial resistance, Hannibas proved competent at heating water and setting up baths for one child after another.

We offered Alessa the first, as she was a lady, and Jer went in last, when the tub was most full. I threw True in after him, and gave the dog a thorough scrub. He got his vengeance, shaking dirty water over me and half the shop floor, to the children's glee. It must be admitted, the fleabane stank.

We had just emptied the bath and mopped the floor when Fisk returned, with two boys from a local cook shop helping him carry bread, soup, and hot meat pies.

"Why does Trouble smell like burning sewage?" The dog was nudging, Fisk who carried the pies.

"Master Michael made him bathe, 'long with the rest of us," Jig said. "And he didn't like it, either. But I thought his name was True."

"So does Michael," Fisk said. "But Trouble and I know better. Call him, and you'll see."

In point of fact, True will go to anyone who calls him by any name, including "that cursed mutt." But the children had some fun discovering this, calling the dog using any name that took their fancy, while Fisk and I set out our dinner. I forgave the commotion when Alessa called True "Kitty," and then doubled over laughing when he came. 'Twas the first time I'd heard her speak.

I thought that Fisk had ordered too much food, until I saw the hungry children tucking in. As we ate, he told me he'd paid the cook shop to send us luncheon and dinner daily. Since I'd brought him six when Hannibas asked for three, I could hardly tease him about the extra expense. Not even when he added, "You know the difference between a bandit and an apprentice? At least with bandits, you don't have to feed them too."

This startled snickers out of several children, but for a moment I still hoped these simpleminded jests hadn't found their way to Tallowsport.

Then Jig said, "What's the difference between a bandit and an apprentice master?"

"I don't know," Fisk completed the formula. "What?"

"A bandit don't call you a lazy lout when he beats you and takes your money."

Even the sensible Hannibas was grinning. "What's the diff—"

"Please," I begged. "Not a whole tribe of you. Fisk is bad enough! No more bandit jokes. Not in my hearing."

They were new enough to our employ that they did as I asked. Though in the days to come, I would hear them whispering behind my back, followed by a storm of giggles as they "sneaked" their jokes past me.

I feared that easy trust would be disrupted when they saw the broken circles that mark me unredeemed upon my wrists. It happened the day after they came to work for us. I'd rolled up my sleeves to keep them clear, as we poured hot wax from one kettle to another, and the laces on the leather guards kept flopping into the wax so I took them off. I was so relaxed in the children's presence by then that I thought nothing of it, till I noticed the widening circle of silence. Jer, holding the other kettle, looked around in puzzlement. Timasus stared at my wrists wide-eyed. Hannibas was scowling...not at me, but at Fisk.

"You didn't tell the chandler that. You didn't tell any of us... that."

"I'm sorry," I began. "'Tis—"

"I told the chandler about Michael," Fisk interrupted. "And I told him the truth."

I wondered what Fisk had told him.

"If the chandler knew *that*," Hannibas said, "he wouldn't have made the choice he did. He'd have... Oh."

"Exactly," said Fisk. "Who do you trust more? Michael? Or Atherton Roseman?"

Hannibas' scowl vanished into a look of troubled bafflement.

"You can trust me," I told them all. "I had some...difficulty with the Liege's law. But what I did was not dishonorable. I swear it."

Timasus snorted. "Ain't like the law gives a flip about us. Don't see why we'd care about it."

As far as the other orphans went, that seemed to settle the matter. But for some time after that, I would look up suddenly and catch Hannibas gazing at me with worry in his eyes.

Those first days, as we cleaned up the shop and started making and selling candles, were interesting in many ways. Hannibas and Timasus took charge of the backroom as if they'd been born to it, while Fisk handled our finances and manned the front room, in his persona of the chandler's timorous nephew.

Fisk was wary of allowing me to become known in this neighborhood, lest someone report my presence to Roseman's thugs, so I was relegated to distant errands, and helping Jer with tasks that required strength and little skill. The children learned to handle the rest with remarkable speed.

Working together, they slowly began to trust us, and Fisk and I learned bits of their past. Though listening to them talk to Hannibas taught us more.

"How'd you lose that eye?" he asked Timasus one day. "Did the Rose's thugs do it, as a lesson t' your parents or something?"

"Nah." Timasus, stirring chips of wax into a melting tub, didn't look up. "'Least, not deliberate. My Pa, he was a baker, and he fell behind on his payments. Like your chandler here, only he really didn't have the money. Second time, they was going t' break his hands. For a baker, can't knead..." He shook his head.

"So what happened to you?" Hannibas persisted. I wouldn't have dared, but after a moment Timasus went on.

"I ran t' try t' stop 'em. Which was stupid, but I was only six. I bit one of 'em, and he threw me aside. My eye hit the corner of a table. It hurt horrible, and I was all wobbly and dazed. Mam wrapped a clean cloth over my face and told me to run 't next door, and I did. But I wouldn't have, if I'd knowed what she was going t' do."

"I heard about that, I think." Hannibas voice was matter-of-fact, but his face had paled. "The Baker's Wife. Killed three of the Rose's thugs with a bread paddle, she did."

"Only two," said Timasus. "According t' what the neighbors said, anyway. But after..."

"I'm sorry," Hannibas said. "She was a brave woman."

The others had fallen silent, listening.

"Brave don't mean nothing with the Rose," Timasus said coldly. "The Rose's guard, the Rose's judicar, the Rose's noose. And all of us, hiding like rats in the walls, trying t' nibble at his great house. Master Michael promised t' help us hit him, in exchange for us saving him from them thugs, and that'll do for now. But one of these days, when we's old enough, when they's enough of us, we's going 't have a chat with Tony bloody Rose. Then we'll see who's nothing but a pack of lousy orfinks."

A murmur of agreement swept the room, and the cold hate in those young faces chilled my heart. I had made them no such promise, whatever they thought, but their lust for vengeance troubled me.

Atherton Roseman must indeed be brought down, before he broke more children's souls.

The next day, Hannibas sent me out to a market nearer the countryside to buy herbs to scent a batch of sickroom candles. Since I wasn't expected back soon, I took a detour to find the headquarters of the High Liege's guard.

I knew better than to go to the town guard. The children, customers, the suppliers we dealt with, all told us that the whole town government was in the Rose's pocket.

But I knew something of the world outside this town, and I couldn't believe the High Liege would appoint a corrupt man to such an important post.

I told the clerk at the outer desk that I wished to see the ranking officer, to make a complaint.

Even when your clothes are splotched with wax, a noble's accent and a confident tone can get you a long way. It took only half an hour to work my way past his subordinates, into the presence of the Liege Guard's commander.

It didn't look like the office of a corrupt man. Fisk has taught me to look for the small luxuries that betray a man living beyond his means. But the inkpot on the desk was plain pottery, and the blue and silver coat of a Liege guardsman, hanging on the rack behind, him was of unadorned wool. No bright gold buttons, no rings on his hands. The day was mild enough he'd chosen to work in his shirtsleeves, and that shirt was ordinary linen, without even a scrap of lace.

He was young for such a post, in his late twenties I thought, despite some lines of care that marred his pleasant face.

"I understand you have some complaint?" he asked briskly.

"I've recently acquired a business, here in Tallowsport, and I've been told there's a special tax, beyond the one paid to the city's treasury."

"There is such a tax." His expression was so guarded, I could read nothing from it.

"Yes, but this one's paid every two weeks, and all other taxes are quarterly." I tried to sound guileless without being too stupid. "Men come to fetch these payments instead of billing you, and 'tis curst high! I couldn't help but wonder if the High Liege has approved this."

"Pay the tax," he said. "That's all I can do for you, sir. Pay the tax, on time, without grumbling."

He put a hand to his throat as he spoke. Under his shirt I glimpsed a thick strap of leather encircling his neck, for all the world like True's collar. He saw me looking at it, and his hand fell away.

"Tallowsport is a rich city with a thriving market. If you're competent at your trade, you'll manage. Don't complain to the

Town Guard, either. And don't come back. There's nothing anyone can do."

He met my eyes as he spoke, his own as bleak and bitter as Timasus', and I wondered what troubled him. But clearly he could offer me no aid, so I thanked him and departed.

I had difficulties enough, without also trying to rescue the captain of the Liege Guard.

CHAPTER 6

Fisk

I tried not to show it to the children, and I certainly wasn't going to admit it to Michael, but I was getting nervous.

Things were going too well.

The thugs had bought my act. Michael's odd work gang, led by Hannibas, had the shop running smoothly. It looked as if we'd make the twelve silver roundels we'd need for the next payment. Even young Will's rescue from the food train had gone off without a hitch.

It was Jack who used to say that when you thought a scam was going too well, it usually was. And Jack had a nasty habit of being right about things like that.

So I took the time, after I'd delivered a batch of candles that had been ordered for a wedding, to stop off at yet another tavern and leave my message there.

This tavern was of a better class than most, matching the wealthy neighborhood here on the rise of land west of the port and north of the river. Some of the early manors built on The Rise, as this upper-class area was called, had a view of both the river and the sea.

The tavern didn't have a view, but the floors were clean, the brass handles on the taps gleamed, and glasses for wine as well as mugs for ale were stacked behind the bar.

I seated myself on a tall stool and ordered the cheapest ale the house offered, since I didn't plan to drink much of it.

When the bartender brought my mug I told him, "I'm looking for a man who lives here in Tallowsport. But I don't know his last name."

"City as big as the Port, that's a problem," the man said pleasantly. "What's his trade?"

Con men have no guild, so answering that wouldn't help me.

"I'm not sure." I let a rueful note creep into my voice. "We were talking horses, you see. And drinking a bit, so I don't remember as much as I should."

The man nodded, with professional politeness.

"He's in his thirties or forties," I went on. "Middling height and build. Brown hair and eyes."

The bartender snorted. "That's four men in this room. Except for the age, it could be you. Any scars, distinguishing marks, mannerisms?"

"Not that I remember," I said. "But his first name was Jack. I think. If you should see him, tell him that I've changed my mind. I want to buy his black horses. He'd probably have a tip, for the information."

The bartender's eyes narrowed in sudden suspicion—this sounded so much like a code that few would fail to recognize it as such. But as Jack had pointed out, they also wouldn't care.

"Does he know how to get in touch with you?"

"No," I said, and left the address of our old rooming house, adding that a note left with the landlady would reach me.

I'd been leaving this message with tavern keepers on and off since we reached Tallowsport. And if things were going as well as they seemed to be, Jack would never get that message. But if he was expecting me, he'd have told a number of barkeepers to pass on that message about the black horses, if anyone ever asked.

There are a lot of taverns in a city this size, but I needed to learn more about what Tony Rose was up to. And I needed to warn Jack to get out.

We came up with this system after one of our cons had gone spectacularly wrong. It was a lost heir scam—easier than most, since the rich mark had no children of his own. This left him free to choose between his wastrel nephew, and the nephew who'd gone missing as a child and had now "returned," conveniently claiming near total amnesia.

I'm pretty sure the old man knew I wasn't his nephew—he just wanted to send his real heir a stern message. And since receiving that message resulted in the heir offering me some really nice family jewelry if I'd agree to vanish again, that suited Jack and me just fine.

It wasn't till after he'd handed over the loot, and gotten out of our reach, that the real heir turned the dogs loose…and sent the local guard after us, as well.

I suppose he planned to say that I'd stolen the jewelry, proving—as he'd correctly claimed from the start—that I wasn't his long lost cousin.

It's impossible for a man to outrun a dog pack, and I'd rather take my chances with the judicars than be mauled. I leapt into the lower branches of a tree and was about halfway up the trunk when Jack—who was supposed to be waiting at a tavern in a nearby town—rode up to the base of my tree.

"Throw down your coat. I'll lead them off."

Even as I stripped, I noted that A) he wasn't where he said he'd be, and B) he clearly hadn't trusted me to bring this off alone—though under the circumstances, I could hardly complain about that.

Jack caught the coat and cantered off, leaning down to trail it against weeds and bushes till the dogs fixed on his horse's scent instead. The dogs had followed him, the sheriff and his men had gone thundering after the dogs, and I was climbing down the tree before I finally realized that C) if those dogs were as vicious as they sounded, Jack had probably saved my life.

By the time I reached the tavern rendezvous our descriptions had been plastered all over the countryside—if I hadn't needed to find Jack, I'd have been racing into the next fief. Instead I was disguised as a beggar so ragged they wouldn't let me in the door. I had to hover in the street outside until Jack—who was not only disguised as a tinker, but carried a full pack and had sharpened several knives before I approached him—finally showed up.

The first thing he said to me was, "We've *got* to think of a better way than this to find each other if we lose contact."

Over the next few months, we figured out the method I was using now. And at the time, it didn't occur to me to wonder if he'd have bothered to come for me if *he'd* been the one holding the loot.

Jack's morals might be lacking in many ways, but some of the orphans' stories were enough to turn even his stomach. On the other hand, he was also capable of turning a blind eye to anything he didn't want to see.

However, Jack was a realist above all, and there was no way this kind of corruption could escape the High Liege's notice forever. Sooner or later the Liege Guard would descend on the town, and then Atherton Roseman and everyone associated with him would go down.

It would happen sooner, if Michael had his way. He was undeniably crazy, but I had long since stopped underestimating what Michael could accomplish when he set his mind to it.

After hearing the orphans' stories, I understood his desire to see the Rose...not just cut, but torn out by the roots. Then burned, so not even a seed of his making could sprout.

Do roses have seeds? Gardening is something I know nothing about, but I knew that I was one of Jack's seeds. Or at least a plant he'd tended, shaped...and dumped horse shit over at regular intervals, too.

I owed him nothing—but I couldn't stand by and watch him hang, either.

I left a generous tip and an unfinished beer on the bar, guaranteeing that my message would be remembered, at least.

THE DAYS until the thugs came to collect their payment also passed with unnerving smoothness. Despite my forebodings, I decided that we'd probably be in Tallowsport long enough to get a reply, and sent a letter off to Michael's sister Kathy. She'd have written to Michael directly, but when he was first cast off by his stiff-necked father, Michael was too stiff-necked to ask her to defy their father's will. So I got stuck writing between them. And that was the least alarming paperwork I had to deal with.

We'd found the evidence against Roseman that the chandler had collected—his neighbors complaints were mostly vague, and all unsigned.

"It's not enough for a judicar," I told Michael. "Much less the High Liege's court."

He didn't look as depressed by this as I thought he should. "Then we shall have to hunt up better evidence."

"Have to? Why?"

Michael said nothing, but his silence was eloquent.

"Fine. Whatever. But I'm *not* going to burgle Roseman's townhouse to get it. You understand that?"

"Of course, Fisk. Whatever you say."

It should have taken him several weeks to figure out an alternate plan, but Michael came up with an idea just three days later—a new record for lunatic schemes. And it didn't involve burglary, so I couldn't object. Much. The only thing that delayed him was the need to wait for the second payment to be collected—and now, time had run out.

I'D BEEN HOPING that the same thugs would come to collect our payment, which might have bought us a few more weeks— though we'd been told they were an "elite" group, who only came when someone gave the Rose trouble. But they might have wanted to show up a second time, make sure I paid.

No such luck.

It was Jack who'd taught me how to deal with bullies without getting the crap kicked out of me, and my act had been too good.

The men—only two—who came through the door two weeks from the day Michael and I had first passed the chandler's shop, were merely slightly tough clerks.

"You have the city tax?" one of them asked.

The other consulted a list and added, "Twelve silver roundels."

"I have it, yes, I do." I fumbled a bit with the cash box, letting them see my hands shake—you have to keep up appearances. "It's not all in silver. I'll have to give you some brass, but the sum is right."

They counted it with a skill that told me I was right about them being more clerks than thugs, roundels, quarts and octs flowing though their fingers with practiced speed.

Then they dropped it into a large purse, checked me off their list and departed. They'd been so professional I almost expected them to give me a receipt, but of course the Rose was too smart for that.

If we wanted evidence, we were going to have to hunt for it—just as Michael had said, curse him.

I went back into the shop, to run over our what-to-do-if-it-all-falls-in-the-crapper plan one more time.

It shouldn't. Michael was more competent than he seemed, and those two had never set eyes on him before.

On the other hand...things had been going way too smoothly.

CHAPTER 7

Michael

The two thugs came out of our shop and went on to the next, with only a glance up and down the street. I was tucked into a narrow gap between two buildings, some distance away, and wearing the drab coat and britches Fisk had found for me. They were most unlikely to see me, lurking in the shadows.

Fisk didn't like my plan. He claimed 'twas too dangerous, that we were moving too fast, and that we didn't know enough. I replied—accurately—that Fisk wouldn't think we knew enough about our mark, even if we'd lived in Roseman's pocket for a year. I then asked if he had a better plan. His lips tightened in irritation, but he turned away without a word. So 'twas my plan we now followed.

I lurked for some time before I had to move on, and might have become bored watching them move slowly from shop to shop—but after a time, outrage seized me.

This was theft. Theft outright, and backed by the threat of violence, as much as any bandit's. But they performed it openly, in broad day, on a busy street, in a good neighborhood. And if those who saw them glanced swiftly away, 'twas more as if they sought to ignore some social embarrassment, like public drunkenness, than daylight robbery.

How had this Roseman managed to corrupt a whole town—the largest city in the Realm—this completely?

His men were so methodical that I waited till they'd turned a corner and gone out of sight before I followed them. I was also able to take my time finding another perch from which to watch, while they collected payment from a cabinet maker.

'Twas only when both their purses were heavy enough to make their belts sag, that they diverted from their pattern, setting off down the street at a brisk walk.

I let them get half a block ahead before going after them, with little fear that anyone would notice me. The outfit Fisk had chosen for this day combined with my scuffed boots to make me look like someone's groom on an errand—a sight so common that no one would look twice. And since Fisk had kept me in the backroom, only going out to make purchases outside our neighborhood, few were familiar with my face.

They turned after another block. And while they kept a cautious eye on those in their vicinity, they never looked back to see if they were being followed at a distance.

This became more understandable when they reached their destination—a treasure cart, its square cab armored with iron bands, its doors and windows barred.

The horse that drew it, a big gray, glowed to my sight even in the sunlit street. In an emergency, a magica cart horse could pull that wagon at a gallop—and it must have cost almost as much as the load it hauled.

Five guards, with swords and daggers on their belts, surrounded the cart. But despite their weaponry, they didn't seem much more alert than the tax collectors. Master Roseman's reputation must be a formidable deterrent.

I had missed luncheon, waiting for the collectors to arrive at our shop, and it had taken them several hours to get this far. I went into a nearby tavern and ordered a sandwich, in case I had to leave in a hurry, and some sweet potato mash that they served spiced, with lots of butter.

I had time to eat my meal, and then linger at the table. When I'd stayed so long I was about to become conspicuous, I went out and found yet another place where I could watch the cart without being seen.

The thugs I'd followed weren't the only ones bringing money to this wagon; I counted eight more pairs of men. Several of them had delivered coins to the collection cart twice, before one of the guards mounted to the driver's seat. He drove the wagon almost a mile before he pulled over and parked, to receive more deliveries.

'Twas an efficient way to deal with coin collected from a large area in a short time. And if every merchant in Tallowsport was paying every two weeks, even if some of them paid less than the chandler, Master Roseman must be unimaginably rich.

It was dusk, and the magica street lamps that made wealthy neighborhoods safer than poor ones were beginning to glow by the time the cart accepted its final purse and rolled away.

The fading light helped me to follow without being noticed, and for the first time since I'd seen the tax collectors start down our block, my heart beat faster.

We had learned where the Rose's town house sat, on top of the rise where the affluent lived. He also had a country estate, not far out of town, and a ship he kept in port for his personal use. What no one seemed to know was where the money went after his men collected it—and that was what would matter to the High Liege. Even if 'twas in some bank, the judicars' accountants had to know which bank to audit.

But the cart passed right by the bank where I thought 'twould stop, and rolled on up the hill to The Rise.

Could Roseman keep his wealth in his own house? If he had thugs enough, and a stout vault, why not?

'Twas harder to be inconspicuous in this neighborhood, but the growing darkness helped. I skirted the pools of light around the lamps, and I was sure none of Roseman's men saw me as they rolled from one patch of brightness into the next.

Then they turned down a side street.

I waited for a slow count of ten, then sprinted to the street and strolled casually across it.

There were no street lamps in this narrower lane, between two high-walled estates. The only light came from the small tan Creature Moon, rising now without its larger companion.

If not for the livid glow of the magica horse, I wouldn't have been certain the cart was still ahead of me. But thanks to Lady Ceciel I was sure, and set off after it.

There was enough light, as my eyes adjusted, to make out the occasional gate set into high stone walls, an alley to my left, a lamp post looming...a lamp post? But it was, its glass case barely visible against the dark sky.

Magica phosphor lamps don't 'go out' unless the moss dries out and dies—or someone removes it. These streetlights had been put out, probably to obscure the presence of Master Roseman's money wagons. One of which was getting ahead of me. I picked up my pace, confident that my soft footfalls would be lost in the creak of cart wheels and the clop of horseshoes on stone.

Hurrying, 'twas harder to avoid pot holes in the street, but I still noticed when the shadowy form of a man stepped out of a recessed gate in front of me. Moonlight gleamed on the blade of a drawn sword.

Grooms on errands in peaceful towns don't wear swords. The largest knife that wouldn't attract attention hung on my belt, but 'twould be no match for a longer weapon. Particularly in the dark, where he could swing for my dim shape and doubtless hit something important to me, while a knife needs more precision to strike effectively.

So I did the sensible thing and turned to run...only to find two more ominous shadows, with swords, behind me.

I knew I was trapped, even before the sword point pricked my back and a calm voice said, "Drop the knife."

I didn't think 'twould work, but Fisk would expect me to try.

"I got a message t' deliver," I said. "I don't want no trouble. Any of you know where twenty-four Seaview Street is?"

I thought my Tallowsport accent was quite passable, but the sword point in my back only pricked harder. "The knife."

Moving slowly, I pulled it from the sheath and cast it aside. Only then did the two men in front of me close in, one to bind my hands behind me, the other to search my person for any other weapons.

"Please, I don't got but a few coins, and you can have 'em. But Mistress is going t' be furious if I don't get her message delivered."

"Don't bother," one of them said. "Or you can go on, if you want, but it won't do any good. The boss has had us out here almost a week, waiting for you. I'd begun to think he was finally going to be wrong about something."

One of the others snickered, perhaps at the thought of the boss being wrong.

But how could he have posted guards to await me a week ago, when I'd only come up with this scheme about four days past? Mayhap they were looking for someone else?

"I think you've mistaken me for someone else." I dropped the accent, since 'twas clearly useless. "What were your orders, exactly?"

"To bring in anyone trying to follow the tax cart," the first speaker told me. "And that's what we're going to do."

And so they did, leading me onward for several blocks before they turned down another dark lane, and then another. I thought about shouting for help, but having seen this town's lack of reaction to a neighbor being beaten in front his own shop, I knew 'twould do no good. I'd lost all sense of direction, but the tall stone wall whose back gate we passed through looked very like the one that surrounded Atherton Roseman's townhouse.

They took me in through the kitchen, and neither the cooks who were kneading dough to rise overnight, nor the scullery maids washing the dishes, seemed surprised to see a prisoner at sword point go past their workplace.

"Where's the boss?" one of the men with me asked.

"Study," a cook replied.

As we entered a well-lit hall, I noted that my captors moved in the strong, lithe way of trained swordsmen—just as you'd expect from men who wore the black and red livery of Roseman's household guard. The rooms we passed held beautiful rugs, paintings, statues and tapestries. But I didn't see the gold- and gem-encrusted opulence I'd expected. 'Twas newer, and less well-worn than the ancient country keep where I'd grown up—but 'twas actually a more tasteful display of wealth than my father's house.

The study, on the second floor, was even more inviting. A pleasant fire warded off the spring chill, bookshelves lined the walls...and all of this welcoming warmth was negated by the man who sat in the great upholstered chair.

The guards hauled me into the room, and pushed me to my knees before him.

The last criminal Fisk and I had dealt with looked like a nervous clerk. Atherton Roseman looked like a thug, even in a brocaded dressing gown, his open shirt collar trimmed with delicate lace. He was big, mayhap taller than I, and nearly twice as broad. Very little of that bulk was fat, either. His hands were blunt and looked as if they should be wielding a shovel, or crushing a man's neck.

He held a thin porcelain cup quite gently, and eyed me with more curiosity than venom.

"You look more like Sevenson than Fisk."

So much for hoping 'twas someone else they sought. It had to be Jack who'd told him, warned him. But it had been over half a year since Master Jack Markham/Bannister/whoever had left us in Huckerston. He had no way of knowing we'd follow him. And the guards said they'd been waiting for me for a week.

"How did you know I was coming?" I asked.

"I know everything," said Roseman. "You've been snooping in my business, Master Sevenson. I don't like snoops."

The threat in his calm voice made words like "death" and "dismemberment" superfluous. But 'twas not right for a knight errant to cower. If I was going to die anyway, be cursed if I'd give him the satisfaction. I raised my head and steadied my voice.

"Others know where I've gone. If I don't come back, my murder will be the first crime you're charged with. Life debts are paid with the noose. You can kill me. I have no doubt you will. But when the law comes, you'll hang for it."

In truth, the law might not avenge an unredeemed man. But no one here had seen the tattoos on my wrists, so I was surprised when Roseman laughed.

"The law's not going to come."

"They will. In the end, law always prevails."

I thought for a moment our discussion would devolve into a childish round of, no they won't, yes they will. Then Master Roseman lifted his massive head.

"Bring him."

I wasn't even surprised when one of my guards went out, and returned moments later dragging Fisk's bound and battered form. He was conscious, but stumbling unsteadily, and the left side of his face was one solid bruise. When the guard released him, he toppled to his knees beside me.

"So," said the Rose. "You still think the law is coming?"

CHAPTER 8

Fisk

Michael looked more pissed at me than at the Rose—a ridiculous nickname for a man who looked like a coal heaver, despite his fancy dressing gown.

"Of all the times to stand and fight," Michael snarled. "Why didn't you run?"

I had to admit, it was a fair question. "What makes you think I didn't try?"

Michael looked a bit less irritated. But then one of the thugs who'd arrived at the shop and demanded I go with them broke in.

"He didn't run. He was buying time for those vicious brats, while they escaped."

Michael was now mollified—but I'd have traded his anger for the sudden interest in Roseman's face.

"That orphan gang? Are you sure it was them?"

"Recognized two of 'em," the man said. "Looked like they was working in the chandlery, though I can't be sure."

"And you let them get away?"

The Rose's voice was mild, but sweat popped out on the thug's brow.

"He put up a real fight, boss. And you know how fast they are. And slippery. They even took a dog with 'em, but they was darting though cracks in fences, and into pipes and—"

The Rose gestured and he fell silent.

"How did you get those little vandals to work for you?" he asked.

"Michael brought them in." I only go with truth when I don't know what else to say, and this was one of those times.

The Rose's heavy regard shifted to Michael, who returned it with more calmness than I felt.

"I simply asked if they wanted a job. But that wouldn't work for you. Do you know why that wouldn't work for you, Master Roseman?"

The scowl that gathered on the Rose's beefy face was so formidable that I was actually glad to see Jack stroll into the room.

He looked the same as he always did, sleek, calm and in control. But he also looked that way when a con was crashing around him, so I didn't take much comfort from it.

"It's not as if they can do you any harm," he told the Rose, confirming that he'd been eavesdropping. Then he turned to me and added, "I got your message."

Jack had always been able to turn gratitude to anger in a heartbeat. I felt Michael's eyes burning into me, without even glancing at him.

"You tried to contact him. That's how they knew I was coming. That's how they knew to go after you. Curse it, Fisk, I told you not to do that!"

I had already realized—when the thugs showed up at the shop—that if I hadn't tried to contact Jack we might not be in this mess.

On the other hand, if Michael had agreed to let Jack go I wouldn't have had to contact him. So I didn't feel all that guilty. This was what came from falling in with Michael's crazy plans. I should have refused. I should have refused to come to Tallowsport at all!

"You're the one who insisted we come here, remember? You were the one who—"

"It would have worked if you hadn't—"

"You shouldn't be too miffed," Jack interrupted Michael's rant. "If he hadn't warned me, you'd both be dead by now."

"That's true." Tony Rose had followed this with the lazy interest of a cat watching mice frolic. "Are you sure I can use them, Jack? They don't seem that bright."

"I know you can use Fisk. As for the other...up to you. But you might take a look at his wrists before you make up your mind."

"Really?" Roseman sounded more interested than dismayed. "No, you don't have to pull up his sleeves. I'll take Jack's word for it. But that's not how I'd have read him."

I wondered how Jack had known about Michael's status— though there were several people who might have told him, back in Huckerston. It was another reminder not to underestimate Jack's ability to gather information. Not that I needed it, just then.

"It doesn't matter," Roseman went on. "I don't rely on other people's judgment—certainly not the judicars'. I judge men by whether or not I can count on them. Can I trust this one, Jack?"

I'd thought it was impossible for my heart to sink any lower. I should have known better.

But Jack hesitated for a moment, and I beat him into speech.

"You won't get any use out of me if Michael's dead."

We'd had this conversation once before, on a rain-swept cliff top—so Jack, at least, would believe I meant it. Because that conversation had ended with a broken gang of wreckers, and him on the run.

"No need for hysterics," Jack said. "And yes, you made that point the last time we met." He turned to Roseman. "You need someone who can run a game, someone your captains won't recognize as a part of your organization. Fisk fits that description. Besides, you appreciate loyalty. Fisk has it, even if it tends to be misdirected."

Michael had been listening to this with considerable interest. "Why do you think either of us would ever help you?"

"Shut up, Michael," I muttered.

"No, really. Master Roseman isn't a fool. He must know we'll turn on him, or at least flee, the moment we get a chance."

"I'm not worried about that," Roseman said. "Because... Here, I might as well show you."

"I'm sure that's not necessary," I said swiftly.

But he rose from his chair with an agility I hadn't expected from such a big man, and walked out of the room. The guards hauled Michael and me after him, which was more than a little inconvenient with ribs as bruised as mine.

Jack brought up the rear, whistling under his breath. I had learned betrayal from Jack, too. So it shouldn't have hurt, this time.

Michael was right. I'd been an idiot.

We climbed the stairs to the third floor, then a ladder to the attic—no small feat, with two bound men, but the guards more or less shoved us up. Michael first, then me.

Usually the lesser servants in a house like this live in the attics. But at the top of the ladder, instead of some housemaid's bleak, neat room, was a magpie's nest, a bandit's legendary lair—or the prop shop of a large theater company.

Half a dozen flaming candelabra cast golden light over swaths of tattered silk, velvet and feathers, and gleamed on broken swords, and in the glass gems strewn over a battered workbench. In fact, this room was mostly a workshop, despite the rumpled bed near the window, and the draughts board, and the giant puppet that dangled from a rafter like a hanged man. Half its strings appeared to be missing.

Roseman looked around. "Come out," he called. "I need work done."

"Too many." I couldn't tell from which shadowy corner the croaking whisper came. "Too many, scaring the rats. Makes my eyes sparkly."

The Rose looked at half a dozen guards, as if they were so common in his life that he'd just noticed their presence.

"Stan and Willet. You stay. And Jack. Everyone else, out."

"But boss..." One of them gestured to Michael.

Roseman snorted richly. "Four of us, against two bound men? I think we can handle them."

Unfortunately, I agreed with him.

The guards departed, and I wondered why the person lurking in the shadows didn't count as a fifth man against us.

Then he stepped out, blinking at the light. His hunched shoulders were wrapped in a shawl, woven out of ribbons in every color imaginable.

At first I took him for an old man. The flyaway, light brown hair might have been gray, the scraggly stubble a sign of senility and neglect. But the face under that wild hair wasn't that of a man much past his thirties. It was his eyes that gave the truth away, darting from place to place, resting for long moments on things that no one else could see.

"Work is a sparrow. Hop hop. Then the snake eats it, and spits the feathers out. Do you want a nice hat? A hat to parade around town, and seduce the ladies?"

Michael's expression was soft with pity. I wondered what we were doing here, with even more dread than I'd felt before.

"I need a pair of collars," said The Rose. "To keep these two from plotting against me. To keep them from even thinking about it."

"Collars? Like I've made before, for the little rats, for the little and the big." The madman nodded to his workbench. "Bright gems, like pretty panther eyes. I can have them for you in just a month."

The Rose frowned. "A month? I need them now."

"Schemes are part of the mind. Of thoughts and prayers and gingersnaps. To make a spell that warns of plotting, I must know them, their dreams, the freckles on their ears. Can't reveal scheming in a day or a week, or maybe even a month. Not for skirts and feathers, not at all, for she's a girl and I don't see in. But not a year, no. The rats wouldn't like that."

Spell? As in human magic?

No one knows whether magic comes to humans who are mad, or makes humans mad when it comes to them—but this ragged lunatic was what Michael feared he might become, if he used the magic Ceciel's potions had given him. I thought that if that was going to happen, it would have done so years ago, but this man's eerie rambling still chilled my blood.

Jack, I noticed, wasn't disturbed by it. And it seemed to make sense to the Rose, which was even more frightening.

"I need it faster than that," he said. "How about collars to stop them from killing me? That blood thing you do for a demonstration, with the rats. It's just a warning system, but if that's all I can get I'll make it work."

"That won't take long, just a sunflower," the madman said. "Only blood is needed for that, no cookie dreams at all."

"Then do it," said the Rose. "But first we'll show them it works." He turned to Michael and I. "This isn't the best he can do, but it will let my men know instantly if either one of you ever kills me. And then they'll kill you. Simple and effective."

I hadn't realized the rats were real, till one of the guards picked up a cage beside the bed and set it on a table near the workbench.

The madman wandered over to the bench, opened a drawer and took out two rat-sized collars, each one studded with a chip of glass.

Atherton Roseman drew on a pair of leather gloves and reached into the cage to extract two squirming rats, which he dumped into a deep kettle on one end of the bench. I could hear them scrabbling for purchase on the slippery metal.

The Rose removed his gloves and held out a hand to the madman. "Do it."

The man sighed. "Might as well only prick you once. Prickory dickory. But not for one of them."

He opened another drawer and brought out two full-sized collars, large enough for a dog twice Trouble's size. They were each inset with a gem so big it had to be glass. They were also unfinished, the leather layers flapping on the ends, no buckle in sight.

I suddenly became very interested in what was about to happen to those rats.

But the first victim was Tony Rose. He held out his hand to his mad henchman, who picked up a knife and made a small cut in the Rose's thumb, then smeared his blood liberally over all four gems.

The Rose sucked the cut, and gestured to one of the guards, who put on the discarded gloves and picked up a rat. Its teeth didn't penetrate the leather, but it wasn't because the rat didn't try. The madman avoided the scrabbling claws by nicking its ropy tail. Rat blood joined Roseman's on the small gems—but not the larger ones.

My thumbs began to feel vulnerable.

Another guard donned another pair of gloves and scooped the second rat out of the kettle. His tail blood joined his friend's.

Then the madman took the small collars in his hands...and held them, doing nothing I could see.

I heard breath hiss into Michael's lungs. He was staring at the madman's hands with utter fascination. And I knew enough about his ability to see magic to guess what he was staring at.

See? I said it could be controlled, if you practiced.

Whether this maker of stylish collars had gotten his magic because of his madness, or been made mad by it, was a question for philosophers. But I was still surprised when— after a considerable struggle to get the collar onto a squirming rat—the blood-stained gem began to glow. Green, oddly enough, beneath the blood.

I looked at the second collar to see if the gem was green glass, mostly because with that much horror prickling up your spine your mind needs distractions.

The stone was too small for me to judge its color, but the one attached to the rat was getting brighter.

"You see that light?" the Rose asked, though everyone in the attic was staring at it. "Those gems are linked now, by blood and magic."

"And life." The creator of the spell wrestled a collar onto the other rat, and the second gem flared like a tiny ember. "Heart beat, blood beat, but don't beat Sally. She's a good girl."

Sally might have been his sister, his lover, or one of the rats, but tears sprang into his eyes.

The Rose shrugged. "Take it as far away as you can, in this room."

The guard promptly carried his rat to a corner, the green light winking like a firefly as it struggled.

Then the Rose gestured, and the other guard pressed the nearest rat flat on the bench. His boss picked up a knife. "Look at the gem on the other one's collar."

Since I had no desire to watch even a rat die, I did so—and wasn't really surprised when I heard the knife blade hit wood, and the gem on the distant rat's collar went dark. I was more surprised, and all things considered, relieved, when the guard came back with the distant rat still alive and wiggling in his grasp.

The madman snipped its collar off, and cast the limp leather strip into a waste bin at the end of the bench. The guard returned the living rat to its cage—seemingly none the worse for its blood-brother's demise.

I wondered if I could get that discarded collar into Michael's hands, and whether it would help if I did. Because we were surely going to need magic to get out of this.

"We've tested those collars at a distance over sixty miles," Tony Rose told us. "When any member of the blood bond kills another, the light in both stones goes out. Doesn't matter how far apart they are. Or who kills who. Whom?"

"Whom," I confirmed. The mad jeweler went behind me, and grasped one of my bound hands. I managed not to wince at the cut, at the feel of my bleeding thumb sliding over leather and smooth glass. "But it's only if Michael or I kill you that the gems go out, right? I'd hate to die because another of your enemies got lucky."

"Oh, I'm not that unreasonable," said the Rose. "If someone else scrags me, your gems will go right on glowing. And you live."

"It can't be made to work the other way," the madman said. "I tried and tried, not lied and lied. Has to be one of the bond who does the—"

Roseman's big hand lifted and slapped him, so hard the madman fell sprawling at his master's feet. Evidently we weren't supposed to know there was anything beyond his or his master's ability. He cowered for a moment, then looked up at the Rose and began to laugh.

Tony Rose laughed with him.

Michael looked away, as if from some obscenity.

I watched, wondering if the lunatic might be turned. If anyone could undo this binding, it was him.

"But when you killed the rat, making the stones go dark, it didn't kill the other rat," Michael pointed out.

"Well, technically, it's not the collars that keep you from killing me." Roseman sounded quite affable about it. "It's my orders to your guards that if they ever see those stones go dark, they're to kill you instantly, no questions asked. That's what will keep you from trying anything... unwise."

The mad jeweler had gone behind Michael now, collecting his blood. We stood in silence as he held the collars and gazed at them—though all I could see was a ragged man, looking at two leather bands. But when he stood, took a needle and thread from the bench, and laid the collar around Michael's throat, the gem began to glow—not green this time, but pale gold. This stone was large enough that I could see small sparks drifting inside it, like bubbles in sparkling wine. Indisputably magic, human magic, for all to see.

And for Roseman's men to see. If either Michael or I killed Roseman, the stones in both our collars would go dark. And assuming Roseman's men would obey his orders after he was dead—which, I noted, Roseman didn't seem to doubt—they'd promptly kill us to avenge their master. If we were ever alone with Roseman, in a place where we could flee together afterward, the stones going dark wouldn't matter...which guaranteed that Roseman would never allow us, unguarded, into his presence.

But there was some hope. I made a mental note to turn the stone out of sight when I went out. Because all these eerie, elaborate precautions indicated that at least one of us would be allowed to go out, at some point, alone. Which also, not incidentally, meant we were going to live. Unless we did something stupid. Which I wasn't going to, though I wouldn't have put it past Michael.

"What if we both run off?" he asked, proving my point. "Or what if one of us runs away without the other? Or cuts the collar off?"

The madman was doing a neat job of stitching the collar closed on his neck.

"The moment that collar leaves your body the stones stop glowing," Roseman said. "But if you both managed to escape at the same time, you could run off, cut the collars, and that would be that."

I noticed that he didn't sound particularly worried.

"But if just one of you gets away...well, without a hostage I couldn't trust the other, could I?"

He didn't need to expand on this point.

"As it is," he went on, "you'll work for me as long as those gems keep glowing. If you work well, they'll keep glowing. If either of you tries to run, or fails me, I'll kill you. And when the other's stone goes out, my men will kill him. And yes, there are ways you could arrange to escape at the exact same time," he continued, answering my thoughts. "But that kind of timing takes a lot of planning—and I'm not going to give you the chance."

With a sinking heart, I watched the madman tie off his thread and cut it, finishing with Michael's collar.

"Take him away," Roseman told the guards.

Michael was foolish enough to struggle, and got tossed down the ladder for his pains. I didn't hear any bones snap and, judging by his furious curses as they hauled him off, he hadn't broken anything important.

The jeweler came up and slipped the second collar around my neck, the leather smooth and stiff. My mouth was so dry I had to swallow before I spoke.

"I'll have to be allowed to see that he's alive and well treated. At regular intervals. Or I might begin to believe that he isn't."

"The collar will tell you he's alive," Roseman said. "Or at least, if one of your guards stares at your throat and then pulls a knife and kills you, you'll know he isn't. As for seeing him, that's going to be tricky. I'm sending him to my country estate."

So much for sneaking down to Michael's cell at midnight to drop a note through the bars. The madman's hands, stitching my collar closed, were dry and deft. And it wasn't too small. It was only in my imagination that it was getting tighter and tighter around my throat.

"I want to see him once a week, at least. I've only got your word for how these collars work."

The Rose gazed at me for a long moment. "I might allow that. If you can earn it. But I don't advise you to assume I'm lying about those gems. I really don't."

"Fisk's too smart to do something that stupid." Jack hadn't turned a hair as all this went on. "He's just wiggling in the trap. But you won't find a way to twist out of this one, lad. So you might as well get over it, and get on with it. Tony's promised me that after this first job, if you work out, he'll put you on salary. There are bonuses for successful jobs, too. Like I've been trying to tell you, this is good work!"

How well I remembered that exasperated tone.

"He could still abandon his friend and run," The Rose pointed out. "I'm not trusting him with anything serious. Not till I'm sure of him."

"Fisk won't leave anyone to die. Much less a friend. He's soft." Jack's lips curled with contempt. "That's why I had to dump him."

That wasn't why Jack dumped me. But...

"He's right," I told Roseman. "If you've got Michael as a hostage, you've got me."

CHAPTER 9

Michael

Riding into Tallowsport on the River Road, at the slow pace of the food train, took a full day. Riding out toward the north, on the Hillboro Road, we reached Roseman's country house in just seven hours.

The guards, four of them, kept my hands bound till we left the city. Once we were out on the country roads—and they were certain there'd been time to stitch Fisk's collar into place—they turned the reins over to me.

The Green Moon was riding high and nearly full, the half-full Creature Moon setting. In this flat open land, 'twas light enough I could have kicked my horse to a gallop and fled. I might even have eluded their pursuit.

But without me as a hostage, they'd kill Fisk. Riding on a sound horse, with my captors not even paying much attention, I was as tightly bound as I'd ever been in my life.

Though I was so furious with Fisk for warning Jack Bannister, that I was almost... No, I wasn't tempted to consider fleeing. But of all the lame-brained, idiotic, futile... And he claimed *I* was too trusting!

If it did nothing else, my fuming passed the time.

'Twas after midnight when we passed through the gates, set in a tall stone wall, and rode up the long drive. Rose Manor was larger than the townhouse, newer, and even more richly furnished—but still with a restrained good taste the High Liege's decorators would have approved.

I didn't see much of the house that night, however. Half a dozen servants, clad in their night robes, came to answer my guards' thunderous knocking. They glanced curiously at the collar around my throat, but the eerie sparkle of the gem occasioned no comment. I was not the first hostage Roseman had sent here.

Inside the house the guards went off to their own quarters, and 'twas a footman who showed me to my bed—not in some noisome cell, but in an ordinary guest room on the third floor. He bade me a polite "Good night."

I sat on the bed and listened to the sound of his retreating footsteps. I expected to hear the approaching footsteps of a guard, who would surely come to watch my door. But I heard nothing.

After a time I went to peer up and down the corridor. No guard. The lamps had been turned low, but I could see that no one stood watch at the top of the great staircase. Even if the front door was locked, the ground floor windows probably opened with a simple latch.

I went over to my window, turned the latch, and swung the glass panes inward with no more effort than 'twould take to open a window in my bedroom at the chandlery.

I hoped Hannibas would take care of the shop. I knew the orphans would take good care of True. Though Fisk, ever practical, had told them that if they had to flee, and couldn't feed him, they were to take the dog to our old landlady, and tell her we'd settle for his care when we returned for the horses.

If we returned for the horses.

Looking out, I could see that the wall surrounded the grounds, though it was several feet lower in back. I could have climbed it without much trouble. But the place was not completely unsecured, for a guard came strolling across the lawn in what looked like an accustomed patrol. He was so unconcerned by the presence of a prisoner that he didn't even bother to look up, to see me watching him.

Were they so sure of these collars? I was a good enough woodsman to slip out of a downstairs window, and creep from shadow to shadow till I escaped the grounds. But I'd not be able to reach Atherton Roseman's townhouse in time to free Fisk before my escape was reported.

Even if I waited till tomorrow, set out as early as I dared, and got lucky and found a horse I could steal—'twould still be past dawn when I reached the city, and they'd get word of my escape near noon. Not enough time to plan and execute a jail break, unless we were both fiendishly lucky. And angry though I was, I wasn't about to bet Fisk's life on that kind of luck.

So I closed the window and went to bed, hoping tomorrow would bring something that offered a better chance of success.

THE FIRST THING I sought in the morning was breakfast, for I'd missed last night's dinner and was hungry enough to eat even jail food.

Instead of that, another footman directed me to the dining room. Master Roseman's thugs were breaking their fast at one end of the long table, and a young woman, a few years older than me with rich brown hair braided about the crown of her head, sat alone at the other end.

She wore a leather collar, studded with a pale blue gem that glowed in a way that was rapidly becoming familiar.

My heart began to pound, and my appetite vanished. But if I wanted to talk to her, 'twas best to appear casual. I gathered a plate of pastry, coddled eggs and ham, poured myself a cup of tea, and seated myself at the lady's side.

My shirt collar was open, so she'd already seen that I was in the same straits as she. When I ventured a "Good morning," her lips twisted in an expression that was nothing like a smile.

"You don't have to be circumspect, sir. They'd not care if you pulled me into the hall for a private chat right now. They know they have us."

Thin fingers rose to touch the collar around her neck, a gesture I had seen before.

"Your...husband? is the captain of the High Liege's guard, isn't he?"

Her eyes flew wide. "How did you know? Is he... That beast hasn't... He can't be dead, or I would be too."

"No, don't be alarmed. I chanced to meet him, that's all, some time before I encountered Master Roseman. He'd turned his gem to the back, but..." I touched my own collar lightly, though I was already coming to hate the thing. "'Tis an unusual ornament, and I noticed."

"Did he appear well?" Her hands clenched on her napkin.

"Yes, though I thought him a trifle brusque with my request. Haven't you seen him recently?"

How long had Roseman been holding her here?

"We're allowed to meet once a month," she said. "For an hour. Sometimes longer, if Gervase has been 'behaving.'"

"Well, now I understand why he brushed off my complaints of corruption in the town. I was surprised at that, in a servant of the High Liege."

I dropped a spoonful of honey in my tea and stirred, hoping a more conversational tone might let her relax, for she was strung as taut as a lute. Small wonder, with her very life dependant on her distant husband's "good behavior."

This time, her smile seemed more real.

"The Liege had heard rumors of corruption in Tallowsport. He sent Gervase because he was certain of his honor and his loyalty. Along with a senior judicar, to look into the matter. When the judicar met with an 'accident,' the Liege believed Gervase' report that it *was* an accident. Because he trusted him." Her lips tightened. "We had only been married for a year."

What had it cost a trusted man to choose between love and honor? I had no blame for his decision, for there was a lady—now traveling with a troupe of players in the northern parts of the Realm—who was...now my dear cousin, and nothing more.

But that had been her choice, freely made—not a criminal's use of extortion and magic.

"Are we the only people here, besides Roseman's guards and servants?"

"Yes, though he brings house parties, sometimes. In spring and summer for horse racing, and hunting parties in the fall. He's usually doing business with his guests, as well. I'm expected to stay out of their way."

"How long have you been here?" I asked.

"Almost two years." She took a sip of tea, and I noticed that she hadn't even tasted the meager slice of toast on her plate.

"'Tis a long time." I looked up the table to where Roseman's thugs ate their breakfast, ignoring us. "You haven't gotten to know any of your guards?"

"I tried at first," she said. "But the Rose's men are as loyal as he claims. He pays well, and he chooses them well too. I didn't find one I could bribe. And my husband's visit that month was cancelled."

It sounded like a small thing, unless you saw her mouth tremble.

"Roseman will pay for his cruelty," I promised her. To her, and the orphans, too. "For all the evil he's wrought, for all his victims."

And if that meant Fisk must grieve for Jack Bannister, so be it. None who served the Rose were innocent.

"Then I hope you brought an army," she said. "And that you don't care much for your...wife, mayhap?"

"Not a wife. Fisk is my friend..."

I hesitated, for I didn't wish to have this woman who needed an ally so badly think me a lunatic. But it had never been more true than at this moment.

"Fisk is my friend, and my squire," I finished firmly. "I'm a knight errant, in search of adventure and good deeds."

Her jaw dropped and she shrank from me, as anyone might from a stranger who made so ludicrous a claim. But then her eyes met mine, searching. I know not what she found, but her whole face brightened as she laughed. And for the first time, I saw why a man might love this woman more than honor.

"Then good luck to you, sir knight. I'm afraid you'll need it."

"My name is Michael." And since I had observed her eyes as well, I added gently. "I couldn't help but notice...do they drug you?"

Those dilated eyes flashed up, and a bit of color warmed her pale cheeks.

"No. Not the way you mean. I don't have the right disposition for a prisoner, I'm afraid. These last few years, I've had a hard time sleeping. Master Roseman is generous enough to provide me with a sedative. Well, my husband insisted, because after a while I was falling apart." She took another sip of tea. "The effects linger, in the morning. By luncheon I'll be fine."

She might also be addicted to laudanum for the rest of her life—yet another hold the Rose would have on her and her spouse.

Generous be hanged.

"My mother is a skilled herb talker," I said, using the country phrase for those who know how to safely harvest and brew magica plants. "She taught me a great deal. Mayhap I can make you a tisane that will let you sleep without so many side effects."

She was so fearful, so unhappy. Without even thinking, I sent a wave of calmness surging through my animal handling gift...and felt the lid slide off the bright pool of magic, which ever since I drank Lady Ceciel's potions has lived somewhere inside me.

Or mayhap 'twas always there, and her potions just uncovered it. Whatever the case, I saw the tense muscles in my new friend's neck relax for the first time since I'd met her.

"I'm Lianna," she said. "And if you could brew something else to help me sleep, I'd appreciate it. Master Roseman's potion works, but it makes me dizzy and I feel so...heavy in the morning."

I had a notion that I could push my gift further, with magic and will, and she'd grant me the trust I needed then and there. But if I did that, I wouldn't deserve her trust. I willed the lid that covered my magic shut. And if part of me was sorry for it, as some of her tension returned, I knew I'd done her nothing but good.

Surely such small bits of magic as this, which I'd been using on and off for months, wouldn't drive me as mad as that poor jeweler.

"You don't believe I'm going to stop the Rose," I said. "There's no reason you should. But we're going to help you, my squire and I."

Which meant I'd best find some way to communicate with Fisk, for I had no doubt he was plotting and scheming just as I was. And the way our luck was running, I'd put high odds on each of our schemes foiling the other if we couldn't coordinate them.

That was what the Rose was counting on, after all. But I know full well that betting against Fisk's cleverness is a serious mistake.

CHAPTER 10

Fisk

No guard was set on my door that night—which told me that even if I escaped, Michael was out of my reach.

And looking out my window at the guards who patrolled the grounds all night, just getting myself out of the house might be tricky. Tony Rose appeared to have an unlimited supply of guardsmen, and I wondered what they were there to protect. We hadn't found out where he kept his money. But the thought of lifting a bit of that vast fortune had barely passed through my mind before I rejected it. Which tells you what a tight spot we were in.

On awakening, I opened my shirt collar to make sure the glowing stone was visible, and then went down to the kitchen to ask about breakfast. None of them followed me, but every guard I passed looked at my throat.

By the time I reached the kitchen my appetite was fading. It all but vanished, when the cooks told me I was to join "the boss" for breakfast.

I followed a tray of jam-filled pastries up the stairs to, not a dining room, but to Tony Rose's office. Unlike the carefully staged study, this was a room where work was done. The massive desk was covered with correspondence, bills of lading, and what looked like the text of a city ordinance. Several changes had been marked in the margins.

The boss was working as he ate, his plate on top of a stack of letters. Jack was still in attendance, and so was another man, with the rugged face and wiry build of a dock worker. His worn leather vest and boots resembled that of the guardsmen, but despite the scars across his knuckles his hands were stained with ink, and he'd abandoned his own plate to take notes for his employer.

Roseman waved me toward half a dozen trays that sat on a chart table, which was almost as cluttered as the desk so the trays rested on scattered city maps, books, and more loose papers.

I picked up a plain pastry and a cup of tea, and listened till the Rose finished giving orders for the food trains to purchase fifty more oxen, and arranged to meet with a rope maker to see if the man could justify the price he was charging for cordage.

The rope maker would no doubt be charging less by the interview's end.

I expected the secretary to rise and leave when he finished making notes, but he put down the pen and reached for his cooling plate.

The Rose pointed to a chair, and I sat.

"This is Ugg Wiederman." He nodded to the stranger, whose mouth was full. "He's in charge of my operations here in the city, just like Jack's in charge of operations outside. First, you take my orders. Second, you take theirs. Got it?"

Jack had said he was "an expediter" for his employer. No wonder he'd felt free to offer me a job.

"Suppose their orders contradict each other?" I asked. If the one who wasn't top dog resented it, rubbing a little salt in that wound might be useful.

"Then you'll take Jack's orders. Your job is at the port, but it deals with outside operations. So Jack's in charge of you."

"Will he be punished if I fail? What a tempting thought."

Jack grinned at me, and for a moment years and betrayal all fell away. I'd forgotten that rare, open grin.

"Jack's not the one who's hostage for your good behavior." Roseman eyed me critically. "I don't mind smart-ass cracks, as long as they amuse me. When I stop being amused..."

I nodded and took a bite of pastry, mostly to show him I wasn't intimidated. My throat was so dry I had to wash it down with a sip of tea.

"So, what is my job?"

Tony Rose was still staring at me, in a way that was cursed unnerving.

"Some of my ship captains are spending more money than they're making," he said finally. The fact that he knew that much about his employees was a warning in itself. "I think they're skimming. Not on the cargoes—I've got clerks with them who keep track of that. But the captains dispose of smaller items for me, in sales that don't usually have receipts. You know what I mean?"

He meant loot from people like the wrecking gang who had sunk so many ships in Keelsbane Bay. Loot from bandits, burglars, and other criminals all over the south coast. Maybe the whole United Realm.

My estimate of the Rose's fortune grew yet again. Knowing that the goods you stole will never be traced back to you is worth a considerable cut of the take.

"Have you sent a clerk to audit their ledgers?" I asked.

"Not yet," said the Rose. "Because I don't employ idiots. They're going to have a second set of ledgers for those transactions—or if they're really smart, no records at all. Skim a bit of profit off the top, tell me they got the best deal they could, and put what they're giving me down in the books. Just a bit of extra coin in their purse, that's all. Though the way some of them are spending, it's more than a bit."

"That's an amateur's mistake," I said. "They should spend it in other ports. Or better, bank it in some other city, under another name, and leave it untouched till they're ready to quit and claim it."

"Yeah, well, they're ship captains," said Tony Rose. "At scamming, they are amateurs. Which is where you come in."

Because I wasn't.

"You want me to find their real ledgers? Assuming they kept them."

"I'm assuming they didn't keep records," the Rose said. "They may be amateurs, but I don't hire fools. I want you to go in as a clerk, new to my employ, running a standard audit. I audit people all the time, so they won't find that suspicious. When you find something wrong in the ledgers—every ledger has something off in it, even if they're honest—I want you to make a big deal out of how you'll report it, and what I do to men who cheat me."

"Ah." The light dawned. "You want them to bribe me."

"Accomplishes two things," said the Rose. "If they come to me and report you, I'll be pretty sure they're honest after all. If they don't, that means they have something to hide."

I thought that even an honest man might not want to bet on the Rose's mercy—but this was one of those times when a smart crack wouldn't be wise.

"If they don't report you," the Rose went on, "once you've taken their bribe you can work your way into their organization. Demand to know what's going on, tell them you can help them get better deals in several ports, offer—"

"I know how to work my way in," I said. "When I know the whole set up, everyone involved, then I report back to you?"

It wasn't a bad scheme. I bet I knew who'd come up with it, even if Roseman thought it was all his own idea.

"You'll tell them you're new to Tallowsport," Jack added, confirming my suspicion. "That I brought you in from the outside. Because no one Master Roseman hires would ever take bribes."

He even kept his face straight when he said it.

Unfortunately, the Rose was watching mine. "That's true, even if you don't believe it. I'm loyal to my people, and I *demand* their loyalty in return. If they're not..."

I was actually glad he chose not to finish that sentence.

"What about your shackle?" I reached up to touch my collar. "It kills the image of trusted clerk, don't you think?"

"Turn the stone to the back and keep your jacket on," Roseman said. "It won't show through thick cloth."

I wondered how he knew that, but he was probably right so I went on, "If I do this, if I find out who's cheating you and how, is there any chance you'll let Michael and me go?"

"Not yet," said the Rose. "But you'll go on breathing. And if you do a good job on this, next time you'll get a bonus."

I took a deep breath and made up my mind. I was going to get us out of this. Somehow, I was going to get both Michael and myself out of this, and bring Atherton Roseman to his knees.

Though how I was going to do it, without taking Jack down too, escaped me.

"All right," I said. "It'll take me a while to study your ledgers, but once I—"

"What?" Roseman asked.

I gave him my best look of mild surprise, the one even Jack had never seen through.

"How can I spot discrepancies in their ledgers if I haven't seen yours first? And it has to be your real ledger, with accounts of everything they're involved with. Or I won't be able to recognize a problem when I see it."

Yet another thing Jack had taught me was how to forge a ledger.

"Pox," said Tony Rose. "You're right."

His eyes turned to Jack.

"Can I trust him not to be stupid about this?"

"As long as you've got your hostage, yes," Jack said. "But you'll have to keep guards on Fisk, and they need to be smart. Not tough. Fisk's no killer."

The word "soft" hovered in the air between us.

"I'll see to the guards." Wiederman had finished his breakfast as we spoke. "I've got plenty who are smart *and* tough."

The boss shrugged and rose to his feet, but instead of going to the shelves near the table, which appeared to be filled with ledgers, he unlocked a door on one side of the room and went in. I wondered if that room had another door that opened onto the corridor, or if this was the only way in. Either way, a locked second office, when you already have a perfectly good unlocked one, implies something interesting inside. Unfortunately, Jack knows me well.

"It's better guarded than it looks. That lock and key are magica, courtesy of Tony's tame madman. You could try to pick it for years and you'd always fail. I tested it for him."

That ended my newly hatched plan for tonight's entertainment—Jack's a better hand at locks than I, though he can't pick pockets at all.

Roseman emerged with an armload of big, leather-bound books. He had to jostle them into one arm to relock the door, and watching him go through those awkward steps confirmed that Jack had probably told the truth about the lock...and that there was something worth seeing beyond it.

No one had only one key, for an important lock. And I could guess where he kept the backup.

Roseman handed the ledgers to a guard. "Take him to the study; he can work there. You don't leave him alone, you don't leave these books alone, and you don't leave him alone with the books. Aside from that, get him anything he needs."

This might have sounded contradictory, if I hadn't known my warden could pick up more guards on our way down the hall.

I wouldn't mind being watched while I worked...all right, it was going to drive me half mad having them all standing around staring at me, but that didn't matter. I didn't intend to do anything to the books, to do anything at all, until I managed to contact Michael. Tony Rose was a smart, cautious man, and the safest and smartest place to keep another magica key would be out of town, in his country house. But more urgent even than that, I had to get in touch with Michael to make sure that my plan—once I had a plan—and whatever lunatic scheme he was hatching didn't trip each other up.

I have learned, over the years, that it's a really bad idea to underestimate Michael's craziness.

CHAPTER 11

Michael

I had been at the estate for three days when Atherton Roseman arrived. When the carriage with the rose crest on its door rolled through the gate, surrounded by a ridiculous number of guards, I was on my knees in the mud.

I'd spent most of those days looking for magica plants. Finding magica is easy for me, since they actually glow to my sight. Ordinary herb talkers must start by looking for plants that grow in the perfect shape for their species, that neither bugs nor grazing animals will touch. Only when they draw very near, will their sensing gift reveal the palm-prickling presence of magic.

I didn't have to look so closely, but there was still the difficulty of finding sleep-inducing plants growing in early Grassan.

Another thing my search taught me was that as long as I stayed inside the wall that surrounded the formal grounds, I could wander at will. But if I let myself out the gate into the wilder part of the estate or its attached farm fields, soon one of the guards would come after me. He wouldn't try to stop me. Wouldn't even approach to see what I was doing. But he'd follow me up hill and down dale, letting me see that if I should vanish, a message would shortly be on its way to Master Roseman.

Fortunately, I'd found a patch of magica chamomile sprouting early in a sunny corner of the kitchen herb garden. The glow around the new sprouts told me that the dried blossoms from the previous summer would possess the magic I needed—and the gardeners and cooks must have been warned of its nature, for a wire mesh prevented unwary hands from plucking it.

It had taken me the better part of the previous day to make the leaf and moss mulch that chamomile prefers for its sacrifice, and the season was early enough that I could churn it into the whole herb bed. I carried the buckets to water it in with my own hands, and those same hands were carefully plucking the dried blossoms when I saw Roseman's traveling caravan coming up the drive.

Harvesting magica isn't a task to leave half-finished, but I picked the rest of the chamomile quickly, then hurried in the back door and up a flight of servants' stairs. I was just in time to look down into the entry, as the Rose and his guards rolled into the house like an avalanche.

Most of the upper servants were there to greet him. Hovering in the shadows, I should have been unnoticed, but his gaze was sharper than I'd expected.

"Master Sevenson." He took in the bundle of greenery in my hands, and my muddy boots and britches. "I'd not have taken you for the gardening type. It's a good thing I brought your clothes along. I expect to see you at dinner."

He turned back to the housekeeper after giving me my orders, and I wondered how he'd come by clothing for me.

But magica must be attended to promptly, so I went to the still room, crushed my dried blooms properly, and then set a kettle on to boil. Only when I'd poured hot water over the strainer, and left the first batch to cool and steep, did I return to my room to find my own pack sitting on my bed. It contained all the possessions I'd left at the chandler's shop, except my sword.

After so many years of traveling, even my best clothing wasn't up to the standards of a man as wealthy as Atherton Roseman—but I'd no desire to please him, anyway.

ONLY ONE END of the long table had been set with plates tonight. Just four, so it appeared that the guardsmen didn't dine in state when the boss was here.

Roseman was already seated at the head of the table, with a rough-looking man I'd never seen before at his right hand.

Mistress Lianna, eyes on her plate like a shy schoolgirl, sat on his left. I'd have liked to sit beside her, to lend the poor woman some support, but the last plate had been laid to the stranger's right.

Roseman glanced at my worn, brown velvet coat. "If that's the best you can do, it's just as well you'll be gone when my guests arrive."

"You're throwing a party?" I refused to give him the satisfaction of asking where I was going.

Lianna's eyes flashed to me in alarm, but I had no assurance to offer her. If Roseman wanted me gone, I'd have to go.

"Yes, I have several guests coming," said Roseman. "The first race of the year is week after next, and they were curious to see how my horses are shaping up. Mistress Dalton here will make herself scarce. But as for you, I've found something you can do for me after all. When Fisk sent for your clothes, his note told the shop boy to keep the place running, and to hire some men who wouldn't run off on him this time. Which made me wonder, how did you come to hire that savage brat pack?"

If it was only me, I'd have risked keeping silent to protect the orphan's hiding place. But Fisk's life was now bound to mine, and he might not be willing to take that risk. He wasn't even willing to sacrifice Jack. On the other hand, one of Fisk's rules is to tell an enemy nothing you don't have to, so I might get away with a small lie.

"They'd heard that your men were driving the chandler out, and came to see if they could help him and his family escape," I said. "The chandler's workers had fled, and the children needed the money. I found them good workers, myself. Very bright and determined."

Pricking at this man would likely do no good—but I couldn't see it would do any harm, either.

The servants brought in the soup as I spoke, but Roseman never took his eyes off me.

"For the honest man I judge you to be, you're not a bad liar. If I didn't have a report from the men who chased you into that alley, I might have believed you."

There seemed to be nothing to say to that.

"I think that's close to the truth, anyway," Roseman went on. "I think they did see my men, and decided to help—not the chandler, but you. They've done it before, you know. Interfering in my business, vandalizing my cargoes, meddling with my collectors."

"Bright and determined," I repeated. "Good for them. But I don't see how I can help you. Or why I should."

"You should," said the Rose, "because even though your friend is working out so far, he'd go right on—maybe even work better—if I break one of your legs."

'Twas not thought of the pain that made my blood run cold, but the thought of how such an injury would demolish any escape plan. Roseman knew it, of course. The grin that spread over his face made Mistress Lianna shudder.

I took a spoonful of soup, though I've no memory of how it tasted. "What do you think I can do for you?"

"I've actually considered burning down that warehouse," the Rose said. "That's how obnoxious those feral little gnats have been. But a blaze big enough to destroy the warehouse might spread to the docks. When I send my men in the front door, even if there are others guarding the side doors, it's always empty. They're slipping out some hole, like the rats they are. A hole into that alley where you 'vanished,' Master Sevenson. You're going to show my men where it is, and then you'll go around to the front door and distract the brats while my men go in the back."

I could try to stall him for a time, tell a few lies…but as long as he held Fisk's life in his hands, I had no choice.

'Twas Jack Bannister who taught Fisk that when you can't refuse, you should play along and find a way to escape the snare later. Fisk had passed this wisdom on to me, and I planned to take some pleasure relating that to both Jack and the Rose one day... Assuming that I *could* find my way out of the snare.

At the moment, Roseman's thugs and I were about to enter the alley behind the warehouse, and I still hadn't thought of anything.

I'd had no chance to contact Fisk. The stranger, a Master Wiederman, had pointed out to Roseman that keeping me apart from Fisk was important. So the thugs who escorted me into town got us rooms at a tavern near the docks, and kept close watch on me. They'd roused me well before dawn, and the eastern sky was just beginning to brighten as we arrived at the warehouse, leaving three men to guard the big double doors at its front. 'Twas likely the children were asleep inside, just as they hoped.

That, at least, was something I could change.

"I don't think this is going to work," I lied, as we turned into the alley. "I bet these children have many different places where they live and hide. They know you've captured me, and that I know about this one. They've probably gone elsewhere."

"Shhh," said Tossman, the thug in charge. "They might hear you."

So they might.

"But even if they've gone elsewhere, I bet they still have guards here." My voice was only a bit louder than it had been, but Tossman's scowl darkened. The eight men who tip-toed beside us stirred uneasily.

"And if they set a trap..." I raised my voice a bit more. "...I bet they set it right here in the alley. We should watch—"

"Keep it down!" Tossman's whisper wasn't much softer than my first comment, and I fought back a grin.

"But if they're setting a trap for us, we'll never see it in this light. We ought to come back after sunrise." My voice was almost loud, now. I inched forward, trying to position the tottering stack of broken crates behind me. "We should come back when it's light, or we might fall into—"

I saw him start to swing, and it took all my self-control not to duck. I'd thought to aim my staggering fall backward into the crates, but his fist hit my jaw with a force that wiped out thought.

A hard hand dug into my arm, the cobbles smacked my rump, and lights like a bonfire's sparks swam before my eyes. My hearing came back first—a series of rattling crashes, and Tossman cursing furiously. 'Twas almost as loud as I'd hoped, but the wood didn't seem to be crashing around me.

My vision slowly returned. One of the other thugs was extracting himself from the remaining crates. "I didn't want him falling into them," he was saying. "It'd make too much noise." Another crate toppled as he spoke, knocking into the building's wall on the bounce.

The man who'd stopped me from falling into the pile hauled me to my feet, and I swayed as the world tilted around me. My jaw hurt even worse when I grinned.

Tossman was beginning to repeat himself, so he finally stopped swearing and took a deep breath.

"Show me how they got you out of this alley. Now." His expression made further threats unnecessary. And he hadn't bothered to lower his voice.

I'd given them all the warning I could.

I led Roseman's thugs down the alley, dragged the bin aside—noisily—and showed them the loose board behind it.

Tossman eyed it, no doubt considering how easy 'twould be for even a child to hit someone's head with a club as they wiggled through the opening. I wasn't surprised when his gaze turned to me—though 'twould be just as easy for me to hit someone over the head after I'd crawled through. He reached out and pulled my collar around so the glowing gem showed, then nodded curtly.

"No point trying to surprise them now. So we're going to forget about fancy plans and just go in and kill them. And since Sevenson was the one who warned them, he gets to go first."

I half expected to be struck down as I squirmed through the narrow gap, but no club descended. Early morning light had begun to seep through the cracks in the walls and roof, showing me nests of blankets scattered over the floor. We had surprised them. There was no sound in the warehouse, except for thumps and grunts as Roseman's men pulled themselves in after me.

I wasn't fooled into thinking the orphans had gone, however. The silence from the shadows between the tall piles of crates was not that of emptiness, but of waiting.

I knew some of these children, and I liked them, but my skin was crawling by the time the last of the thugs had joined me.

I had no scorn for the wary looks the others cast into the dim passages between the stacks—even though they had clubs, and knives drawn.

"We stick together," said Tossman. "This way."

He led them down the central aisle, past several stacks, then plunged abruptly into one of the dark corridors between them. After a startled moment, his men rushed after.

I hesitated, but if they should catch one of the children, I could do nothing to hinder them out here. I followed them in, around the mostly square pile of crates, kegs and bundles, and out on the other side. We stepped into the central corridor again, a bit breathless, with nothing to show for our detour.

Tossman glared around him.

"I told you," I said. "No one home."

"Piss on you," Tossman said.

A chorus of ghostly giggles proved me wrong. The thugs spun, searching for the source of the sound, weapons raised. But they also stepped closer together.

"They's hiding up in the crates," one of the thugs said. "We'll never catch 'em up there."

Even a grown man, climbing a tottering stack of boxes, could be brought down by a crate pushed down on top of him, or a small hand reaching out to grab his ankle.

Tossman turned and started toward the center of the warehouse.

"Soon as we see one of 'em, we'll surround the stack he's on. Then we'll unload the crates till we nab him."

Those towering piles of cargo had been assembled using the blocks and tackle that dangled from the rafters above them—a labor that usually took at least four men, two to pull on the lifting rope, and another two on the pile to maneuver the crates. Which left only four men to "surround" them. But 'twas not my expedition, so I held my peace. If they were wise, the children would never even show—

'Twas at just that moment a girl with tangled dark hair stood up on a keg, and hurled half a brick at us. It struck the man next to Tossman on the shoulder, but any sound he made was lost in the others' shouts as they rushed to the girl's pile and started around it...and a hail of stones erupted from the other side of the corridor.

One hit my back, and another my knee. Children they might be, but they threw cursed hard! They'd the advantage of height, too, as they proved when the thugs swarmed toward the stack that held them, and started to climb.

Several were knocked down by stones that struck their heads and faces. The rest were half-way up the pile when a second hail of stones flew from the crates on the other side of the warehouse.

'Twas hard to dodge, stranded on a pile of crates, and more men fell. No doubt adding to their bruises as they bounced down the stack. Blood streamed down several faces, four more men were limping, and another clutched an arm that looked to be broken. And still children popped out of crevasses between the crates to send stones flying in among us. I dodged one that might have cracked my head, and was struck in the back once more.

But since I'd not been climbing up with the others, not many stones were aimed at me.

"Out of this," Tossman shouted. "The front doors! Now!"

They were already half way through the warehouse, and there seemed to be fewer children in the outer stacks, but the thugs still ran a gauntlet of stones.

I followed, moving a bit slower than they. One man, struck in the head, went down. Two of his cohorts grabbed his arms and dragged him on, shielding their heads with one arm as they ran.

I was using both arms to protect my head, and several stones bounced off them, and off my ribs. But despite the pain, and the panic that came with it, I slowed my pace still more.

Tossman was hammering on the door, screaming orders to the men outside.

Dawn light flooded in as the doors swung open, and thugs hurtled out into the street. A barrage of stones followed, banging on the wooden walls like a drum roll, and the doors closed.

I stopped in the center of the corridor. Two stones whizzed past me, clattering across the floor. Another struck my thigh.

Slowly, I pulled my hands away from my head and held them out, empty, weaponless.

One more stone sailed past, but I kept my arms down and stood still. 'Twas one of the bravest things I've ever done, for a stone to the head can kill a man. After several long moments, where the only sound was my own heartbeat thundering in my ears, I heard the muffled thumps of someone climbing down from a pile, and light footsteps behind me.

I turned, slowly still, for to alarm them could mean my death... and then relaxed as I saw Timasus coming toward me.

He might only have one eye, but the mind behind it was sharp enough to make up the difference. He studied the glowing gem at my throat and grimaced.

"Got Master Fisk too, do they?"

"Yes." Roseman had held hostages with these collars so often that even the children knew of it. I wondered what had become of the others so ensnared, but I hadn't time to ask that now. "I can't talk long—if I don't go out soon, they'll be even more suspicious. If I give you a note, can you get it to Fisk?"

"Might be we could," Timasus said. "Iffen that message told us how we could hit the Rose."

"What? I just warned you about this ambush! Surely that pays any debt I owe."

The boy was already shaking his head. "That's not the agreement. You said you'd find some way for us t' hurt Tony Rose. And you hasn't! So why should we do more for you?"

It appeared I had no choice with them, either. "Very well. If you deliver messages between Fisk and me, I'll find some way for you to strike at Master Roseman. They think they have me trapped, so they talk in front of me—and Fisk is probably learning even more. But you must take care when you approach him. Roseman hates you. You've evidently done him some damage."

"All we can," said Timasus cheerfully. "And you've got a deal. We should be able t' reach Master Fisk when he leaves the house. Inside we can't, but the next time he comes out we'll get your note to 'im."

"Thank you." 'Twas all I'd time to say, but relief swept through me like a lightning bolt. I may even have matched Timasus' hungry grin, as I reached into my pocket for the small slip of paper.

CHAPTER 12

Fisk

It had taken me almost a week to study the Rose's ledgers. There were nearly a dozen ships he wanted me to audit, with transactions going back for decades. Even looking over the last five years took a long time...and I didn't just study the last five years. By the time I'd finished, I knew where the goods the captains fenced for Roseman came from, where they were selling them, and how much money they might have skimmed.

The one thing I hadn't learned was where the Rose's profit went. The totals were set up to be copied into another account book—but like the books that dealt with the "city tax" he collected, or any other scams he might be running, those were ledgers I wasn't allowed to see.

Every night, Roseman put the books I was working on back in that locked room. Every morning they were brought out again. There was no entrance into that room from the corridor, which made it doubly secure. I thought there might be a window, but I couldn't be certain—and the nightly guard patrols made burglary from the outside dicey.

I'd never been allowed even a glimpse past the door, and judging by the sums I was seeing, from just a small part of Roseman's operations, it could have been a mammoth vault. But something about the sound when it closed told me it wasn't a closet or a vault, but a decent-sized room. I was more and more convinced it was an office. The real office, where the real work was done.

Which was, no doubt, why Roseman kept the magica key on his person at all times.

I couldn't get into that inner office, but as I worked with the ledgers of his fencing operation a plan began to form. I couldn't see any way for Michael and I to escape from Roseman without help, and—though I hated to admit it—the most effective source of help would be the High Liege's Guard. The best way to get the guard to come, would be to give the nearest honest commander…not just evidence, but evidence of so much corruption, and so much power, that he'd be willing to bring the better part of an army with him. If he just sent a few investigators the Rose would know who'd betrayed him…and Michael and I would die.

Most of that evidence was stored behind a lock Jack said was unpickable—and now that I'd met the Rose, I was even less eager to burgle any place he owned. But I could still start gathering evidence.

THE ROSE and Wiederman left town for some meeting. It was disguised as a party, but from the way they talked it was a meeting, and an important one—and he took his magica key with him. Soon after they'd gone, I told Jack I was ready to start talking to ship captains.

"And I hope you realize that if I show up with a procession at my heels, they're going to know I'm not really a trusted accountant."

I gestured to the hallway, where my oversized guard unit milled. Though they were guarding the ledgers more than me. With Roseman gone the account books were stored in Roseman's outer office, to which Jack had a key.

"Of course." Jack shut the outer-office door, and locked it. "You'll have one guard, known to the captains, to affirm your identity when you present Master Roseman's letter of authorization. After that…" His eyes lingered on the glowing stone at my throat. "I have every faith in your good sense, my lad."

I wasn't his, or a lad. Not anymore.

I KEEP AN OUTFIT in my wardrobe that will let me pass as a clerk. And one that will let me pass for a dock worker, and another that would let me pass for a rich man's valet—no mean feat, when you live out of a traveling pack. When Roseman's men brought our possessions from the chandler's shop, my case of lock picks was missing, along with Michael's sword and both our knives. My backup picks, beneath the thin false-bottom of my pack, had escaped notice—which told me that Jack wasn't the one who'd searched our gear. But I still wasn't surprised when a servant arrived in the morning, bringing a coat and britches that would let me pass for the kind of accountant the Rose would employ. Jack was a stickler for details.

I went down to breakfast in my new clothes, and had just finished eating when Jack came in, carrying a letter sealed with Roseman's crest. It was, unimaginatively, a rose. And the thorns weren't as prominent as I thought they should be.

"Ready?" he asked. "Excellent. I'll walk part way with you."

My guard for the day joined us in the entry hall. He wore the Rose's black and red livery, and didn't look as thuggish as most of them did. His name was Kitchell, and he told Jack that he'd delivered several messages to Captain Rigsby.

"Rigsby's the one you suspect?" I stopped at a mirror to turn the leather collar so the glowing gem was concealed by the collars of both shirt and coat, and that my shirt was buttoned high enough to hide the leather strap. Eagerness to get out of this house for a while made my hands tremble—which was silly, since I'd be coming back this evening.

"One of them. In fact, Roseman thinks he's the ringleader," Jack told me. "I'm not so sure myself. He has a wife and young children living in the Port."

That did make this kind of shenanigans less likely.

"Are you certain the captains are chiseling?"

Jack opened the front door and we stepped out onto the portico. Only a short walk across the yard now, and the gatekeeper was already unlatching the iron gates.

"Not certain," said Jack. "But the boss knows what prices those goods should fetch almost as well as I do. If they're not skimming, some of his captains are really bad bargainers."

"Or the market for small swag could have declined in some cities," I said. "That happens, particularly if business is bad for a while."

"So it does," Jack said, as we went through the gate and into the street. "But this smells like a scam—and if someone tries to bribe you, we'll know where to start looking. The only reason Roseman hasn't gone after them already is that he wants proof. He won't take down a man who might be loyal without it."

"How very ethical." It was an illusion that I was breathing free air now. Air is air, even if you're in a jail cell—much less comfortably housed in a rich man's mansion. I drew deep breaths of it into my lungs.

Kitchell fell in behind us, as a well-trained servant will when his superiors are talking. But we'd gone down the rise and half way to the docks before Jack spoke again.

"Here's your letter of authorization." He handed it over. "Master Roseman wrote it before he left. He introduces you as a clerk who worked for him in Ralling, who was obliged to relocate suddenly. It explains why he'd trust you, even though he doesn't really know you."

"Good enough." Ralling was an inland town, where Jack and I had once spent several months before we were obliged to relocate very suddenly indeed. I probably knew the town better than a ship captain would.

I expected Jack to leave then. There was no harm to the scam in his walking with me—he was supposed to be my superior. But there was no purpose in it, either.

"I know you're trying to find some way out of this," he said abruptly. "You and your friend."

There was no point in denying it, so I didn't.

"Give it up, Fisk. You'll get yourself killed, and take your friend down with you. Roseman may not look it, but he's not just tougher than I am, he's *smarter* than I am. You're way out of your league."

"Caught you trying to scam him, did he? I wondered how you ended up working for someone else." I let contempt seep into the words, and color rose in Jack's face.

"I keep trying to tell you, this is a good job. If your friend would settle down to it, the Rose has use for swordsmen too. You could both come out of this alive and employed, if you had any brains."

He left then, before I could come up with a retort. I'd known the Rose was smart, but smart enough to catch and cage Jack was very smart indeed. I was sufficiently distracted by my thoughts, and the way Kitchell was coming up behind me, that I didn't see the ragged little girl till she crashed into me. But I still felt her fingers slip into my pocket. I started to reach for that small deft hand and then froze, staring into Alessa's wide pale eyes.

"'Scuse me, sir. I didn't see you."

"That's all right." I strode on, before Kitchell had a chance to do more than glare. She was indeed "good with her hands." And there was no way I could ask, even obliquely, how she and the others were doing. I didn't even dare to touch my pocket, to see if she'd taken something out...or more likely, what she'd left there.

I did walk a little faster.

CAPTAIN RIGSBY was a ruddy middle-aged man, with a thick mustache and a suspicious expression.

"Master Roseman is welcome to check my accounts, at any time." It was the only thing he could say, after all. "I'll take you to the chart room, set you up there. Would you care for some ale? Tea?"

"Tea, thank you. Kitchell, you can wait for me at the tavern."

Kitchell scowled. He'd been preparing to follow me below, but he couldn't insist without giving the game away. To follow me into the chart room and watch me work was not how you treated a trusted clerk—which I'd have pointed out to him, Jack and the Rose, if any of them asked.

So I was free—after the second mate escorted me below, brought the ledgers to the chart room, and then a pot of tea, ink, paper, and offered to fetch me "anything else, for Master Roseman's man."

"Nothing but a chance to get to work," I told him, and he took the hint and departed.

Just in case, I sat down at the desk and opened the first ledger before reaching casually into my pocket.

It could have been anything, but a note was the most likely. He hadn't signed it, but I recognized Michael's untidy scrawl: *Must bring HL's troops to take down R & guards. Need evidence! How?*

He might as well have signed it—and could he possibly have written anything more incriminating? But that was Michael.

I took some time to consider my answer, then turned to the ledger where I hoped to find...not the evidence we needed, but maybe the beginning of way to get it. I'd seen enough of Roseman's ledgers to know that his ship captains could probably supply that evidence, if I could win their trust.

I worked through the morning, and declined an invitation to join the ship's officers for luncheon, though I welcomed the sandwich the cook sent in.

It was late afternoon, and sunlight slanted through the windows when I closed the last ledger and asked if Captain Rigsby would join me.

"Your man, Kitchell, he's been aboard twice now to ask if you need anything," the captain told me. "If you've gotten through that stack already you're a hard worker, Master Fisk."

"He'll wait," I said. "And judging by these books, you're a hard worker yourself. I only found three small errors—the largest of which is in Master Roseman's favor."

I let him relax for a moment, under my pleasant smile, before I went on. "Then I found this..." I opened one of the ledgers, and pointed to an entry near the bottom of the column. "This isn't an error, Captain Rigsby."

After one glance, the color drained out of his face. But he tried to bluster his way out of it.

"Three crates of dried woad to the dyers guild in Tillsport. Did I make some error adding up the price?"

"No, you entered the price for three crates. But looking at the cargo you added on later, you had room in your hold for thirty crates. Which also explains why you sold so little other cargo there, and so much more at the next port. Raw woad fetches a good price, but it is bulky." I shook my head, sadly.

"It's not my fault some clerk dropped a zero when he entered the number of crates," the captain said. "This is a simple error!"

"It might be, if he also hadn't added the price of just three crates to the tally," I pointed out. "When you turned your profit over to Master Roseman, your books balanced. That would take, not just a few errors, but an outright miracle. It wasn't a bad idea, but there's no way you can pass this off as a mistake. Everyone makes mistakes," I put all the sympathy I could into my voice. "Perhaps you could persuade me that...oh, that you weren't happy with the state of the hold's caulking, so you decided to sail with a lighter load till you were certain it was safe?"

The captain's hand fell to the place a sword hilt would have been, if he'd been wearing one. Though even if he'd had a sword, he couldn't use it—not with a guard waiting for me, and all the Rose's men knowing where I was.

"I didn't think anyone who worked for the Rose could be bribed," he said cautiously.

"I can't." It was time to give up the game. Or rather, pass over the journeyman round and get to the master levels. "But it's nice to know I could have pulled it off, if I'd wanted to."

"What?" His confusion was understandable.

"Roseman wants me to get you to bribe me," I told him. "Then I'm supposed to work my way into your confidence till I've identified all your cohorts, and learned exactly how you're cheating him. Then he'd move in."

The man's eyes were all but popping out of his head by the time I finished. "But he... But I... Why are you telling me this?"

"Because I need your help."

I reached up and turned my collar so the glowing gem showed. The captain stared at it curiously.

"I've heard of those. I thought they were supposed to keep anyone who wore them from even thinking about treason."

Was that what the mad jeweler had needed more time for? Thank goodness for the Rose's impatience.

"This gem doesn't care what I think," I said. "But if I get killed, or cut the collar off, both stones go dark—and whoever is guarding my friend will kill him."

"I don't have any way to help you out of that," the captain said. "I might try, if I could do it without risking my family, but—"

"That's not what I want from you," I said. "Though if it all goes wrong, having quick transportation out of here available for me and my friend wouldn't hurt."

Rigsby was already shaking his head so I went on swiftly, "But I'm beginning to work on another idea. One that would make it so you'd never have to worry about Tony Rose again. The first thing I need is enough hard evidence to convince the Liege Guard commander in Gollford to send troops to take over this town. Enough men to fight, not only Roseman's men, but also the Liege Guardsmen stationed here, since the Rose evidently owns them too. Though how he managed that, I can't imagine."

The High Liege's men really were unbribable. Jack tried it once—we were on the run for two months, after.

"You don't know?" Rigsby glanced at my throat. "The guard captain the High Liege sent when the last one died—old age, they said—the new captain came to town with a pretty young bride. Now the bride lives on the Rose's country estate, or so they say, and the captain wears a collar just like yours. He keeps it turned, but after a while... Well, word gets around."

"Hmm. All the more reason for Gollford's troops. But I need evidence that Roseman has committed massive, serious crimes. Have you, or any of your friends, kept a record of the goods you've fenced?"

This was the moment of truth—I could have been saying all this to get my hands on those records, to take them to the

Rose. Until he handed them over, Rigsby could deny that he'd admitted anything. His gaze darted around the room, seeking some escape. It settled on the glowing magical noose around my neck.

"I don't keep anything, but some of the others do. I'll name no names, not without their consent. But I think I could get that evidence."

"That's just the first part," I said. "For the next part, I'm going to need at least three of you, maybe four, who'd be willing to let me turn you in to the Rose."

"What? I thought you wanted to help us!"

I'd actually said that I wanted them to help me. But a bargain has to be more or less equal, if it's going to stick.

"I've got to give the Rose something," I pointed out. "Or he'll know I'm playing him, and kill us all. Surely a few of you have enough salted away that you're ready to run by now. If the Rose trusts me—which he will, if I'm the one who turns you in—I should be able to give you at least a day's warning. But on that day you'd better be running, and beyond the Rose's reach."

"Oh." The captain stood and paced to the windows, overlooking the bustling docks. Pushing would only make him push back, so I waited.

"You know, I grew up in the Port. My father was a sail maker. I could have taken the shop, but it was always the sea for me, so his partner bought me out. That's how I got the money to buy this ship. It was a good town then. And it wasn't so bad, when the Rose first started taking power. The city government actually ran better for a while."

Anything I could learn about the Rose interested me. "What changed?"

"I don't know, not really. But about ten years ago, maybe a bit more, the boss started talking about some big plan. Really big. Then he stopped talking about it, but that's when the city tax began. Other things, too. We'd been disposing of a few trinkets, here and there. Then the number of valuables he had us handling grew and grew. It's gotten so bad, our buyers really are dropping their prices. They say the market is saturated. And it's always harder to sell jewels with blood on 'em."

I waited.

He took a deep breath, and made his choice.

"You can turn me in. I started skimming because I wanted to get my family out of this town. Raise my children where the law is guardsmen instead of thugs, and justice is real."

I wasn't sure justice was real anywhere, but I let that pass.

"But I'm going to need that day's warning," Rigsby went on. "I have to be sure I can get my family onto my ship and sail before the Rose can stop us."

"You can't tell them," I said. "No packing. No saying goodbye to your daughter's best friend, who goes crying to her mother, who tells her husband, who just happens to be a drinking buddy of one of the Rose's men."

"I won't warn them," he promised. "My wife knows what I've been trying to set up. The children love to come aboard—they won't make a fuss."

"Can you find some other captains who feel the same way? Who could be relied on to keep it quiet till I'm ready to turn them in?"

"We've been cheating the Rose for years." Rigsby smiled sadly. "We can all keep secrets."

They hadn't done it all that well—the Rose had sent me to nab them.

"I'll need to forge some evidence against you," I said. "I've got to show the Rose something. Can you give me some blank receipts, manifests, that kind of thing? I've got access to the Rose's ledgers, so I can figure out what to fill in."

"You don't need me to write them up?" He went to a cabinet and began pulling papers out of a drawer.

"You were too smart to keep a record," I said. "We'll leave it at that. I'm thinking more about papers other people might have given you, cargo lists you wouldn't have been able to alter easily, things like that."

While he gathered the blank papers I needed, and others to disguise their presence, I composed a note to Michael. One that would be less compromising than his, if it fell into the wrong hands.

People talk about a man's handwriting, or a woman's, but in fact you can't always tell gender from people's penmanship. And I can forge most people's writing, anyway.

Once the ink had dried, I crumpled my note and then tore off the top half, so it looked like part of a letter blown out of the trash. The remainder said:

...thought Roberta's playing was quite good. Unlike most girls that age. Why some women think that men will be attracted by bad music, I shall never understand. The Key to the Door of a man's heart isn't talent—and without that Magica Key no girl stands a chance. I'm sure you understand. People living in the Countryside have more understanding of the true Keys of the heart. But even if Roberta plays decently, someone has to get that girl out of those gaudy necklaces she favors. So inappropriate for her age—she might as well be wearing the chandelier! Someone should drop her a hint—but that's so hard to accomplish without offending. Any idea how it might be done? It's going to be necessary, if she ever wants to marry and get out of that house. I shall be at...

The page ended before I had to make up another name.

I left the ship shortly after that, carrying an armful of ledgers, notes and bills to "study" later. Kitchell joined me as soon as I left the ship, scowling over how long I'd been out of his sight. This didn't worry me—or it wouldn't, if he hadn't expressed his disapproval by walking only a few strides behind me.

I spotted Alessa soon after we left the docks. She had enough craft not to approach me, but skipped down the other side of the street without even glancing in my direction. She would then turn and follow us, waiting for me to drop my reply...which was going to be curst hard with a guard glaring at my back.

As Jack used to say, if the situation doesn't work for the scam, then change the situation.

I gave it two more blocks, then stared looking for something I could trip over, which wasn't hard to find—in this rough neighborhood there were plenty of loose cobbles. I rammed my toe into one and then, naturally, flung out my hands to break my fall.

Papers flew everywhere.

Unfortunately, the neighborhood wasn't quite rough enough. Three passersby stopped to help me gather them, and Kitchell, who'd started forward, stopped.

"These are Master Roseman's papers!" I said. "Very important. Don't touch them!"

The mere mention of Roseman's name had them backing away. I turned to Kitchell. "What are you waiting for? Help me pick them up or they'll blow away!"

There wasn't much wind, which was lucky—the papers had scattered over half the street. I'd proclaimed Roseman's name loudly enough that no one stepped on them, and Kitchell hustled to gather them up. By the time we departed he was walking beside me, carrying an armload of ledgers and notes... and just one piece of paper had been left behind, tucked into a shadowy niche between a rain barrel and a step.

I'd have worried about someone else finding it, but I'd developed considerable respect for Alessa's craftsmanship.

Back at the townhouse, I'd have plenty of time to forge evidence against Captain Rigsby, and also to copy any evidence of Roseman's crimes. As long as I didn't have the ledgers the guards paid little attention to me, and the Rose himself was gone.

As for Jack, he'd never enjoyed "paperwork." Indeed, the fact that I had some clerkly skills was one of the reasons he'd picked me up in the first place.

When I was finished, I'd take the real evidence back to Rigsby, to hide until I had enough to send to the High Liege's men. As for the fake evidence, against Rigsby and his friends, I had no fear it would be disbelieved. The difference between a ship's captain and a bandit is that the one's called a pirate instead.

Though Rigsby would probably have been an honest man, if not for his boss. The Rose had told me to win the captain's trust. By offering to rescue him from The Rose, I'd done it in just one day.

If Jack wasn't the one I was scamming, he'd be proud of me.

CHAPTER 13

Michael

I had hoped we might linger in town for a time, which might have given me a chance to get Fisk's reply. But fear of the Rose overcame bruises. We left the man with the concussion and his comrade with the broken arm at the healer's, and rode back to Rose manor that very afternoon to report our failure.

Tossman, perhaps thinking that the Rose would blame him for his failure to control me, said nothing of the slight disturbance I'd created in the alley. So, although he glared at me a great deal on principle, Roseman was forced to accept a simple victory for the orphans.

Seeing how furious that made him, I resolved to tell them all about it if I ever got the chance.

Except for seeing him at meals—which had a sad effect on my appetite—Roseman's presence in the house made little impact on my days. Lianna was sleeping well with my potion of magica chamomile, so I'd no need to find other herbs, but I still continued my walks about the countryside. In part, this was because I liked walking in the countryside, even with a guard trailing at my heels. But mostly 'twas to allow the orphans a chance reach me.

I exchanged a few words with anyone I met on those walks, so my guard thought nothing of it when I strolled up to a boy who sat by the stream, fishing. And in truth, I was almost upon him before I recognized Jig under the ragged straw hat.

"Did you mange to contact Fisk?" I tried to look like I was making casual conversation, and I must have succeeded, for my guard came no closer. "I can't talk too long. Roseman's here now, though I think he's leaving in a few days."

"We know. We always try t' know where he's at." Jig pulled his hook from the stream, saw that his bait had vanished, as it does when fish are clever, and made a sound of disgust.

"I think they's magica fish in this creek. Been here two days now, and all I catch is little ones.

"Are you using worms?" I asked, drawn in despite myself.

"Cheese. It works as well and it's easier come by." He pulled a cloth-wrapped nugget from his pocket and rebaited the hook as he spoke. "If you was t' climb up that rock pile down the stream there, and admire the view for a while, you might find a bit of paper under a stone at the base of that little oak. And if you wanted to reply to it, you could just leave a bit of paper in the same place, and someone would pick it up when there's no one around at all."

"What a clever way to pass messages." I put my hands in my pockets, so the guard could see I had picked up nothing from my new friend.

"Yah, but if you want t' use it, then it's time to make good on your promise. None of your notes is going nowhere, unless they's a plan for us t' get at the Rose along with it."

I should have known this was coming, but the firmness in his voice still took me aback. "Something that could strike at

Roseman, without getting us all killed, is going to be tricky. I'd need time."

"You've had time." Jig pulled his line from the water, and shook his head over the empty hook. "You want your notes delivered? This is the price."

It seemed that my time had run out.

"Very well. I'll think of something. But it *will* take time— several days at least. How are you staying here, without shelter? Without arousing suspicion?"

The hat tipped up, and he sent me an amused glance. "I got friends in this neighborhood, Master Michael. They're too scart of the Rose to take me in, but they'll let me stay in the barn and help out with the animals now and again. Most of us got folk like that, kin or friends, who'd take us in if they dared." He rebaited his hook once more. "They felt really bad about what happened to my father."

His father had been a town guardsman, who'd refused to carry out the sentence one of the Rose's judicars had passed on an innocent man. The flogging was still carried out, by another of the town guard. And two weeks afterward, Jig's father had "fallen" into the bay and drowned. A story that quite failed to account for the bruises that covered his body when 'twas pulled from the water.

"I'll find a way," I promised. "Somehow, I'll find a way."

I wasn't talking about a simple strike against the Rose, either.

To AVOID casting suspicion on my conversation with the young fisherman, I waited till the next day, when no one was nearby, to scramble up the small, rocky hill. The view from the top was worth the climb, and it made perfect sense for me to sit under the tree and admire that view. Away from the great river's floodplain, low hills rolled into the distance. I thought I could see the sea on the far horizon, though I couldn't be sure.

I resolved to make that climb a regular part of my walks, and waited again till I was alone in my room before I finally read the note—though by then I was half-mad with suspense.

It took some moments to translate Fisk's circumlocution. I was clearly the recipient (female) of the letter, but what was this key—a magica key?—that he considered so necessary? People wealthy enough to own two homes often kept spare keys to some strong box or vault in a different establishment—it made things harder for an untrustworthy servant or a thief, though 'twas also more annoying to reclaim it if the master key was lost. This key Fisk sought clearly unlocked something important, but what? And why was he being so cursed cryptic? Any note found in my possession would be suspect, and without a better description of this key how was I to find it? But he was right that any plan for escape, or for foiling the Rose, must hinge on one or both of us being able to get out of our collars without getting the other killed. If I couldn't do that, there was no point in worrying about keys or anything else.

I'd already put it off too long. 'Twas time to try magic.

"I DON'T KNOW what's wrong," I told Lianna, who had appointed herself my assistant. We were working in the herbery, a room rich with sunlight and the welcoming scents of bruised greenery and damp earth. Almost no one came here besides me—though if anyone should happen by I had a drawer open, ready to sweep my work off the bench before it could be seen. If I got no better results than I had so far, 'twould scarcely matter.

I had asked Lianna for some bit of jewelry to experiment on, and explaining what I wanted it *for* had resulted in a tale that lasted several hours. She was the first person besides Fisk to learn that I had some ability to work magic, and she didn't seem nearly as horrified as I'd expected. That might have been because she'd been wearing a magica gem around her neck for several years now. Or mayhap she simply thought me deluded or mad—as a self-proclaimed knight errant, this is something to which I'm well accustomed.

My utter lack of success was no doubt adding weight to the deluded and crazy side of the scale, even now.

I tossed the faceted glass oval onto the workbench where we sat, and it clinked against its twin. Once she'd learned what I wanted the stones for, instead of a small tasteful stone, she'd fetched me two crystal pendants from some chandelier swathed in sheets in the attic. Lianna, it seemed, possessed a finding Gift—once she had a clear idea of what I wanted, if 'twas nearby she could locate it. 'Twas a rare Gift, much valued by those who sought precious metal or even underground water, and she'd kept it secret from Roseman. But 'twas valuable for other things as well, and I congratulated myself and her on my choice of allies. I'd asked her about finding the key, without much hope that she could do it from so vague a description, but she said she'd try as soon as Roseman departed. The gems she'd brought me were an excellent match for the stones in our collars, and would have made near perfect replicas...if only I'd been able to make them glow.

"Your sleeping potion works wonderfully," Lianna consoled me. "I've completely stopped taking laudanum."

She looked the better for it, too. Her eyes were bright, and her nerves didn't seem so fragile...though that might have been because the time for her husband's visit was approaching.

"Any competent herb talker can harvest magica," I said. "And any competent healer would have had you taking it long ago. This..."

I stared in disgust at the harmless bits of crystal. "'Tis as if my magic only comes in times of danger or stress, like fighting a fire or falling off a cliff."

Or mayhap 'twas my fear of ending up as mad as Roseman's jeweler that kept me from using it unless my life was in peril. Though I'd once summoned it to calm her, as well—which made as little sense as all else that came with this strange, unwanted Gift.

"Then what about the man who made these," Lianna touched the collar about her neck. "He may have been mad, but he was directing his magic with conscious thought. Even if he couldn't make mine work like Gervase's did."

"What do you mean?" The stone at her throat glowed as surely as the sun. "Don't they both go out if one of you dies, or sheds the collar?"

Or killed Atherton Roseman. 'Twas a thought that lingered in my mind more than I liked. I understood, too well, why the orphans had demanded their price.

"Yes, but Gervase's collar is worse than that. They had to let him go on being captain of the Liege Guard, you see. Or the Liege would simply send someone else, and *he* thought too many deaths would be suspicious."

She seldom used Roseman's name if she could avoid it, and his presence in the house left her tense and oppressed. If nothing else, helping me had given her something positive to do. But I was recalling the conversation between the Rose and his jeweler on the night my collar had been created.

"Roseman wanted the collars to go dark if either Fisk or I even thought of betraying him, only the jeweler said 'twould take too much time. But surely they couldn't do that!"

"I'm not sure if they could or not," she said. "But since Gervase couldn't help but think about destroying him all the time, that would have been useless. But that poor madman did somehow manage his spell so that if Gervase ever acts upon his desires, if he ever starts to do anything he knows might harm that man, then both our collars go dark."

"But how could a...a glowing stone know what he intends? Or what he does? How can a bit of glass know anything?"

"How could it know if you killed the Rose?" She smiled sadly. "I'm afraid the answer is: ''tis magic.'"

"And I have some access to magic, which is why Fisk thrust this task on me. But I've no idea how to make it do this."

"Well, the jeweler couldn't either," she said. "Not always. Or I couldn't be helping you now. He blamed it on my being a woman, said my mind was too alien for him to reach or some such thing. But it could simply be that his magic failed him. Or he couldn't control it. And it might be that his magic is of a different kind than yours, too."

"Or it could be that he knows what he's doing, and I don't," I finished ruefully. "But I won't give up. Though if danger can get this gem to glow, we should be able to light up a chandelier!"

It made her laugh, as 'twas meant to, but I wasn't lying. Fisk was right—one of us had to be able to get out of these curst things without killing the other before we could even escape. Much less bring down the Rose.

A FEW DAYS LATER, one of Roseman's carriages rolled up to the gate—and this time Lianna was waiting in the hall when the doors opened, quivering with eagerness. For behind Jack Bannister came the captain of the High Liege's guard.

Despite Roseman's presence, despite Bannister's smirk, she shot forward and into her husband's arms.

They did not kiss, but simply clung to each other with a desperation painful to witness.

"Where's my hostage?" I asked it more to pull attention away from them than because I thought 'twould do any good. "You promised that Fisk and I could meet every few weeks."

"I'm breaking it," said Roseman easily. "At least for now. Master Fisk is doing good work for me, and I don't want him to stop. Master Markham here," he gestured to Jack, who went by so many last names there was no point in keeping track. "He'll go back and assure Fisk you're still in one piece."

"As if either of us would take his word." But I knew that Fisk was still alive—because without him, they had no further use for me.

"He's fine," said Jack. "If a bit frustrated. He's still trying to plot his way out of the snare, I think, but he's not having any luck. He'll settle down eventually."

"As you did?" I asked. "Like a tamed cur?"

The Rose laughed, but Jack's grin only widened. And 'twas true—I delivered insults only because I couldn't do them any harm that mattered.

And I needed to think of a way to cause such harm, or the orphans wouldn't bear my message to Fisk even if I found some way to escape these cursed collars!

Lianna and her husband had already slipped out, followed by at least six guards, so I departed as well.

I COULDN'T avoid the dinner—they sent a servant to fetch me.

From sheer cruelty, they'd put Lianna and her husband on opposite sides of the table. They'd placed me next to her, mayhap attempting to make Dalton jealous in addition to the rest of his woes. But since she spent the whole meal trying to eat him with her eyes, 'twas wasted effort on their part. As for Dalton, I'm not sure he even knew I was there.

Since there was no one present to impress, Roseman was conducting business at the table, a secretary in attendance since Wiederman had departed in the carriage that had brought Jack and Lianna's husband. Evidently one of his two henchmen had to be in the city at all times.

"We've got eight of the riders on our payroll already," the secretary was saying. "But that still leaves three who might try to beat Red Thorn. And two of their horses are pretty fast."

"Deal with it however you must." Roseman was spooning gravy over a thick slice of lamb. "If you run into trouble let Wiederman know. I won't place any bet till it's settled."

"Of course not," I said. "That might entail real risk. Requiring real nerve."

"I never take risks," Roseman said. "I never bet, unless it's a sure thing. You should know that by now, Master Sevenson."

I started to say that a gang of children was still beating him, but I had no desire to provoke him into action against the orphans. They were all too eager to do that on their own.

My hesitation left a silence, which Jack broke. "And you shouldn't be so contemptuous of fixing races. Unless you're prepared to despise Fisk."

"Fisk is a better man than you think him," I said. Though I'd no doubt he'd have fixed a race, back in the day when he was Jack's apprentice instead of my squire. "He's changed."

"He was always too soft," Jack said. "It was the one bad habit I couldn't break him of."

"Was that why you two separated?" Roseman asked. "You never told me why you dumped him."

"It wasn't exactly that," Jack said. "Though the scam would have worked if he'd played his mark the way he was supposed to."

He had the attention of everyone except the lovers now, for Fisk hardly ever speaks of his past.

Jack was one of those who relished an audience, and he took a sip of wine to make us wait.

"It was a lost mine scam. We already had the first payment in our pocket, and the heir's father was *not* a man you wanted to cross. But Fisk let the heir get out from under his control, and the whole thing was about to come unraveled."

He took another sip.

"I had to throw the law a bone, as it were."

"You left him." Even knowing what I did of the man, I could hardly believe it. "You left your partner to take the blame while you ran. With this 'first payment,' no doubt! Fisk could have been years working off such a debt. He could have been flogged or maimed."

"Well, he wouldn't have been hanged," Jack said. "Because we didn't kill anyone. All else can be survived, or escaped from eventually. And he clearly did escape, so no harm done."

None but the harm such a terrible betrayal must have done Fisk's heart.

"He wouldn't have been hurt." Jack must have read my curst, open face. "Or he shouldn't have been. I taught him right from the start to never trust anyone. This was just the final lesson."

No wonder it had taken me so long to win Fisk's trust.

The Rose laughed aloud at Jack's so-called wit—which would have told me a great deal about what kind of man he was, except I already knew it.

He went on to discuss a few more details of the horse race he was fixing, and some other business as well. But horses are something I know a bit about, and as I listened a plot that solved at least one of my problems was born.

That night, I wrote a detailed letter, not for Fisk, but to the orphans.

And Lianna was delighted to give me a small but nearly-full bottle of laudanum to send with it.

CHAPTER 14

Fisk

Roseman's men intercepted Kathy's letter. I should have expected it, since I'd told her we'd be in Tallowsport long enough to get a reply. But I'd forgotten all about that...until Wiederman came in, snickering, and handed it over. Once I'd read it, I understood why.

You can joke about slaying monsters all you want, she'd written. *But I haven't been writing to you all these years, without being able to tell that you're not really joking. Take care. For yourself, as well as Michael.*

"Roseman wants you to reply," said Wiederman. "Tell her your monster turned out to be a mouse, or something stupid like that. Markham or I will read it before you send it."

I'd already noticed that he and Jack used each other's last names, and wondered how I could use the animosity between them. But I wrote a letter to Kathy, as commanded. Knowing that Roseman would probably read it made my prose stiffer than usual, but she should be reassured to learn that our dragon had been captured by the town guard, as soon as Michael's antics had drawn their attention.

I felt no more guilt deceiving her than I would have cheating a mark, back when I was with Jack—less, because this was for her own good. I just hoped she couldn't tell that I was lying through my teeth—the last thing any of us needed was for Kathy to turn up, looking for her brother. Which was yet another reason to get on with the plan...

ROSEMAN AND JACK soon returned, but in the week they were absent I recruited three more shipmasters who were willing to let me sacrifice them to the Rose.

One, who had no family to worry about, had already departed on a scheduled voyage—with no intention of coming back. Another was about to visit his mother in Gittings, which hadn't been planned, but he went there often enough that no one would find it odd. Rigsby and the fourth man were prepared to flee at a moment's notice, Rigsby and his family by sea. The other's cousin had been put in the stocks. It took more than a month before his neck was right again. He'd agreed to pretend to leave by sea, but then slip ashore and carry my evidence to the High Liege's guard post at Gollford.

Once I managed to acquire evidence.

The problem was that even if I proved the Rose was fencing an enormous amount of stolen goods, that wasn't enough to bring the High Liege's troops down on him. Proof of the wide spread "city tax" would probably do it...but I still hadn't gotten my hands on those ledgers!

I knew what I needed to do, but this was more risky than a normal burglary—and they're risky enough! I kept trying to find some other way. But I also knew that sooner or later I'd encounter a captain who'd give my game away. Two had already reported to the Rose that I'd tried to get a bribe out of them, but since that was what I was supposed to be doing the Rose told them he'd take care of it.

Those who didn't hate and fear Roseman were surprisingly loyal, which made what Michael and I were trying to do even more dangerous.

I was studying yet another ship's books—a task that became more boring the more I did it—when a guest rode through the gate and up the short drive to the town house.

This had happened before. I was told to dine in the kitchen, or in my room, when the Master had dinner guests. But this man arrived in the daytime, and I pressed close to the window to watch him dismount and walk up to the door. Some country baron, from the look of him, prosperous and respectable.

Had he come, as the mayor of Casfell had wanted his baron to come, to complain about how the food trains drained the countryside? I still hadn't figured out how the food trains could pay two brass roundels and a oct for a bushel of carrots, and sell them in the Tallowsport market for a tin ha' the bunch.

The baron looked like someone who might have come to quarrel with the local dragon, righteous determination spread over fear.

I heard the big door open below me, and soon the sound of many feet passing my study on the way to the boss's office.

Interrupting one of the Rose's meetings might be a bad idea...but I needed to learn something, curse it.

I spent twenty minutes searching through the papers on my desk—ship's papers, not the Rose's crooked ledgers—to find something I could plausibly ask him about. Then I left the study and walked down the hall toward the small mob of guards who hung about the Rose's office.

One of them stepped in front of the door as I approached.

"I need to ask the boss about something," I told him. "It won't take long."

"He's got a guest," the guard said. "He isn't to be disturbed."

I could hear their muffled voices. But they didn't seem to be behind the door.

"Well, maybe Wiederman could help me. Is he—"

"He's in the meeting," the guard said. "You'll have to come back later."

Someone's voice grew louder for a moment, and I realized the sound came, not through the door, but through the wall to the left. This stranger had been taken into the Rose's secret office!

"Ah," I said. "I'll do that."

I went back to my study and back to work. But I left my door open.

I was watching as they came back down the hall, Wiederman showing the baron out. He no longer looked grimly determined, but stunned. His collar had been pulled loose, and he was turning his hat in his hands as if he didn't know what to do with it. But he didn't look angry or...well, he did look frightened. In fact, he looked terrified, but not as if he'd been browbeaten into submission. This was the feverish exuberant terror of a man about to take some great risk for a great gain—not quite sure it would work, but committed to try.

You never want your mark to look like that. They should look relaxed, trusting, certain the bait you've promised will come through.

Which either meant the Rose was a bad scammer...or this wasn't a scam.

I closed the door and went to the window to watch the baron ride away. He'd put his hat on backward, and didn't even notice that the plume fell over the brim in front of him.

Whatever had happened at this meeting, it was big...and there was only one way to find out what it was. Somehow, I had to get into that second office.

THE LAST MARK I'd seen come near that state was Herbert Twylinger. Herbert was a nice kid, in an awkward hapless way. If his father had spent more time with him, and less time making a fortune in the fur trade, Herbert might have been more competent...and Jack and I wouldn't have been scamming him.

As it was, Herbert was pathetically grateful when I slowly struck up a friendship. And he felt honored, truly honored, when I finally confided the secret business that had brought me to his town...that my uncle, a roving prospector, had found the lost Hanged Man's Mine.

It had been lost because its discoverer, another prospector, who'd never had a fract to spare, had come into town after one of his long excursions in the wilderness and gotten roaring drunk. In that state, he'd killed a man in a bar fight—and debts of blood and death are repaid in the same coin. If the judicars hadn't been meeting just two days later, he might have had time to think things over and made a different decision—or maybe not. They said his years of lonely wandering had made him odd, secretive and suspicious. But no one knows why he went to the noose without telling anyone *why* he'd been celebrating so wildly.

It was only after his death that the innkeeper cleared out the room he'd rented for a week—probably hoping to sell the man's worn out gear for a few copper roundels. It was almost a week later that the maids turned the mattress, and discovered half a dozen tight-stitched bags of gold nuggets stashed under the bed.

That had been almost a century ago, but people were still looking for the Hanged Man's Mine. Although there's no way to prove it, my personal belief is that con men have made more money by claiming to have found it, than its unlucky discoverer would have made had he lived to mine out the seam.

Jack played my uncle, a rough, solitary miner much like the hanged man, and he produced a handful of real—and cursed expensive—gold nuggets to back up his story. I was a green clerk, who he'd brought in only because I was family, to buy the land where the mine was located from its oblivious owner…but the owner had demanded far more money than our not-so-wealthy family could pay.

Poor, rich Herbert positively begged us to take him into partnership. And in his defense, Jack's performance had been brilliant, right down to the dirt—not under this nails, which would have been too obvious—but engrained in the roughened skin of his hands. He told Herbert that he'd fallen from the trail above a mountain ravine, and found the mine as he struggled to escape from the chasm. It might even have convinced me, if I hadn't known the truth.

It was hours later, behind the locked door of our rented rooms, that Jack brushed back the straggling hair, combed the bushy beard, donned a nice silk dressing gown, and fell out of character and into himself.

"My word but that boy's credulous. I could have told him an earth sprite led me to that mine, and I think he'd have bought it."

"He's not that bad." My urge to defend Herbert to Jack was stupid, but I felt it anyway. "He wouldn't have fallen for your story if he hadn't watched me spend the last two months trying to buy that worthless mountainside. For a while, I was afraid the baron was going to sell it."

"The land around it's prime timberland," Jack said. "We're offering a bit less than it's worth, even if it wasn't in the middle of his estate."

"But Herbert has no way of knowing that."

"He could, if he asked around," Jack said. "He's an idiot."

"He's trusting his friend." I kept my voice fairly neutral, considering that I was the friend who'd won his trust.

"Which proves he's an idiot. You should never—"

"—never trust anyone," I chimed in, finishing the familiar sentence.

Jack laughed, the rich rare laugh he never offered anyone but me. Warmth, friendship, and yes, trust, washed away the shame of what I was doing to a lonely clumsy kid, who thought I was his friend.

I already had a friend, partner, and teacher, all rolled into one. Still grinning, he lifted his glass in a toast to all the money Herbert was about to steal from his father's vault—money that would not go to buy land, that had no mine on it, anyway.

I can't say Jack didn't warn me.

IT WAS SEVERAL days later, and Jack was "holding" the first third of our land payment. This was all Herbert could raise by raiding his own accounts, and selling an heirloom ring for which his mother would never forgive him. In a rare rush of caution, he asked to see the mine before he broke into his father's vault—trying to be sensible and adult about the big deal that would finally make his father proud of him.

I'd pointed out to Jack that the money Herbert had scraped up was already a decent haul. But Jack said that while I was drinking and riding out with Herbert, he'd been digging that accursed hole, and he wasn't about to let his work go to waste. He gave me good enough directions that we might even find it on the first try.

I was actually enjoying the ride, into the mountains on a sunny summer day, and ignoring most of Herbert's excited babbling, till he spoke the fatal words.

"...and then we'll buy the land, as soon as my father's assessor signs off on the mine. He'll be impressed that I checked before I—"

"Wait, whose assessor? I thought you weren't going to tell your father anything till the deal was done. To surprise him."

"Yes, but part of the surprise will be the mine assessor's report!" Herbert's face brightened, imagining the glorious moment. "That way he'll *know* that for once I got it right! He'll be so—"

"Where is this assessor now?" I demanded.

Jack had salted the empty hole he'd dug to fool an ignorant rich boy—not a mining geologist.

"He's meeting us at the mine," Herbert said. "Didn't your uncle tell you? He said I was smart to think of it, and he was glad his new partner wasn't a fool. He even wrote down the directions, so the assessor could find it…"

The next time we stopped at a stream, I told Herbert I had to relieve myself and that I might be a while. Walking over the mountains into the next fief took four days, but while Herbert Twylinger was a nice, credulous kid, his father Bertram was the kind of man who might bribe judicars to flog a thief— even one who hadn't succeeded in robbing him.

I had plenty of time to think about that, as I tramped up to a ridgeline and down into the next valley, over and over again. My riding boots weren't designed for walking, and my blisters broke, bled, and then just went on bleeding. I ate every berry I found, hoping like crazy they weren't poisonous, but too hungry to care. At least it was summer—if it hadn't been, I'd probably be dead.

But what I thought about wasn't my survival—no matter how painful it may be, walking a long distance is mostly boring—I thought about the fact that any pursuers would have *my* description. Jack had been well-disguised the few times he'd been in town, and Herbert was the only one who'd spoken with him for more than a few moments. I had lived in that town for months, and there were dozens of people who could identify me. Some of them might even be able to draw.

I spent a lot of time trying to figure out whether Jack had intended to run from the start, leaving me to bear the brunt of Bertram Twylinger's anger. (In fact, the man put a bounty hunter on my trail, and it took the better part of three months to lose him.) Or had Jack stayed so carefully in the background—spending weeks digging a mine, of all things—just as a precaution? A backup plan, in case of need…and then he'd needed it.

Or maybe he'd just suddenly learned that the jig was up, and realized that it would be safer for him if the pursuit went after me.

Whether he'd planned it or not, when everything came crashing down he'd fled—without me. If Herbert hadn't mentioned it, I'd have walked right into the assessor's arms. An assessor who would probably have known this was a scam before we even reached the mine. Who'd have been ready for me, when I wasn't ready for him.

I should have noticed that this time Jack was holding the loot.

In the end, the thing that bothered me most wasn't that Jack had abandoned me to take the fall, or that he'd lied to me. It was that, thinking I knew him through and through, I hadn't been able to *tell* that he was lying.

So maybe I ought to test his claim that this magica lock couldn't be picked.

SINCE I HAD no excuse to put it off, I waited for two hours after the servants went to bed, pulled my backup picks from their hiding place, and then slipped out of my room and down the stairs to Tony Rose's office.

The lock on the outer door was good enough it took me fifteen minutes to get through it. I'd begun to wonder if I could, when the hook snagged on the last pin and tugged it over. The door swung open with oiled ease.

The curtains were open and moonlight poured through the window—unnecessary, because picking locks is mostly done by feel. I locked the outer door behind me, ensuring privacy, and went to kneel in front of the door that mattered.

I have no Gifts at all, no way to sense the presence of magic. To me this looked like a perfectly ordinary lock, the metal of its faceplate cool and smooth under my fingers.

I took a settling breath and slipped the L wrench in. I half-expected a bolt of lightning to flash out and scorch my hands, but nothing happened. After a bit of probing I found the plug, applying just enough pressure that the pins would stay turned once I flipped them.

I chose a simple hook pick—my favorite for testing an unknown lock—and started feeling for the pins...and I couldn't find them. Or I would find them, turn them, and they promptly turned back. Or maybe I just imagined that they'd turned in the first place, because if you keep torsion on the L wrench they *can't* shift back again. But somehow, they did.

It was like trying to work with, not a metal mechanism, but some living thing that squirmed in resistance to my probing—although nothing about it was soft or living, and I could have sworn that I both heard and felt those pins click over.

My knees were aching on the hard floor, sweat rolling down my spine, when I finally sat back and rubbed my cramping hands.

Since I was alone in the outer office and might never get another chance, I searched it. With guards patrolling the grounds around the house I didn't dare strike a light without pulling the curtains, and I didn't want to pull the curtains in case they noticed. That meant I had to take every ledger, every piece of paper, over to the window. After a while, even reading by the light of two moons, my eyes were as tired as my hands.

All for nothing, too. Except for the ledgers I'd been working on, all the paperwork in this office related to the legitimate business of a legitimately wealthy merchant. A man with influence in the city, maybe a few councilmen who regarded him favorably, but nothing worse.

I wondered if all this legitimacy resulted from the fact that Roseman only worked on honest business in this room, or if this office was deliberately set up to take an audit from a Liege judicar on a moment's notice. Because except for my ledgers, it would have passed one.

And that other office was locked tighter than most bank vaults.

How like Jack, to have told the complete truth the one time I wanted him to be lying. The only way into Tony Rose's secret room was with the magica key that belonged to that lock…or the spare key, that he probably kept in his country house.

It was up to Michael, now.

CHAPTER 15

Michael

As soon as Roseman and Jack departed, I asked Lianna to try to use her finding Gift to locate the magica key Fisk wanted. I'd little hope she would succeed. 'Tis one thing to locate a missing earring or a lost dog, which is what most female finders I've known do with their Gift. The men, at least those who aren't born to run some estate, are in great demand to locate buried veins of gold, iron, or tin. They soon become attuned to those metals, and know what they're looking for.

But once I'd told her what I knew of the key, Lianna simply closed her eyes for several long moments and then started walking. She had to open her eyes to see where she was going, but they seemed unfocused. Sometimes she would stop and close them, hesitating a few seconds before moving on. To my surprise, she passed the door of Roseman's office. The room was locked in his absence, but I thought I might be able to open the window latch with a thin blade. However, Lianna ended in a room some way beyond the office, staring up at the ceiling. We had to retrace our steps and climb the staircase to the second floor, whereupon she led me straight to Roseman's bedroom. This door wasn't locked, and since there was no one in the corridor we went in. Lianna crossed the room to the right side of the dressing table and laid her hand on a section of the intricately paneled wall.

"It's here," she said, with a simplicity that left no room for doubt.

'Twas the work of moments to discover three carved rosettes near that spot, which pulled off to reveal three dials numbered one through thirty…but there I stuck.

There was obviously some safe or compartment behind the panel, and the dials would each have to register the correct number to open it. Had I dared spend the better part of… how many hours? days? standing in Roseman's bedroom methodically trying all the possible combinations, I might eventually find it.

Fisk could probably have opened it in minutes.

But Fisk was gone, and one maid coming in to dust could destroy all hope of bringing down the Rose.

I would have to discover the combination the hard way.

Now that I needed his presence, Roseman didn't return to Rose Manor until two days before the race. The servants were preparing for several days before they came, and Roseman himself arrived a day before his guests, to make sure all was in readiness. He brought Jack with him, leaving Wiederman behind. Did that mean Wiederman was more important to the running of his criminal empire? The race was evidently cause for a real house party, instead of a business meeting in disguise.

Having no reason to watch the man arrive, I made a point of not being in the entrance hall. Her husband wouldn't be with him, so Lianna was avoiding Roseman too. But he sent for both of us to come to his study, soon after he came in.

"I'm having guests here for the next few days," he announced as we entered. "Mistress Dalton knows to avoid being seen, and I'll expect you to do the same, Sevenson. Though you may both come to dinner tonight."

That "may" was pure formality, and I nodded acquiescence to his orders.

"That's all." Roseman reached for the stack of papers on his desk, dismissing us from his thoughts as well as his presence. He clearly thought us helpless, and with good reason. Even if I got the key, and figured out some way to break the hold of our collars, 'twould still not bring the man down. How we could manage that I still had no idea, but I did know what to do next—Roseman's dinner with his guests would give me a chance to try for the key. And after I laid hands on it, I still had to get it delivered.

"So, how do you become invisible for days at a stretch?" I asked Lianna, as we departed the presence.

She grimaced, looking more relaxed away from the man she so hated. "Mostly I stay in my room. You'd better pick up a stack of books tonight, or you'll be horribly bored. When I do go out, I dress myself as one of the lesser maids. The servants know who I am, of course, but they understand. And he's usually only here a short time."

"It sounds tedious," I said. "Is there any way I could get to this race?" The orphan's price had been paid when I delivered my plan, but I was terrified to leave its execution solely in their hands. 'Twas my scheme, and any disaster that befell the children would be my fault. If anything went wrong, I needed to be there in order to fix it.

"The estate where they're holding it is twelve miles away," said Liana. "I heard some of the gardeners lamenting that they couldn't walk there and get back in time for work, even if they set out well before dawn."

"Then I shall have to accompany Master Roseman." Despite all the dangers, I felt more cheerful at the prospect of action, and my expression must have revealed this, for alarm flickered over Lianna's face.

"He'd never agree. Even if you begged him to take you."

"Oh, I won't beg," I said. "With a man as paranoid as Roseman, that would be fatal. But suspicious people are easy to manipulate. More than those who aren't so suspicious, though they'd never believe it."

"I suppose you learned that from your criminal squire?"

I had told her about Fisk.

"In a sense," I said. "I learned it, because sometimes I have to manipulate Fisk. He's as paranoid as Roseman—though in a nicer way."

FOR ALL HER NERVOUSNESS Lianna was willing to assist, and that night at dinner she expressed a timid interest in going to see the race.

"I know your guests and Master Markham will be going in your carriages, but some of the upper servants plan to drive out in the wagon. I was wondering if I might go with them."

Jack, who had taken Wiederman's place at the table, raised a skeptical brow.

Roseman's gaze turned to me. "What about you, Sevenson? Do you also want to go to the race? Fisk is still back in the city, you know."

"I have no desire to go," I said calmly, and went on eating a rather nice pheasant.

It took a bit more prodding on Roseman's part, but by the meal's end it had been agreed that I'd go with him to the race—dressed as one of his guards, so they could keep an eye on me—and thus prevent whatever I was planning to get up to here, in Roseman's absence.

Honestly, he was easier to handle than Fisk.

But before I could profit from that small victory, I still had to fulfill Fisk's request. 'Twas time to try for the key.

I FREQUENTLY FIND that efforts intended to accomplish one thing end up accomplishing something else entirely. Roseman had ordered Lianna and me to stay out of sight while his guests were present...which meant no one would consider my absence for much of the day remarkable. And even in the country, a gentleman must dress for dinner.

Most of the company arrived in the early afternoon, and since the horse Roseman was running had already been sent to the estate where the race was to be held, he took them out to show off the rest of his stable. I had only to wait till his valet went down to share a cup of tea with the other servants before I sneaked into his room and secreted myself under the bed.

I had already ascertained that I had a clear view of the dials from there, as well as considering other possible hiding places in the room. The view from the wardrobe was better, but the odds of my being found in it were ridiculously high. In fact, beneath the bed was the only place I thought I might go undiscovered and still see the numbers on the dials—or at least the direction of their pointers—when the compartment that held the key was opened.

There were also were several boxes pushed beneath the bed, which held lightweight summer coats, some hats for which there was no more room in the wardrobe, and a set of matched dueling swords, all of which would further serve to hide me. Finding the space not only cramped, but somewhat dusty, I'd taken the time to clean it long before Roseman's return.

Now, sliding into the narrow space between the boxes, making sure that none of them pushed from beneath the bed skirts to attract attention, I was glad I had. This was, mayhap, the one moment in my life when a sneeze might mean my death.

I was also glad I'd taken the precaution of hiding myself early in the afternoon, for Roseman's valet kept popping in and out. He was a small man, with an irritating habit of whistling under his breath when he thought himself alone. Why he hadn't mended his master's coat and polished his boots earlier I didn't know, but when he was present I didn't dare even to turn my head.

In his occasional absence I could turn onto my back, or stomach, or side, and ease my cramping neck. After the first half-hour, lying on a hard wooden floor becomes increasingly uncomfortable. On the other hand, listening to the valet bustle about his work my pounding heartbeat gradually slowed, for he came and went without ever suspecting my presence.

When dinnertime drew near, I seized on one of his errands to position myself in the way it was most comfortable for me to see the dials. I'd had plenty of time to arrange the boxes and the bed skirt so I had a clear view of that section of the wall.

But the sound of the Rose's footsteps set my heart pounding.

"The maroon velvet, I think," he told his man.

"With the gold lace collar, sir?"

"No, that's too fancy for a country dinner. The shirt with pointelle lace, collar and cuffs."

Did that mean he wasn't going to wear jewelry? My every aching muscle screamed in protest.

They went on to discuss britches and stockings at most tedious length, while the valet brushed his master's hair and assisted him into his clothing. Finally, Roseman said, "Looks good. A ring do you think?"

"The emerald, sir? A bit of color, to brighten up dark brown and gold?"

"Won't that be a bit much, for the country?"

No it won't! I thought at him, as hard as I could. *You need to show off for the neighbors, intimidate your guests, display how rich you are...*

"Well, sir, you are a great man," the valet said.

I could have kissed him.

Roseman laughed. "All right. The emerald ring."

I'd expected the valet to get the jewelry, but 'twas Roseman himself who went to the wall, pulled off the concealing rosettes...and stood right in front of the dials, blocking my view as he turned them.

The section of paneling that swung open was below the dials, and I had only a moment, as he bent to sort though the jewel boxes in the hidden compartment, to note the places all three pointers rested. Then he closed the door, turned the dials again, and even replaced the rosettes before returning to let his valet put the final touches on his attire. I closed my eyes, ignoring the valet's fawning flattery, fixing the location of all three dials in my mind—which might have been harder, if it hadn't struck me to think of them as times on a clock face.

Not long after that Roseman departed, and I lay on my back listing to his man putter about, putting away brushes and the stockings that hadn't been chosen.

Finally, *finally* he left.

Mayhap I should have waited. He could have returned at any moment. But the thought of Roseman returning to this room, of creeping out as he slept atop me—which I had once considered an acceptable possibility—was now too much to be borne.

I squirmed from beneath the bed, replaced the boxes I'd shoved aside, and dragged myself to my feet, my joints creaking like an old grandfather's.

My fingers shook as I pulled the rosettes off their dials. I'd have little chance to conceal myself if anyone came in, and I dared not open the door to try to hear footsteps. My best hope now was speed.

The first dial had rested at 12:04 or mayhap 12:05—'twas hard to be precise, but I turned the pointer to that position, ignoring the number it settled on.

The second dial had been set at 12:45 precisely. I was sure of that one. Almost.

The third dial I turned to 12:36…and nothing happened.

I reached down and pressed my hand against the panel that had opened trying to shake it—it felt like trying to shake part of the wall.

I tried the third pointer at 12:37, and then 12:35, to no avail.

My nerves screaming for haste, I turned it back to 12:36, and turned the first dial to 12:05, then changed the last dial back and forth, clicking though all the positions I thought it might have occupied. Nothing. Straining my memory, trying to figure out how my position on the floor might have affected my view, I turned the first dial to 12:06 and tried the last dial in several positions again… and on the third try, my straining ears heard a faint click from the wall below.

I had to press on the narrow edge of the panel to one side of the pivot hinge to swing it open. Inside lay a nice collection of gentleman's jewelry, though not as much as I'd have expected from someone as rich as Roseman—mayhap he kept the bulk of his finery in town. I got to see most of the collection, because the glowing key lay at the very back, with no more concealment than the clutter of cases that filled the compartment.

It slipped into my pocket like the lethal secret it was, and my pulse hammered as I closed the door and spun the dials. I had no memory of where they'd pointed before I turned them, and I could only hope Roseman wouldn't remember either.

I strode quietly over to the door and pressed my ear to it. I heard nothing, but through a plank this thick that meant little. I eased the door open a crack and peered out—the space I could see was empty, but the hallway on the other side wasn't visible.

Boldness would serve best now.

I swung open the door and stepped out, casually, as if I'd every right to be in that room. As I closed it behind myself, I glanced down the other half of the corridor...and my knees weakened when I found it empty.

With all the guests at dinner, that was the most likely outcome. And despite the fact that no one could know where I'd been, I scuttled down the corridor to the servant's stair. By the time I reached my own room I was drenched in sweat, and breathing as if I'd run a mile...but I had the key in my possession.

If Roseman had no need for it, *if* he didn't notice its absence, *if* he didn't notice that those dials weren't in the position he'd left them...then the dangerous part began.

THE LOCAL LORD who owned the estate where the race was to be held was no friend to Roseman, or so I gathered from the servants' commentary. I wondered at that, till I realized that such an arrangement would divert suspicions of foul play. The agreement of the owners was that the horses would be housed here, fed the same food and given the same treatment, for a week before the race—mostly so that, if one of the horses was magica, the other grooms would have time to notice. The estate also had a long race course around their broad pastures, and stabling to house the horses that were to compete.

All the local gentry, and most of the country folk who lived nearby, had gathered to watch the event. Stands had been erected, as if for a tourney, and the rest of the crowd spread out on each side of the line that would both start and finish the course. Beyond the rope, that held the crowd back, the inner part of the course was lined with blue flags, and the outer with red. If a horse passed outside one of those flags, it had to go back and pass inside it or be disqualified—and sober-looking judges stood by each flag, particularly in areas where the course passed out of sight.

Not being part of the gentry, or even a real guard, I went with the rest of Roseman's guardsmen to stand beside the part of the course the horses would race past on their way to the finish. We'd have a poor view of the start, and almost as poor a view of the end, but we'd be able to watch them jockey for position in this final stretch.

To my surprise, Jack came up and stood beside me.

"The Rose doesn't think a dozen guards are sufficient to keep an eye on me?"

"After you were angling to get here so obviously? No, he doesn't. I'm here to remind you that if you make too much trouble Fisk will be the one who pays the price. Well, he'll be the second person to pay."

The indifference in his voice nettled me. "And how is Fisk? He's not dead." I touched the collar, concealed beneath the collars of my shirt and coat. "But 'twould be nice to know he's not chained to some dungeon wall."

"Fisk is doubtless scheming away, even as we speak. It won't get him anywhere, but it keeps him happy so I don't try to stop him."

"You must have been a very bad teacher, to be so sure his schemes will be fruitless."

I had hoped to touch Jack on the raw, but he only smiled absently. A squad of stablemen where walking over the final yards of the track, tossing out any stones they found. The course master, who owned the estate, was arguing about something with the judges near the finish line.

If the Rose's bought riders did their job, when the horses passed us 'twould be Red Thorn in the lead, while the others tried to hold back their mounts but still make it look like a race.

Chant is a destrier, not a racer, but I couldn't help wishing myself in the saddle on so fine a day—even in a fixed race, and one I couldn't win even if 'twas honest.

I wondered how Chant and Tipple were faring in our landlady's care for so long. Had the orphans been able to keep True? Or had they taken the dog back to her, as well? Fisk would be paying for their keep, but the animals were so much a part of our roving life I couldn't help but miss them.

Though not as much as I missed Fisk.

"How could you?" I asked Jack. "How could you betray him into such a deadly trap?"

That got his attention. "Like you've never taken Fisk into danger?"

"Nothing so perilous as..." Several inconvenient memories surfaced. "Well, I never involved him in anything against his will! If he went into danger with me he did so in full knowledge, by his own choice."

"If he'd just let go of you, he wouldn't be in danger." Jack sounded more exasperated than repentant. "Or I should say, when he lets go of you he won't be."

I stared at him. "I thought you knew Fisk. His ethics may fall short, by some folk's measure, but he's utterly loyal to those he cares about. He won't abandon me. Ever."

"Then I still have something to teach him," Jack said. "But if I were you, I wouldn't...ah, it's beginning."

The horses were led out to the course. Grooms clad in household livery held their lead reins, and the riders wore ribbons in household colors around their arms.

I saw at once that the orphans had failed to get the laudanum into Red Thorn's feed. The big chestnut pranced his way to the starting line, ears pricked, eager to run. I thought for a moment the whole scheme had failed...until I saw his rider sway in the saddle.

Others had seen it too. Roseman himself came onto the course. The crowd had gone so quiet we could hear him protesting that his rider was sick, clearly sick, and he should be allowed to replace him.

Jack cast a curious glance my way, but I ignored it. Having been under the eyes of Roseman's guards from the time we left the house might have been uncomfortable, but it had its advantages.

We all heard the course master say that the owners had agreed that no rider could be substituted after the fifth day before the race. Master Roseman had insisted on that rule. Did Master Roseman wish to withdraw his horse?

The Rose cast a fearful scowl at his rider, sagging in the saddle, and declined to withdraw.

I had been hoping he'd accept, and let the man get to a healer. How much laudanum had the orphans dosed him with? Surely not the half-bottle I'd recommend for the horse, or he'd be dead by now!

Whatever his rider's state, Red Thorn was ready to run. The horses gathered at the line, the flag went down, and they all burst forward in a mass of bouncing rumps and flying clods of grass and mud.

The rider seemed a bit steadier in the saddle, as the pack galloped into a dip and out of our sight. I hoped he'd be able to stay in the saddle—I didn't want his death on my conscience, even if his survival meant the Rose might win.

The horses were out of sight for several minutes and the crowd relaxed, moving around and speculating about who'd be in the lead when they returned. Scramble and Morning Thunder were held to be the fastest, but a few people murmured that Red Thorn might have "advantages."

"I don't know how you did it," Jack murmured. "And that's impressive."

"How could I have done anything? I've been under constant watch since before we arrived here."

"Which means you have a confederate."

I snorted. "Or more likely, that Roseman has more enemies than just me."

Jack shrugged, but he was still watching me when the horses galloped back into view, on the far side of the pastures, and a chorus of groans and cheers greeted them.

Red Thorn was in the lead, running at an easier gallop than you'd expect in a race. But the others were all many lengths behind, and despite his slack pace, that lead widened.

Stillness spread through the crowd, broken by angry muttering as it became clear that the other riders must be holding back deliberately.

I knew what was happening, for horses like to run together, not away from their fellows. They can be competitive, and try to outrun others, but they don't like to leave them too far behind.

And Red Thorn's rider was too befuddled by drugs to insist that his horse run full out.

The chestnut stallion was only loping in the final stretch, and the others were over twenty lengths behind him, when the reins fell from his rider's hands, and the man toppled from the saddle.

Because I'd been half-expecting it, I was moving before anyone else, leaping over the rope and sprinting toward him. He squirmed feebly, so at least he wasn't dead.

Red Thorn, confused, trotted back to sniff at the rider who was behaving so strangely.

Then, as I'd known they would, the other riders realized that with Roseman's horse clearly out of the race, they were free to try to win.

I didn't look up as the thunder of hoofbeats erupted. No time to carry the fallen man out of harm's way, for the whole herd would be on us in seconds. Magic boiled up within me as I snatched Red Thorn's reins, and pulled him between his rider and the pounding hooves that rushed toward us.

I channeled that molten flood of power through my animal handling gift, into a single thought with all my will behind it: Stand.

Red Thorn's body froze in place, as if it had turned to stone. But he turned his head to look at me as the avalanche of heaving flesh pounded toward us...swerved around his huge, solid body and ran past.

Clots of mud pelted me, and covered the rider's back as the race hurtled by, but that was the only harm we suffered.

I pulled that brimming flood of power back into its well, and sealed it closed. Red Thorn, released from its grip, started to sidle and I let him go to trot after the others.

The crowd was roaring, so someone had won. I was more concerned for the man on the ground beside me.

"Can I get a healer here?"

The man who climbed over the rope to join me was younger than I'd expected, but he seemed competent, checking the rider's bones and neck before rolling him gently onto his back. Eyes dilated to blackness blinked up at us.

"This man's been drugged!"

"Do tell." The Rose's icy voice came from behind me. He was attended by Jack, most of his guards, the course master, and a number of interested bystanders. His grooms were capturing Red Thorn.

"How could this happen, as protected as this race was supposed to be?" Roseman was talking to the course master, but I still shivered.

Jack's expression merely thoughtful, though the gaze he turned on me was very sharp.

"The horses were protected," the man said. "I could hardly keep the riders prisoner. I've no idea where your man went before the race, or what he ate. Or drank."

"He's not drunk." The healer's hands found pulses in the rider's wrist, throat, behind the knee. "I'd guess it's laudanum. Something in that family, anyway. And not magica, thank goodness, or he'd be dead."

"Will he be all right?" the course master asked. "Can you rid him of it?"

"Too late for that," the healer said. "It absorbs pretty fast, and he clearly took it awhile ago. But his pulse is steady, if a bit depressed. He should be all right. Though it will be days before he's—"

"Taken how long ago?" Roseman asked. "If anyone saw who drugged him..."

His grooms had brought up the horse. One of them stepped forward.

"Uh...boss?"

"Yes."

"I didn't think much about it at the time. But we've seen several children hanging around, and they didn't seem to be with any—"

Roseman spun to his guards. "Get them! Bring them to me!"

I turned to go with the others. Jack put his hands in his pockets and said nothing, but his gaze followed me, even as the course master said, "Children? Why would a child try to drug your rider? Or anyone? How could they..."

The guards' leader ordered our search of the estate. He cast me an annoyed glance—I was one more thing he had to keep an eye on, in the midst of this new task. In the end he assigned me to the group searching the stables, the place I was least likely to escape from. At least, escape unseen. I might have stolen a horse, but I couldn't go galloping off quietly.

It made no difference to me where I was sent. They would find me.

And I made sure that neither Jack nor anyone else was watching when I finally managed to wander off by myself, searching a long row of stalls and pens where the horses and livestock that belonged to the estate were housed. But the whispered "hey" came, not from an empty stall, but from the rafters above the goat pen.

I looked up and saw Jig, peering down from one of the big beams.

"Don't look up. Someone might wonder what you's staring at."

I looked down. Several bored goats gazed back at me.

"I told you to dose the horse. How much did you give that poor man?"

"Well, we had to guess about that. They was guarding the horse, see? We figured he was about a quarter the horse's size, so we gave him about an eighth of that little bottle. Couple of big spoons, it was."

Lianna had taken a single teaspoon of the stuff.

"That horse is seven times his weight. You could have killed the man." I was hard pressed to keep my voice down, but the fault was mine, putting such a weapon in inexperienced hands. "Did you even consider that?"

"Yah, we thought about it. But he works for the Rose, so we didn't much care."

The sincere indifference in that young voice was chilling, but he added, "Will he die?"

"The healer says he should be all right," I admitted. "But 'twas still a terrible risk. You must promise never..."

I didn't finish, for 'twas a promise they would either refuse to make, or break whenever they got their hands on one of the Rose's men.

'Twas then that the thought first occurred to me, but I thrust it aside as ridiculous.

"I've got the key," I told him. "And a note for Fisk as well. I'll tuck them behind the tack box here, and you can come down and get them when it's safe." I slid them into their hiding place as I spoke. I'd kept a careful eye out for Jack, and Roseman's guards, but 'twould be safer for Jig to wait till the search died down before he descended. "I trust I've paid enough for their delivery?"

"That you have, Master Michael. More'n enough. We hurt the Rose good today, didn't we?"

Hatred brimmed in that simple question. Who was I to deny them their victory?

"Yes, you've hurt him badly. Not only did you cost him a lot of money, you revealed to everyone here that this race was rigged for him to win. Whatever reputation he might have had, 'tis now in tatters."

"Good."

"Not entirely—he knows you were the ones who did it."

"Even better," Jig said.

"Mayhap it feels better to you, but he's angry enough to do something about it, and he knows where your warehouse is. You'd better clear out of there, for a while. And be extra careful. Promise me."

"We always are."

The scrabbling sounds that came from the rafters as he left were no louder than a squirrel might have made.

CHAPTER 16

Fisk

oseman and Jack had departed for the country, to attend a race in which the Rose had a horse running. And from the sounds of it, a lot of money riding on the outcome. I only hoped their presence wouldn't put a crimp in Michael's plans, and it evidently didn't—a key, wrapped in a brief note from Michael, found its way into my pocket just five days later.

No luck on the necklace yet, was all it said, and I cursed his brevity even as my fist clenched around the key. It looked like an ordinary key to me. It's wards a bit more complex than some, but that was to be expected for an important lock. Where had he found it? Was he sure this was the right one? Of course, Michael could not only sense, but see magic—and how many magica keys could Roseman have? I still wished Michael had written a bit more… But he hadn't, and I'd now run out of excuses.

It was time to burgle Roseman's office.

I DID IT that very night. Both Roseman and Jack were gone, and I had no idea when they'd be back, but doing this in their absence struck me as a really good idea. It took less time to pick my way into the outer office this time. The curtains were still open, letting in the moonlight—though tonight the Green Moon showed only a sliver, and even the smaller tan Creature Moon was only half full.

Not great for reading...and I hoped to be doing a great deal of reading.

I went over to the forbidden door, put Michael's key into the lock and turned it. I should have been pleased when it clicked smoothly open, but instead fear shot through me, and set my heart pounding even harder.

At first glance, the room beyond looked much like the outer office: a large desk, with its back to the window and moonlight shining on the papers that covered it—but not enough to read by. Several chairs were scattered about, and there was a bench against the wall opposite the desk. Cabinets and shelves filled the wall opposite the door.

I went first to the window, and made sure that none of the guards who patrolled the grounds were looking up, before I closed the velvet curtains. There was a chance that one of those men would be alert enough to notice that curtains that had been open weren't—but hopefully not much chance.

I locked the door and pushed a rug up against it to block any light that might show beneath. If someone came in, the opening of the outer office door would give me some warning—though what I'd do with that warning was a question I prayed I wouldn't have to answer. If I got caught in the outer office, I could claim I'd had a sudden thought, wanted to check the ledgers, and found the door unlocked. It wasn't a great lie, but it might be enough to let me live. At least no one could come in after me...but if someone suspected my presence, and I was trapped in this inner office, I'd be done for.

I lit a single candle, and was turning to the papers on the desk when a large map on the wall over the bench caught my eye. At first I'd taken it for some kind of art—a tattered patchwork, as if some quilter had stitched together scraps of odd shapes and sizes. A map of Tallowsport made perfect sense in this office...but the Port only took up about six inches of a map that was almost four by six feet. The rest was filled with those odd shaped patches, darker around the port and lighter toward the rest of the Realm.

Looking closer, I saw it was a detailed map of the estates that covered the Erran River Plain, all the way to Gollford. The ones near the port bore marks in red or blue, most of them covered with slanting red lines, a few with blue Xs. The Xs became more frequent away from the port, and the estates on the outskirts were more often marked with a single blue or red slash. Each estate had been neatly labeled in black ink with the name of the man who ruled it, and those under the red stripes bore a number. The numbers seemed almost random, ranging from eight to over a hundred, though the larger numbers were usually on large estates. Many were marked with the same round numbers, twenty, forty and sixty being most common.

The back of my neck prickled with primitive warning, but I didn't understand what it was warning me about. I chose one name from the map, one of those with red lines all over it: Baron Flaxom, twenty-eight.

The Rose's filing system was excellent—I only had to open three cabinets, all of them stuffed with papers, before I found the Fs.

Baron George Flaxom had promised twenty-eight men— which didn't sound that important, until you remembered it was inked on the map. His estate paid the High Liege a hundred and twenty gold roundels a quarter, which meant it was prosperous for such a small place. The only way the Rose could know his tax rate was if the baron had told him. There were some calculations detailing how much the baron could save if he paid only eighty-nine roundels a quarter.

There were a lot more notes about the prices the food trains would be paying on his estate, prices that were much lower than the one we'd traveled with had paid. I went back to the map and looked—yes, we'd been buying food mostly in areas marked with a single slash, red or blue.

The last entry in the baron's file was a note that ten crossbows, twenty pikes and thirty swords were to be sent to the baron's estate as soon as the production schedule would permit.

I turned back to the map, noting how many red striped patches there were, and how few blue Xs.

Atherton Roseman was about to raise a third of the river plains in rebellion.

Even as my mind grasped it, a part of me howled in protest. The High Lieges had kept peace between baron and baron, lord and lord, for over two hundred years. But it hadn't always been like that.

The first battles of the great war that had brought the Realm under the Liege's rule had been fought on the plains. The first battles of the new war would be fought here as well, if the Rose had his way.

I stared at the map but I barely saw it, as evidence began to click into place. It took a long time, checking back and forth between map and files, but eventually it all became clear.

The Rose paid extra for food in the areas he planned to subvert, draining the land of workers—men who might become soldiers when the war started. When the barons came to him to complain, he brushed them off. Those were the blue

Xs, the men too loyal to the Liege to be subverted. And how could they complain to anyone that their farmers were being paid *too much*? But those who weren't so loyal, he seduced into joining him. That map wasn't just his battle markers, it was a recruiting tool. "See how many of your neighbors, your friends, have joined me already?" He promised to pay their farmers reasonable rates, so they could keep their people on the land. Promised to significantly lower their taxes, once they were paying them to him instead of the High Liege. Promised to arm the men they were training for his army, when the time came...

No wonder he'd told Rigsby he was planning "something big."

My heart was racing, my palms wet with sweat. I don't consider myself easily frightened, but this...

It was at that moment I heard the door of the outer office open, and Wiederman's voice saying, "...if you're doing this because you just want to come inside and warm up, I'll go looking for two new guardsmen in the morning."

The Rose would kill anyone who knew this secret, no matter what excuse they offered. And when I died, so would Michael.

A quick pinch extinguished the candle. Did Wiederman have a magica key? Almost certainly not, but I wasn't prepared to bet my life on it. Patrolling guards or no, I was at the window, swinging it open, even before I heard the soft click from the inner door's lock.

I all but leapt out that window, kneeling on the sill to pull the drapes back before I closed it. I was standing on the sill when I heard the door open and multiple footsteps came into the room. I'd have sworn Roseman kept that key with him at all times—why had he left it with Wiederman? Or was there more than one spare? To *that* room?

If they caught me out here, the answer would very shortly

cease to matter. At least to me.

These men going into the house must have put a hole in the patrol patterns, for there were no guards below me at the moment. But I'd watched them long enough to know that would soon change. Several feet below the window sill, a narrow ledge ran around the outside of the building for most of this floor. Back when I was a child burglar, it would have seemed like...well, not a roadway, but at least a precarious trail. Now, it looked like an excellent way to fall to my death.

"See?" said a strange voice, doubtless a guardsman. "Nothing here. I told—"

"I swear the curtains in here were lighter than the others," another voice protested.

My faint hope that they'd leave without checking the window disappeared, even Wiederman said, "No matter. You're right to bring it to my attention, even if it's nothing. Check the window. Maybe the curtains in here are lined with lighter fabric."

I stepped off the sill and down to the ledge. It was about four inches wide, and held most of my foot when I turned it sideways. I started slinking along it as the second guard said, "They're lined sir, but I dunno if its lighter than the others or not."

His voice faded as I moved away from the window...or maybe the thunder of my heartbeat drowned it out. The stucco covering the wall was too new for cracks. My fingertips clung, uselessly, to its rough surface as I sidled down to the next window—which was locked, curse it! I didn't dare stop there, and the corner of the house was almost within reach. There was a drain pipe strapped securely to the wall, good, solid rich-man's iron, not flimsy tin. I heard the whisper of well-oiled hinges as the window opened, grabbed it, and swung myself around the corner.

"There's nothing here, Master Wiederman." The man sounded

as if he was right next to me—he must have opened the window and leaned out. "But I swear this window looked brighter than the others. Liffer should come by soon. We can ask him if these curtains are lighter."

And when Liffer and his partner arrived, the guard's first call would draw their eyes up to where I perched. In a dark vest and britches, against a pale wall, even if the moons weren't full. Not to mention the magical gem glowing like a lantern at my throat. And no use turning it to the back—in the dark, it was bright enough to show through the collar of my shirt.

I missed Wiederman's reply, if he made one, but the odds were excellent that when they left they'd latch that window behind them.

Memory of the old days, and the feeling of that strong iron pipe, gave me ideas. I took a step back to the corner, and climbed, not down to the well-patrolled garden, but all the way up to the wide ledge that ran beneath the attic windows.

Swinging myself up onto it was something I hadn't done in years, it was a lot harder than it sounds, and I was more agile the last time I'd tried it.

I hate burglary.

After I finally rolled onto the vast two-foot-wide ledge, I lay on my back for a long time, gazing at the dark sky, listening to the guards call back and forth, and waiting for my heartbeat to slow to a reasonable rate.

All those guards, flooding the house and town, acting as thugs and collectors and who-knew-what else, they weren't a sign of ostentation or paranoia—they were *soldiers*. They were the core of the Rose's army.

And the crimes he was committing, the city tax, the stolen goods he fenced, rampant corruption...they only served as cover for his real plan.

No wonder Jack admired the man. I was awed at the scope

of it myself. Even the stocks had a concealed purpose, helping Roseman quell the population of the countryside he planned to rule. When their barons rose against the High Liege, no one would dare rise against the barons—or their new Liege.

The food trains, traveling on public roads in plain sight, were the heart of the scheme. They drained the countryside so that the High Liege's taxes pinched more and more, and changing their rates offered barons relief the moment they signed on with the Rose. They brought labor into the city, too, to make arms for that growing army. That was probably worth even the prices Roseman paid... Of course! There was no hidden treasury, brimming with money from the city tax and all his loot. He spent it on the cheap food that kept his labor force working and happy. The whole city of Tallowsport, the most prosperous seaport in the Realm, brimming with labor and industry, was his vault.

It was so crazy it might just work. No one who hadn't seen that hushed room, read the papers it contained, would ever believe it. I actually gave the rebellion a fifty-fifty chance of success. Though the High Liege would *not* be happy to see Tallowsport, and enough land to feed it, slip out of his tax base.

On the other hand, no Liege had demanded the old, feudal levy of men and arms for over a century. How would hard-headed, independent barons, like Michael's father, react to a sudden command to produce a large number of men at arms and their officers. Not to mention horses, and food, and tents, and cooks... And if the Rose should win his freedom from the Liege's laws and taxes, how many of them would start to think; "If Atherton Roseman can do it, why not me?"

What's the difference between a traitor and a bandit? The bandit never pretended to be on your side.

Any possibility that the Rose might let Michael and me live, and go on working for him if he won, was irrelevant. Because as soon as he knew what was really going on, Michael would do whatever he had to in order to prevent it. Even if he got us both killed, trying.

So I'd better come up with a way to stop it before Michael did.

The core of the answer was simple—evidence of the real plot must be sent to the High Liege before the Rose was ready to start his war. When would he be ready? I had no idea. In fact, I had no idea how to go about executing most of this "simple" plan, and the odds of my success ranged somewhere between impossible and are-you-kidding-me?

I had no desire to climb down that pipe, even if it wasn't for the soldier-guards lurking in the garden below. As for leaving the pipe to slide along that ledge, trying to cling to smooth stucco with my fingertips...no.

Instead I crawled along the wide ledge, trying and mostly failing not to look down, till I came to an attic window. It was already unlatched, and the hinges didn't squeak, but I guess the mad don't sleep soundly.

"Come to pay me a visit, have you? Tea and crumpets? Jammy tarts?"

The jeweler sat up in bed, his rumpled hair flattened on one side. His amiable expression combined with the wild roving gaze in an effect that went well with the hair.

"I've been meaning to come talk with you for some time." I swung my legs over the sill and stepped into the room. "I'd have brought refreshments, but I don't know what you like."

"Ravens in a clear sky, and fish that bite." A part of me kept thinking of him as an old man, though he wasn't. "Hearts and flowers, beating hearts, fluttering in my hands... I don't get visitors, not unless they want something."

I could see why.

"I must admit, I was wondering if you could figure out

some way to change the spell on my gem. So it would keep glowing even if I took the collar off."

His face sagged, his lower lip pouting like a toddler's, and I added swiftly, "It's not that we don't like them. But I'd like to take it off, just sometimes, and those gems are so beautiful it would be a shame if they went out."

Petulance vanished in a cackle of laughter.

"I knew it was that, of course I knew. They all come to me, curses and wishes both. But I won't do it. Why should I?"

"You could do it to get back at Tony Rose," I suggested. "How long has he been keeping you prisoner? Wouldn't you like to tick him off?"

Even if he'd been sane, I wouldn't have dared to say, "get free of him."

"Me? Hurt the Rose?" Surprise rang in his voice. "Why would I want to do that?"

"Because he uses your magic, and you get nothing in return. He keeps you locked up here."

"He keeps me safe! Safe from those who want my magic, digging it out with their dirty fingernails. Poking, poking through the bars of my cage, drinking my blood to try to steal it."

He was so agitated that he got out of bed and started to pace, his nightshirt's hem ragged around his knobby knees. I'd have liked to think this was the rambling of madness, but remembering what Lady Ceciel had been willing to do, to risk, to give humans magic...

"Someone else held you prisoner?" I asked gently. "Did they make you drink potions?" It might have been Ceciel who'd held him, though she lived on the other side of the Realm. If it was her, I wasn't going to tell Michael. He was sufficiently alarmed by his abilities as it was.

"Drink something? They drank me! I was the source, the

origin, a garment they wanted to wear. Like a clock, tick tock, get the screwdriver, get it open, look at its guts how they spin."

His expression made the words even worse.

"They studied you."

"Master Rose took me from them, keeps me here with the other little rats, keeps me safe, feeds me. All he wants in return is a little magic. Doesn't even beat me when I can't *perform*."

I nodded understanding, wondering who'd held him and why they'd treated him so cruelly.

"I see why you don't want to tick off the Rose. I won't ask again. Sorry to have troubled you. Oh, one more thing...how do you feel about Master Wiederman?"

"Sticks and snakes and one wall-eye. Can't stand the man."

I let myself out the trap door and climbed down the ladder, leaving him pacing and muttering. If even half his tale was true—and I'd no reason to doubt it—that man would be genuinely loyal to his master. But at least he wasn't likely to report me to Wiederman, and might well have forgotten my presence by the time his master returned.

What would become of him when Roseman was gone? Because, whatever careless kindness he'd shown his pet madman, the Rose had to go down.

Before he set the whole eastern part of the Realm on fire.

I went first to my own room, but there were no guards waiting to slaughter me, so despite my desire to leap into bed and pull the covers over my head I went back to the Rose's office. And this time, I took a thick blanket from my bed, to make sure no light would show.

I tapped softly on the door, to make sure no guards had been posted inside. The outer door's lock took longer than it had the first time, because my hands wanted to tremble.

Wiederman had clearly dismissed the guard's report

tonight—but who knew what precautions he might decide to take in the morning? It had to be tonight.

I hung my blanket over the window, making certain there were no cracks around it before I relit the candle—but I had to have light to find the files I needed and write clean copies. One file might be explained as some odd kind of business deal, six, seven, eight of them were damning.

Knowing what the Liege's judicars would want most, I wasted twenty minutes looking for a master list of all those who'd promised the Rose their allegiance, but I didn't find it. Judging by the map, it might have taken too long to copy anyway.

There was probably a full hour of darkness left when I decided I had enough evidence, and I took the time to set everything in both offices back where I'd found it, refiling all the papers carefully in place.

Inner door, securely locked. Outer door, unlocked but closed. You'd think I'd have been numb to terror by then, but my heart was still pounding as I crept back to my bedroom and tucked my copied files in among the stacks of ship's papers.

Tomorrow I'd take them with me, and have one of the captains hide them—so they wouldn't be found by some housemaid and get me killed.

I did not sleep well.

THE NEXT MORNING at breakfast, Wiederman eyed me suspiciously.

"I'm sending an extra guard with you today, Master Fisk. And I think I'll put a guard on your door as well."

"What for?" I asked.

"You don't look like you slept well."

"And that's a reason to put guards on me?"

Wiederman said nothing, but his eyes were sharp enough

to cut glass.

"Fine, have it your way. If you want to have someone following me out to the jakes, that's up to you. But it's a waste of a guard."

I ate the rest of my breakfast as if nothing else was happening, and then went back to my room to change into accountant clothes. Eventually my hands stopped shaking enough to let me shave.

I'd already concealed the copies I'd made among my ship notes—and since they were all in my writing, anyone who wanted to search for them would have to read through the whole thick stack to pick them out. If Wiederman was going to do that, he'd have done it already.

I had the evidence to convince the High Liege's commander in Gollford to send enough troops to take the Rose down. I had a messenger, in the captain—and I'd give him those damning copies this very day. I'd even figured out that he could leave a letter with the chandler in Hinksville, asking him to send me a message when the Liege's troops passed through that town, which should give us half a day's warning before they got here.

Because the moment those troops arrived, the Rose would know that Michael and I were behind them. Whichever of us was in his reach at that moment would die—followed shortly by the other.

I even had some idea how to create enough confusion, that if the Rose was out of the way the others might not kill us. Not without their boss's orders, anyway.

But Tony Rose would give those orders in an instant...unless he was dead or incapacitated when the troops arrived.

And I had no idea how to accomplish that.

THAT AFTERNOON, safe in the chart room of one of my conspirators, I wrote several long, incriminating letters.

CHAPTER 17

Michael

I thought Roseman would leave immediately after the race, but he spent several more days in the country settling his racing debts. His losses were larger than I'd expected. Although he put on a face of rueful amusement, jesting with his friends about jockeys who rode with the flu, his eyes were so bleak that the men he paid exited his office with the quiet tread of men sneaking past a sleeping wolf.

'Twas the morning he planned to return to Tallowsport, and I was seating myself at the breakfast table when Roseman looked up from his plate and said, "Sevenson, you're coming with us. There's an…entertainment back in town I want you to see."

"I haven't packed." Anything Roseman called "entertainment" in that tone of voice was something I wanted no part of, but I kept my voice level and a flicker of reluctant respect crossed his face.

"You're still coming."

That settled that and I began to eat, more hastily than I'd have preferred.

Lianna looked nervously between us, clearly understanding that something was going on—and she must have decided that she wanted in on whatever it might be.

At first she said nothing, but she looked brighter and more eager every time Roseman spoke of leaving. After a time, he had to notice it.

"So, Mistress Dalton. Are you going to miss your friend here?"

"Not at all!" she said, far too swift and emphatic. "Well, of course I will, but I like the country."

'Twas enough to make a duller man than Roseman suspicious, and a frown gathered on his brow.

"I couldn't see my husband in the city, anyway," Lianna babbled on. "So there's no reason for me to go. At all. Is there?"

Lianna never babbled. Roseman stared at her thoughtfully. The disastrous race had made him more paranoid than usual, and he must have suspected she was playing him. But if she was, was it safer to leave her behind or keep her under his eye?

"All right," he said finally. "You'll come too. You won't like it. You'll stay at the inn with my men, locked in your room. Your husband won't even know you're there."

Lianna looked down, concealing her expression from all of us. But when Roseman added, "You'll travel in my carriage," her eyes flew up, with so much dismay in them that he nodded in satisfaction and returned to his meal.

Lianna and I had to leave the table early so we could pack, but we reached the courtyard before the guards came to fetch us.

To my considerable relief I was given a horse and allowed to ride with the escort, instead of accompanying the master in his carriage. Seven hours in cramped quarters with an angry Atherton Roseman was something no one should have to endure—but Lianna had made her choice. And if she was willing to endure traveling into town with him, she'd earned the right to be in on the finish.

I soon came to regret my inadequate breakfast. Roseman had brought a hamper to eat in his carriage, and the riders had brought dried beef and fruit to eat as they rode, but no one had warned me we wouldn't be stopping at mid-day. By the time we reached town, I was so hungry I was thinking less about Roseman's "entertainment" than about getting a luncheon—or an early dinner!

'Tis unworthy for a knight errant to be so concerned about missing a meal, but starving me was such a petty revenge for the Rose to take that I was almost reassured—mayhap his "entertainment" would be equally petty.

Several of the guardsmen closed in around me as we drew near the city, but I paid that little heed. I assumed that we'd be lodged at an inn once more, to keep Fisk and me apart. Had I known I'd be coming back to town, I would have schemed to meet with him—which was likely why Roseman had given me so little warning, for they must know we would try to escape given the slightest chance.

'Twas not until the coach turned east toward the docks, instead of west toward The Rise, that I realized the promised entertainment was at hand.

I asked the men who rode beside me where we were going. We hadn't spoken often during that long ride, but some ordinary words about weather and the road had passed between us. 'Twas alarming when they shot me grim looks, and said nothing.

I had realized what our destination must be long before we reached the orphan's warehouse. But 'twas not till I saw the bundles of wood piled around its walls, and the empty kegs of oil and pitch, that I kicked my horse to run. The beast managed mayhap one stride before the men around me grabbed my reins and dragged him to a stop.

Shouting for the children to escape, I flung myself from the saddle, but several guards had already dismounted and I ran

only a few yards before they seized me. I probably shouldn't
have tried to fight.

I was on my knees, my hands pulled up behind my back,
my head still ringing from a blow that had sent hot blood
spilling down one side of my face and silenced my warning
cries. Roseman emerged from his carriage and strolled over
to me. I can't remember ever feeling more helpless than I
did then.

"I can't prove that you helped those brats drug my jockey."
His voice was conversational, almost light. "Jack Markham's
certain of it, but even he can't figure out how you could have
made it happen. And I won't condemn a man without proof.
But I thought you might find it…instructive to see what
happens to people who cross me."

"They won't be there." I had warned Jig, told him specifically
that Roseman knew about this warehouse. Surely the children
had moved out days ago. Long before the guards, before the
carts of wood and pitch arrived.

"They might not," Roseman admitted. "My men surrounded
the place, covering that alley exit of theirs as well as the front
and side doors, before they went in and extracted the most
valuable goods. They didn't see a sign of the brats. But it's not
easy to watch your home burn, even if you're not in it. And
if they don't have this bolt hole to retreat to, maybe they'll be
easier to catch."

I thought any children in that warehouse could easily have
hidden from Roseman's guards. And if they were in there,
they'd not be able to hide from the flames.

The fire brigade was standing by, I noticed, and the walls
of the nearby buildings looked damp. But I remembered the
contents of that warehouse. Not much of it had been all that
valuable, but taken altogether…

"You're about to burn up a small fortune."

"A medium-sized fortune, for most people," Roseman said. "I'm not most people. You should remember that."

I cared even less about the money than he did. "There might still be children in that building."

"I hope there are. It should make the rest of them less annoying."

The chill that traveled down my nerves at his words was nothing to the horror that swamped me when he picked up the torch.

They finally shoved me flat against the pavement, and bound my wrists and ankles to stop my struggles. They did nothing to stop my shouted warnings, as Roseman walked around the building applying flame to all that piled kindling.

If any children had come running out, into the arms of Roseman's waiting guards, they'd have achieved nothing but a cleaner, kinder death. But I went on shouting, even when the Rose came back to the front of the building and flung open the loading doors.

His guardsmen stood ready to catch anyone who emerged, but no one did. I allowed myself a cautious flicker of hope, even as flames started climbing the wooden walls and smoke billowed out in acrid, eye-stinging gusts. If anyone was in there, they'd have no choice but to run out at any moment... any moment...

And they didn't. They'd heeded my warning and moved out, before the Rose's men had turned up to surround the place. I should have known they would. My clever, cautious orphans hadn't survived the Rose's enmity this long by taking careless risks.

Roseman had realized the truth as well. Angry disappointment turned down the corners of his mouth as he approached me once more, turning his back on the roaring inferno that had once been both a working business and a home.

"I bought all the goods in that warehouse," he said. "And the building, and the land it sits on...just for this."

A raging vortex swirled behind him, making his point quite eloquently.

"I'm loyal to men who are loyal to me. This is what happens to my enemies. So when I tell you to find those brats, and then give their location to my men, you *know* what will happen to you and your friend if you don't."

"I have no idea where they went." To my shame, my voice held the desperate honesty of real fear. "I don't know how to find them."

"You'll figure it out." His casual certainty was more terrifying than any threat. "I'm not so unreasonable as to expect instant results. But I do expect results."

He removed Lianna from his carriage—she was pale, and had wrapped her arms about herself despite the heat. Then Roseman drove off, leaving us to the guards. They'd probably been ordered to make us watch till the warehouse had burned down, but after a few hours it became clear that complete destruction would take a long time. The fire brigade had succeeded in keeping the neighboring buildings safe, so there were no further distractions, and they eventually grew bored and took us to the same inn where I'd been kept before.

And it seemed that despite their own woes, someone was keeping track of my whereabouts. Soon after I arrived in my room, a rock with a note from Fisk wrapped around it came flying through my open window. When I looked out, there was no one in sight...so I untied the note and read it.

Dinner that night was a well-sauced saddle of mutton, with mashed turnips, pickled beets, a salad of spring lettuce, and a dried cherry tart.

I wasn't hungry.

CHAPTER 18

Fisk

Soon after Tony Rose returned from the countryside, I got Michael's reply—and swore. I'd told him everything I'd discovered, including my tentative plans, but all he said was, *I can do it. When?*

Come to think of it, putting a detailed plot to murder Atherton Roseman on paper might not be a good idea. With the inventories of a ship I was investigating spread over the desk before me, I wrote back:

Are you in the city? Our first friend here will send word when the baby's ready to come. We should have roughly four hours after that, before the event. You're in charge of bringing the proper jewelry to commemorate the occasion. Are you sure *you can do it?*

Two days later, a small grubby hand slipped the reply into my pocket. It was larger than I'd expected, enclosed in a folded letter addressed to *My dear cousin, Lieutenant Elliston of the Gollford Guards.* If the recipient believed it, the contents of that letter would fetch the High Liege's troops almost as quickly as the rest of my evidence. I wondered who Lianna Dalton was.

Michael's note was a lot shorter.
I'm here in the Port. And I'm not sure of anything.
Send for the troops.

I SENT my messenger off to Gollford the next morning, and
he promised to make sure the chandler read my letter when
he passed through Hinksville. And that the chandler would
send his warning to the inn and Captain Rigsby's house, as
well as Roseman's townhouse.

One of my ship captains had already departed on his
scheduled voyage. I sent another a note that his mother had
taken ill, and would like to see him.

I told Rigsby he had four days, give or take a day, to get
ready to grab his family and sail the moment he got word of
the blessed arrival.

I'd have spent those four days working on my forged
evidence, but I'd finished with it long ago. It would be more
convincing if the ink wasn't damp, so I stifled the urge to
tinker with it.

Four days dragged by. Then another. I was beginning to
think my messenger had fallen and broken his neck, or gone
on a drunken binge, or just decided to keep on riding, and not
bother to drop off my evidence on his way to the other end
of the Realm.

But a few hours after dawn on the sixth day, while I lay
sleepless, staring at the ceiling, the sound of galloping hoofbeats and shouts reached my ears.

As the rider drew nearer, words emerged. "It's coming, it's
coming, Tilda's baby's coming. It's on its way, it's coming, the
baby's on the way."

It was a young voice, maybe an apprentice, who could be
forgiven for excitement and enthusiasm even at this hour.
I hadn't known if the chandler could be trusted with the

details—but it was nice to know that if he couldn't, I'd been right about his wife.

Just to make sure, the boy galloped around the Rose's block, passing this house twice before going on to spread the word elsewhere.

I got up at the usual time. I dressed in my usual clothes, and took all the ships' papers down to the study, sending to the kitchen for rolls and tea. I had some trouble forcing the rolls down but I didn't let it show. I was about to go ask for an audience with the Rose, when a guard showed up and said the boss wanted to see me. Now.

I put on a slightly startled expression, and picked up my papers and ledgers before I went with him.

Roseman was in his office, and for once the luck was running my way—both Jack and Wiederman were with him. And of course, the usual mob of guards.

The boss looked up as I came in, studying the glowing gem at my throat.

"You're now on gem watch, Master Fisk. Your friend slipped away from my men over an hour ago. He's proved...trickier than I expected."

"Maybe your men just lost track of him," I said. "Michael won't leave me."

"If he turns up in the next few hours, we'll know you're right," the Rose said. "If not..."

"He will."

And his timing was perfect, too. Any signs of nervousness I showed would be put down to fear that Michael had skipped on me.

"I was about to ask to see you, anyway," I went on. "Late last night, I found the final clue."

Roseman's attention, which had begun to drift, returned to me. "You've got them all? You're sure?"

"There aren't that many," I said. "And three of them have departed since I began investigating, which tells you something right there. The reason it took so long, is that it's not the captains that are skimming from you...well, they are, but it's not just the captains."

"What do you mean?" The words were quiet, but there was an ominous weight beneath them. No one cheated the Rose.

"Except for a few small matters, the captains' books balanced," I said. "They didn't always get the best prices—all the stuff you're dumping in port cities really is depressing the market for valuables. But for the most part, they've sold what your ledgers say you've given them, and brought back the price they were paid, minus the cut you agreed to."

"Then why is Rigsby's wife always wearing new gowns?" the Rose demanded. "Why are Conning's stables almost as good as mine?"

Because they were idiots.

"Because they're not just selling the goods you gave them," I said. "They're getting loot from another source, and getting a bigger cut for it than you're giving them. I suspect they're selling it first, for higher prices, but I can't prove that."

"But where would they get more loot? It all goes to..."

Roseman's gaze was already turning aside, because the loot didn't go directly to him. It went to Jack.

Jack had his features under control, but I thought he paled slightly.

"I've always reported every item that came to me." His voice was impressively steady. "It's Wiederman and his clerks who parcel it up to send to the captains. He's the one who keeps those ledgers. If something's gone astray, that's where."

"If anything is missing," Wiederman put in angrily. "You've only got his man's word for that."

"Let me show you what I found." I put my papers on the desk, and opened a ledger for the boss.

I'd been careful, just a hint of other goods here, a larger than expected profit there. The best of it was an offer for "two pearl necklets, one with an ivory cameo, and a man's seal ring," none of which appeared on the Rose's ledger for that voyage. The paper was crumpled, as if someone had thrown it at a trash basket and missed, and some helpful clerk had found it, smoothed it out and filed it.

A splendid job, if I said so myself. After Herbert, I'd stopped scamming the innocent. That didn't mean I hadn't kept my hand in.

Jack cast me a couple of suspicious looks, but even he couldn't be sure. He'd begun to sweat now, a light haze of perspiration that made his face shine.

Wiederman, who had less practice in commanding his expression, was visibly frightened. "I recorded all the stuff he gave me to record. If something else went to the captains, it came from Markham."

Even the guards, four of whom were in the room with us, were growing tense. Several hands were already on their sword hilts.

I was tense too, for a different reason. I was betting my life and Michael's that Roseman's dedication to loyalty went both ways. That he wouldn't condemn a man who might be loyal to him, unless he was sure.

Because right now, they were both doing a really good imitation of a guilty man.

"I had no contact with the captains," Jack was saying. "I turned the goods over to Wiederman. Disposing of them was his job, using men he recruited."

"You could have made contact with them secretly," Wiederman snarled. "And it's your man who's bringing all this forward, trying to discredit me!"

"It might equally discredit me," Jack shot back. "If I was trying to pull something, Fisk is the last person I'd bring in. If he was working for me, don't you think the evidence would point clearly to you, instead of to both of us? Unless this is some trick of Fisk's, for purposes of his own."

They looked at me. I shrugged.

"The captains were cheating you for years before I got to town. All I did was figure out how they're doing it. Why would I risk my life, and Michael's, lying about anything?"

How to betray a friend, without a twitch of remorse, was the final lesson I'd learned from Jack.

"Tony, I've been with you for years," Wiederman said. "From the start. You can't believe—"

"And I brought in the man who found proof you're being betrayed," said Jack. "Wiederman argued against it."

"Enough," said the Rose. "I don't know who's skimming, but—"

A soft knock interrupted him.

The guardsman who opened the door looked nervous, from which I gathered that our voices had carried into the hall.

"I'm sorry, boss, but you said you wanted to be told when Sevenson turned up. He just came in, and he says he needs to talk to you. Says it's urgent."

Roseman looked from me, to Jack, to Wiederman, and back to me.

"I don't know who's betrayed me," he said. "But I'm going to find out. For certain. And when I do... Take all of them," he told the guards. "Lock them up in the cells. I'll do my own investigating, and then we'll have another chat."

Wiederman continued to curse Jack and protest his innocence as they dragged him down to the cellar, but Jack didn't bother to argue.

I said nothing to anyone, going where the guards directed me. I'd guessed they'd search us, so I wasn't worried when they did. If I'd known there were cells in this house, I'd have crept down at night and hidden a few picks in them before they even thought to set a guard on my door.

It was possible that Jack had done that, and I'd look for them, but I doubted I'd find anything. He was always more cocky than I, certain the con would go our way. That we wouldn't need the escape plans I "wasted my time" creating.

The cell was an empty store room, stone walled, with a stout, iron-barred door that allowed the guards to make sure the stone in my collar kept glowing. There weren't a lot of places to hide even a lock pick. Most people don't know this, but it's possible to be bored and terrified at the same time.

There was nothing else for me to do—it was up to Michael now.

Except for one thing. The job of getting Jack out of the noose was mine alone.

Michael would have said that I owed Jack nothing, and he was right. But there were too many bright memories mixed with the bad, too much he'd taught me. For better or for worse, Jack had made me the man I am, every bit as much as Michael had.

I owed Jack nothing...I also owed him everything.

CHAPTER 19

Michael

The guard who escorted me to Roseman's office was agitated, which I took to be a good sign.

I hadn't been in that house since the night I was captured, and I'd never seen this room. There was nothing extraordinary about it—except that a man richer than my father ever dreamed of being had an office that looked less rich. And my father isn't an ostentatious man.

If the Rose was subsidizing the sale of cheap food for this entire vast city, 'twas a wonder he wasn't in rags.

Neither Jack nor Wiederman was in attendance, which I took as a further sign that Fisk's plan to create chaos was working.

Unfortunately, Fisk wasn't there either.

"Where's Fisk?" I asked, before Roseman could speak.

"You should be worried about that. If you'd been gone a few more hours, your friend might not be anywhere at all. Ever."

I had turned my collar so that the stone showed when I approached the house. Now I looked at the window behind the desk—even with the sun shining outside, I saw a faint reflection of its golden glow.

But his threats made the weight in my pocket feel a bit lighter.

"I had to go alone," I said. "I was following a lead. I've found the apothecary who sold the drug the children gave your rider."

"Does that help us find them?" Roseman was already reaching for a pile of papers on one side of his desk. Some of them bore Fisk's writing. "I'll send someone to follow up, later, but right now I've got—"

"Later won't work," I said. "He's too frightened. And you can't send someone else, because he'll only talk to you."

Anger dawned in Roseman's face, but his voice was still mild. "Why should I waste my time talking to some—"

"He says he sold the drugs to someone he's seen with you," I said. "He thought the man was in your employ, though he's not sure of that. The man didn't give his name, but the apothecary says if you come in to him, he can describe his customer. And he's afraid, because what if the man you send—"

"Is the man who bought the drugs." Roseman's fist clenched on a piece of paper, crumpling it. "Do you know what happened here this morning?"

Knowing what Fisk had intended, I could make a fair guess.

"No. How could I? I've been talking to apothecaries."

"No one talked to him, boss," the guard who'd brought me there put in. "We didn't even tell him, when he asked where Fisk was."

"Where is Fisk?" I let my voice grow sharper. "What's going on?"

"Fisk is in a cell," said Roseman. "With a lot of guards keeping an eye on him. Markham and Wiederman, too. I don't trust anybody. I especially don't trust you."

I shrugged. "The apothecary won't talk to anyone but you. He doesn't want to end up "silenced." He wants you to come with me, alone. I was thinking that if you recognize the description, the man he saw might lead us to the children. But if you don't care enough to spend a few hours pursuing it, that's fine with me."

The shrewd eyes, so unexpected in that broad face, went to the stack of papers.

"If the answer was there, I'd know it already." He turned to one of the four guards who'd taken up stations around the room. "Who hired you to work for me?"

"Well, I'm under Captain Jonat, who negotiated the contract for all his men," the guard said uneasily. "But it was Wiederman who recruited us. I think Wiederman hired all us guards. But Captain Jonat says it's you we work for. And we do. Honest."

He swallowed, and managed to stop babbling.

"So I really can't trust anyone," Roseman murmured. "Not until I get this figured out." His gaze fastened on the glowing gem at my throat.

"If you didn't hold Fisk, I'd be the last person you could trust," I told him.

"But I do hold Fisk," he said. "And I'm still not fool enough to trust you. Get Phearson and Moult," he told a guard. "They'll go with us."

"But they're... Are you sure, boss. They're good men, and loyal. We're all loyal. But you'll have to tell them what to do. We never assign them to do anything without a partner."

"That's why I want them," Roseman said. "Because they won't be plotting anything on their own."

"The apothecary said if you bring any of your men he won't be there." I had to fight to keep my voice neutral. Guards coming with us was the one thing I hadn't figured out how to deal with—except by convincing the Rose not to bring them.

"It won't be Phearson or Moult he sold the drugs to," Roseman said. "And if he can describe the buyer to me...well, that might solve my problem right there."

That problem would certainly be solved when the Liege's men arrived—and by the time they did, I had to have Roseman locked down or Fisk's life would be forfeit. I *had* to get those guards out of the way!

When Phearson and Moult showed up, I understood their selection better. Phearson was a big blocky man, and Moult was short and blocky. Neither face displayed the signs of quick intelligence.

Told that they were to accompany Master Roseman and me, they said "Yes boss." and showed no curiosity about anything else.

We left the house swiftly, with no time for me to leave something behind that one of them could be sent back for. Or to get into the medicine chest, and steal something to slip into a beer they wouldn't have time to drink.

Walking down to the port, I considered trying to push them in front of a passing carriage—though 'twould be both too obvious and impossible, since Roseman walked with me and they trailed behind.

The presence of these two could demolish all our plans. Between them, they might be strong enough to break the chain, and they could certainly defend their master. Or stop me from escaping, or break my neck for the Rose. Which would bring Fisk to his death in turn.

If Lianna could manipulate Roseman into bringing her into town, surely I could figure out how to get rid of two guards! She was currently locked in her room at the inn, under guard, but here in town where she'd wanted to be. I'd even found a way to make use of her presence. And I wasn't too proud to steal a stratagem from a lady.

"It's a good thing you're bringing them along," I told Roseman. "You're right, no one would ever use them in any conspiracy."

Roseman snorted. "Unless ,the conspirator was looking for a henchman who would never realize that he'd been used. Is that what you're about to say? Don't push your luck, Sevenson. They're coming."

This man wasn't a fool. What else to try?

We were walking down the wharf now, with all its usual bustle and chaos. A man in front of us pulled a cord that dragged a big hook and tackle back against a warehouse, then looped the draw cord loosely around its cleat.

I was on the inside, while the Rose walked by the water. It would take only a moment's distraction.

When we reached the tie-off I came to a sudden stop, staring as hard as I could at the ships out in the bay.

"What?" The Rose turned to look too. I reached behind me and fumbled the rope off the cleat till just one wrap and my grip held the heavy hook in place.

"Nothing," I said. "I just thought... No, it's nothing."

Roseman's suspicious gaze turned to me. "What are you up to?"

"Nothing." I let the line go and walked on, keeping Roseman's attention on me. I fancied I could hear that rope unwrapping from its final loop, whipping though the rings that held it—but that might have been my imagination. "I thought I saw one of the Liege's—"

Several men shouted in alarm, as the big hook and its tackle swung down into the street and over the water.

We both spun, and I saw that my hope had been misplaced. The massive weight hadn't come near the guards who followed us. It didn't hit anyone at all, though it did knock the top crate off a stack into the water.

"That's vanilla bean!" a clerk shrieked. "It'll be worthless if it gets wet!"

Vanilla extract sells for a sliver roundel the cup.

"Reward?" I shouted helpfully.

"Yes! Get it out of there."

Along with half the men in hearing range, I started forward, but Roseman held me back. "Not you, Sevenson."

But the guards, accustomed to doing whatever those around them did, had already joined the men who rushed to hook the crate, cast a rope around it, get it ashore before it sank.

I stood still, not resisting the firm grip on my arm, and let desperation pull the cover off of my magic. It flooded out, eager as always. I had channeled magic through my animal handling gift some months ago, to make Chant more than what he was. 'Twas harder, though not impossible, to make these two men less. To make them slower, clumsier—so much so that those they sought to help cursed them for dullards, and tried to thrust them aside. Clumsy enough that no one thought it odd when Phearson, reaching out to help haul the dripping crate ashore, toppled into the bay.

I felt a flash of concern, but he rose sputtering to the surface and 'twas clear he could swim. Once the crate was back on the dock, several men helped Moult—who moved more swiftly now that I'd released him—to pull Phearson from the waves.

Roseman had roared with laughter when his man splashed into the bay—though in fairness, half the bystanders had laughed along. Now, staring at Phearson's huge dripping form, he frowned.

The man looked most pathetic. His hat was gone, his hair plastered to his skull. His sodden coat, the black and dark red of Roseman's household colors, dripped like a small rainstorm on the cobbles at his feet. It must weigh twenty pounds. He pulled off a boot and poured the water out, setting it aside before he reached for the other. One toe protruded from a hole in his sock.

"Put them back on." Roseman turned his scowl on me. "You're not winning this easily."

"I was standing right beside you when he fell in."

"Humph."

We had to wait while Phearson dragged his boots on, and as we continued down the street we could hear the flop and slap of his wet clothing. And more distressing to his master, a scatter of muffled chuckles.

No one dared laugh at the Rose to his face, but they were ready enough to laugh behind his back. A hint of color darkened his cheeks, growing deeper as we went on—though whether it sprang from embarrassment or anger I couldn't say.

Eventually we reached the apothecary shop I'd chosen, because 'twas not too far from the stockyards where our trap was set. And also because the only apothecary who worked there was an elderly widow. I'd told them the apothecary I'd spoken to was a man, so if this should fail they'd know I'd been lying, and no innocent herb-grinder would be blamed.

"You'd better let me go in first," I told Roseman. "To let him know you've brought two men. I can convince him they're loyal to you, and that neither could be the man to whom he sold the drug."

"I'll send Phearson around to the back of the shop," Roseman said. "To be sure the man doesn't bolt, if you're not convincing."

I shrugged and waited while he gave Phearson careful orders. He had the man repeat them, to be sure he understood. Then we all watched him walk down the alley that would take him to the shop's back door.

He'd stopped dripping, but his coat swung and clapped about him in a way that was quite comical. Glancing back to the street, Roseman caught sight of several stifled grins.

His glare scattered the crowd for yards around us.

I waited till I was certain Phearson would be in position, then went into the shop. I spent a few moments talking to the proprietor about any need she might have for magica herbs, and the price she'd pay. 'Twas likely our purse had grown thin, paying for Chant and Tipple's stabling, and we'd owe whoever cared for True as well. Finding and harvesting magica herbs is a way I can bring in quick money, though this time of year most plants would be too young.

After a few minutes I returned to Roseman and Moult.

"He's not there. His clerk says that the animal doctor called him down to the stockyards, to look at some case and make rec—"

"An animal doctor?"

"Apothecaries provide their medicines as well. They don't know when he'll be back, but we can wait—"

"I'm not going to stand here all day. He'd be at the stockyard south of the docks?"

I shrugged. "They didn't say where. The clerk said something about a sick barn."

"I know where that is."

Anyone who'd dealt with the sale of livestock would, and I'd gambled that a man who'd made his fortune trading in this city would know it as well.

"It's not far." His gaze fell on Moult. "Why are you just standing there? Go get Phearson."

"Yes, boss."

Watching Phearson's clothes flapping around him as they walked toward us proved the final straw.

"You go back to the house," Roseman told him. "You're calling too much attention to us."

"Sorry, boss." But the man stayed in front of us, swaying from one foot to another.

"What are you waiting for?"

"The sergeant, he told Moult and me we're supposed to protect you. Follow behind the boss and make sure no one bothers him, he said. I can't do that if I go back."

Roseman took a deep breath and controlled his temper. "You're also supposed to obey my orders, right?"

"Of course, boss. Always."

"Well, I'm ordering you to go back to the house. I'm only going to talk to some snitch of an apothecary, in a public yard. If we get attacked by a savage sheep, Moult can protect me."

A full grown ram can knock a man off his feet, but Phearson must not have known much about sheep for the indecision on his face vanished. "Right."

He strode off, still followed by concealed smiles, and Roseman turned to me.

"The stockyard. And he'd better be there. You know where it is?"

"No. I've only spent a few weeks in this town."

"Then follow me."

LEADING THE WAY reassured him, as I'd known it would. When we approached the yard, it bustled with men and livestock—indeed, we had to stand and wait while a drover and his dogs brought a herd of twenty cows into a pen.

But as we went further into the maze of pens, rife with manure and flies, we saw fewer and fewer people, and the only sound was the lowing and bleating of the milling beasts. They weren't the only creatures destined for slaughter…but 'twould not be today. When I'd come here earlier, to leave the chain and shackle, I'd made the orphans promise me, upon the memory of their parents, that they'd hold Roseman alive till the Liege Guard came for him.

In exchange, I'd promised them the Rose would hang.

The high, planked walls of the pens cut off our view of the nearby streets, but they might have been in the next fiefdom for all it mattered. A cow, mayhap bitten by some insect, banged into the fence beside us and Moult jumped.

Roseman didn't even glance aside.

The sick barn, where diseased animals could be separated from their herds and treated or put down, was at the far end of the stockyard, near the marshes that had grown where the river met the sea. The filled pens grew fewer and the air clearer as we approached.

Moult and Roseman took deep breaths of the sea-scented air, but my heart pounded with dread. Fisk's life hung on these next few moments, for if the stone in my collar went dark he would die within moments. The orphans' lives were at stake as well, for Roseman wouldn't rest till they were dead, and so were the lives of all who'd die in Roseman's war.

I wondered when the Liege Guard would arrive. Over four hours had passed since the young lad dashed into the inn where we stayed, and ran down the corridor shouting that Tilda's baby was coming. My estimate was that a mounted man could beat walking men over that distance by a good five hours, but that depended—

Roseman threw open the sick barn's doors, and gestured for me to go in.

"Master Horton?" I called. "Are you back there?"

Roseman and his guard followed me in, and started down the long corridor between the stalls. There were half a dozen sheep in one big pen, and their restless movements covered any sound someone else might have made.

"Master Roseman is with me," I called. "He brought just one guard. I know you said not to, but this is a most trusted and loyal man."

No answer came from shadowy depths of the barn.

"He's afraid," I said. "I promised you'd come alone."

"Poxy fool," Roseman muttered under his breath. "Stay where you are, Master Apothecary. I mean you no harm, and I'll pay well for your information."

"You sure?" The voice was a sort of gruff squeak. To me it sounded exactly like a child trying to sound like a grown man.

But it might have sounded like a man, his voice high-pitched with fear.

'Twas enough for the Rose. He started down the aisle, ready to learn who had betrayed him. He would soon know.

Moult followed his boss, paying no attention to the fact that, before I fell in behind him, I lifted the wooden latch bar from the door brackets and took it with me. I waited till he came up beside a rough wooden pillar, its foot buried in dirty straw, before I brought the latch bar down on the back of his head. It made less noise than I feared, a sort of muffled thump, all but lost in the slithering crash of his fall.

"Are you all right?" I knelt beside him, feeling around the base of the pillar. I'd had no time to fasten the chain into place when I dropped it off that morning, but I trusted in the competence of my young allies.

"What's the matter?" Roseman came back, and stared at the fallen man.

"I don't know. He just collapsed. Help me turn him over."

Roseman bent to do so, and I clapped the shackle around his wrist. The click of the lock as it closed was the most chilling sound I'd ever heard.

"What under..."

As he spoke, I rolled out of his reach. Then I leaned in and grabbed Moult's arm, dragging him out of Roseman's reach as well. Injured or not, I couldn't leave him here to free his master...or threaten the children. Or be threatened by them.

The Rose straightened, sliding the loop of padlocked chain up the pillar till he could stand.

"I don't know what you think you're doing, Sevenson, but if you kill me your collar will go dark. Fisk will be dead in minutes. *Minutes.*"

"I'm not going to kill you," I said. "And they've promised me they won't, either."

And even if they broke their word, *I'd* still not have killed him. Which meant that Fisk would survive until the balance of power had shifted, and we could save ourselves.

"When I get loose," Roseman growled, "you're going to watch your friend die. Then, when your stone goes dark, I'll finish you off even slower than I'm going to kill him."

"I have no doubt you would," I said. "As it is, I'd best get back to Fisk before the troops arrive."

I got a grip on Moult's collar, preparing to drag him out. He was heavier than I'd expected, limp as he was, but his chest still rose and fell. I'd tried not to strike too hard.

"Troops? What troops?" The chain rattled as Roseman yanked on it. "Stop being an idiot and let me loose. I'll let you both live, if you do. I'd have to lock you up for a while, but you can survive this. My men know where I went, and people in the street watch me. They'll be able to track me down."

"I'm sure they could, eventually." The fear hadn't appeared yet. His expression held only the exasperation of a man putting up with a temporary inconvenience, on his way to certain victory. "But it will be the High Liege's men who come to retrieve you. Not yours."

Now his expression changed. "The High Liege doesn't know I exist. You're lying."

"The Liege probably doesn't, yet." I started dragging Moult toward the door. "But his commander and judicars in Gollford do. Fisk and I sent for them."

He pulled at the chain, harder this time. "My men will kill Fisk the moment they turn up. He'll be dead, do you hear me? Dead! The moment some yard hand comes to tend those sheep I'll be free, and you'll wish you *died* before you tried this stunt."

"No doubt I would," I said. "But no one will come here. The children will stop them."

"The…"

I saw his face changed then, terror dawning as he realized what I meant, and who his guards were. His eyes swept over the empty stalls.

"Hey." His voice wavered. "Hey, I'm rich. Really, really rich. Maybe we can make a deal?"

"I doubt it. In fact, I'm leaving you in the hands of those who'd never be tempted by anything you can offer them... unless you could bring their parents back."

I dragged Moult down the aisle and out of the barn, leaving Roseman staring into the shadows, his face sickly with fear.

And not without reason.

"Timasus? I know you're here."

I latched the door shut behind me as I waited for him to appear, and eventually he scurried around the side of the great barn.

"He'll start yelling soon," I said. "You're sure no one will hear?"

"Naw, we've stayed here long enough 't know how they work. They fed them sheeps in the morning. There won't be nobody near this place till tomorrow." His voice was sure, but his eyes were too wide for his thin face and his shoulders twitched.

"So the Rose will be here, alive, when the Liege's men arrive. Right? I needed your help to find a place he could be held, but remember what you promised in exchange?"

"Yah, yah. I know what we said."

But his gaze shifted aside as he spoke, and instinct screamed for me to check his pockets for weapons. 'Twould do no good. I had to have a place where Roseman could be held, by guards who'd bow to neither bribe nor threat. The orphans were the only ones in Tallowsport who had that much courage...and that much hate.

"I'm coming back in just a few hours," I said, dragging Moult down the dusty path between the pens. "I'll be back, and I expect to find Roseman alive when I get here. You gave your word. Your honor depends on keeping it."

But Timasus had already slipped away, and I knew that honor would be a fragile barrier against the sweeping flood of vengeance.

I'd better get back here quickly. Not to save Roseman, who'd deserved whatever fate he might meet at his victim's hands—but to keep the children from having his death on their conscience.

CHAPTER 20

Fisk

Down in the cellar, we couldn't hear what went on in the world above. But after several nearly eternal hours had passed, a couple of new guards came down the stairs, wearing breastplates and grieves. They took the place of the six men, who'd been detailed to watch three prisoners locked into cells, and sent them to arm.

Wiederman clung to the bars and demanded to know what was going on. They looked at him, but said nothing.

Which probably meant that the Liege Guard had arrived in the city, but wasn't at the house yet. In their boss's absence, Roseman's guards were preparing for trouble, but still clinging to the last orders they'd been given. Hopefully the last order Roseman would be able to give, though how Michael planned to accomplish that...

Whatever he was doing must have been working so far— though the guards glanced at my throat occasionally, no one tried to kill me.

More time passed, perhaps half of one of those interminable hours, before we heard the door at the top of the stairs open and a rumble of boots coming down. The first man who hurried into the room was one of Roseman's captains, and he went straight to Wiederman's cell and unlocked it.

"The Liege Guard has invaded the city," he said. "They're marching on this house—be here in minutes. We may be able to hold out, but someone's got to assume command till the boss gets back. You're in charge of city matters, so we figure that's you."

He swung the cell door open, but Wiederman stood gawking at him. "Liege troops? Are you sure? Why?"

"Come see for yourself." The man gestured impatiently toward the stairs.

But Wiederman's eyes turned to me, fastening on my neck.

"Not my fault." I lifted my collar, displaying the glowing gem. If it winked out now, I was done for.

"Later." Wiederman turned and dashed up the stairs. All but one of the guards followed.

The guard who remained looked nervously at Jack and me, fingering the hilt of his sword. He was about my age, and had probably never seen combat in his life.

In these peaceful times, most haven't. Not even sell-swords, unless they dabble in banditry.

"They're probably going to need you up there," Jack said helpfully. "And it's not like we can chew through the bars with our teeth."

"I've got orders." But his eyes strayed to the stairs more and more often.

Time had stopped creeping. It was only about ten minutes later that a faint sound reached us, a distant, clattering roar. To me it sounded like the kitchen of a busy tavern during the dinner rush, with pots banging and shouted orders.

Our guard was standing at the foot of the stairs, gazing up, when the door at the top opened. The sounds of battle grew louder, and Michael came pelting down. He'd acquired a sword somewhere, and a coat in the Rose's colors, and turned his collar around to the back. Even if the guard had seen him on the night he was captured, or on his brief visit this morning, odds were high he wasn't paying enough attention to recognize him.

"They're rushing the house," Michael said crisply. "We need every man to push them back. Get to your unit."

The guard raced up the stairs with Michael behind him. Then the door at the top closed, muting the noise once more, and Michael came quietly back down.

"I got the keys from Roseman's office." He tried the first one in the lock of my door as he spoke. "It's chaos up there."

"Are Liege troops really attacking the house? With enough men to take the town?" I'd set it up, and I still didn't believe it.

"I don't believe it," said Jack. "Where did they come from? How could they know about us?"

Michael, who had finally found the right key, ignored him and answered me. "They've got a sizeable force out there. Enough to take the house, but Roseman's guards got their defenses organized in time to beat back the first assault. There's going to be a blood-bath here, and I don't see how to stop it."

Michael would always want to stop such a thing, but there was a particular urgency in his voice that I didn't quite understand.

"We'll find a way," I said, as the door swung open.

"Hey," said Jack. "What about me? I could help you stop it. I could help you both get out of here. Hey!"

I followed Michael up the stairs to the kitchen. Men ran through it, and more were watching at the windows with crossbows in their hands. Looking past them, I saw that the Rose's men still held the kitchen garden.

Troops in blue and silver livery crowded the windows of the house across the alley. I'd never seen the High Liege's uniform so close before, since I preferred to scam the local law.

"Where's Roseman?" I asked softly. In the bustling confusion, no one paid us any attention.

"I captured him. I left him under guard."

"Then he'll probably be here any minute! There's not a man in this town he can't bribe or—"

"I didn't leave men guarding him." Michael's voice was thin with guilt, which made no sense...until, suddenly, it all came together.

"The orphans? You gave him to the *orphans*?"

I stopped in front of a mirror—my gem still glowed. And since he'd turned his collar to the back instead of cutting it off, Michael's must be glowing too. But they'd only stop glowing if Michael had actually killed the man. The jeweler had said nothing about setting him up to die.

"But they're just kids!"

My voice had risen, and several men looked at us. I pulled Michael into the hall and we started up the stairs.

"What choice had I? Everyone else is too terrified of Roseman to act, even if I'd had some way to organize them! The orphans were the only allies I could reach." I'd never heard him sound so distraught, not even when Rosamund left him.

"Don't worry about it—you've probably just made up for every gift day they've ever missed."

"They promised they wouldn't kill him. That they'd leave him alive to face the Liege's justice."

"And if you believe that, I've got some swampland to sell you. It's not like they're sheltered innocents, you know. They've been living by crime for months, some of them for years. Judging by what Timasus said when you hired them, this might not even be their first murder."

"I have to get back there, Fisk. I have to get back before they do something that can't be undone."

I thought that ship had already sailed, but remembering when I was that young...

My mother died of a fever, and for years after I'd hated the whole world. If there'd been one person responsible for her death, and I could have killed them, I'd have done it in a heartbeat. And maybe hated the rest of the world less.

"*They* won't be grieving," I told him. "I don't see why you should. Can you prove the Rose is dead?"

"I'm still hoping to prevent that," Michael said. "Besides, I thought the whole point was to keep it secret."

"That was then." I pulled him into the study. Except for two men, standing by the windows with crossbows, it was empty. And I'd become so accustomed to having guards around that I barely bothered to lower my voice.

"How did you get into this house?"

"There are rumors all over the city that the Liege has sent an army," Michael said. "I went running into the inn, and told my guards that Liege troops had come for the Rose and he wanted every man back at the house, now. They left Lianna locked in her room, but I managed to slip the key under her door. She'll go to her husband, and he'll add his men to the Liege's force. They're going to take this house, Fisk. Maybe on the next push. They'd just arrived here when they launched it, so their first attack wasn't coordinated. The next one will be."

"Has anyone been killed yet?" It was always harder to make a deal after that.

"I don't know. Several wounded, on both sides, but I'm not sure if anyone died."

"Then we'd better start now."

I went out to the hall and waited till a guardsman rushed by—I didn't have to wait long. I grabbed his arm and dragged him into the study.

"We need to talk to all the captains," I said. "Or at least, most of them, and we need to do it without Wiederman knowing. How many can you bring back here?"

"I'm taking a message to Captain Bussy now," the man said. "But why should he talk to you? Aren't you a prisoner?"

He looked pointedly at my collar, and then looked at Michael. His eyes widened.

Michael turned his collar, displaying the glowing stone.

"Roseman is dead," I told the man. "We didn't kill him, as the collars show. But with him gone, all of this..." I waved my hand at the windows, where the guards had dropped all pretense of not listening. "This is a waste of lives. *Your* lives. Unless you think Wiederman can win this fight, and then make himself Liege of the Erran Plains."

The guard snorted. "Not likely. He's a secretary."

"Then you'd better get your captains in here, so we can come up with some way to get everyone out of this with a whole skin. Right?"

"We're all going to hang for traitors, anyway," the guard said. "I'd rather go down by the sword."

He sounded just like Michael. I clutched my hair, and tried not to sound too exasperated. "That's the kind of thinking that will *get* you killed. I admit, you'll probably spend several years working off your indebtedness—but that's better than dead!"

The man frowned. "I don't see how you could make that happen."

"I don't expect you to. Which is why I need to talk to as many captains as you can bring to this room."

He finally realized that I might have a plan, and was at the door so fast I almost didn't have time to hiss "Without Wiederman!" before he vanished.

Michael eyed me warily. "What are you up to?"

"Nothing. You want everyone out of here alive. I want us out with our hides intact. Fighting a pitched battle won't achieve anything. You know that, I know that, and they know it too."

I gestured to the guardsmen at the windows, in case he'd forgotten them.

In the end, eight officers gathered in the study.

"There's five not here, but they're busy. Three of them agreed to abide by what we decide. The other two are loyal to Roseman. Though if he's dead... Can you prove that?"

The man who spoke was one of the oldest present, with graying temples and a weathered face. He was probably twice my age, and could doubtless both out-fight and out-run me. I hoped he was too smart to try to out-wit me. Besides, Michael's forlorn hopes aside, I was pretty sure I was telling the truth.

"If he's not dead, he's being held prisoner till the Liege's men come for him," Michael said. "Either way, he won't be back. If he was free, don't you think he'd be here now?"

Me, I thought there was an even chance he'd have run for it, but that wouldn't occur to a commander.

Moving slowly, Michael drew his knife and cut off his collar. It took some work, for the leather was thick. The moment it left his neck the stone went dark. From the looks on their faces, I knew my stone had gone dark as well.

He wouldn't have dared to do it if the Rose was free, and they all got the point.

"Alive or not," I added, "his plot is finished. All that remains is to get out from under the consequences, as well as we can."

A younger man, with bronze buttons on his coat and a bristling mustache, glanced at the windows—beyond which lay an army, intent on killing us all.

"Just how do you propose to do that, Master Fisk? Last I heard, high treason was one of the few bloodless crimes you can hang for."

"Ah, but there's treason and there's treason," I said mildly. "There's actually plotting to take over a huge chunk of the river plain, and there's simply being hired by a traitor. A traitor who probably didn't even tell you what he was up to, until you were in too deep to get out. Most of your men probably don't know anything about Roseman's real scheme even now. You had to protect them from him, right?"

They each looked at the others, uncertainty sitting oddly on those stern faces.

"That's about half-true," one of them said. "But I don't see those men out there buying it."

"Well, they certainly won't if you fight them to the death." I resisted the temptation to tear my hair. "Wiederman and Markham are the ones they want. If you offered them Wiederman, and promised them Markham in exchange for decent terms of surrender, that should go a long way toward convincing the judicars that you never wanted to rebel against the Liege."

While they argued, Michael cut the collar off my neck. The back of the blade was cold and smooth against my skin, and when the collar fell away I drew a great breath into my lungs, as if it had been strangling me—though it had never been at all tight.

"But who's going out there to tell them that?" The officer with the mustache gestured to the street. "Suppose they don't think they need to negotiate? Suppose they just arrest the negotiator and Wiederman, and say, 'Two down, a few hundred more to go?'"

"They might," I admitted. "So you probably want to send Michael out to do your negotiating."

CHAPTER 21

Michael

All the officers turned to stare.

"Why me?" I asked. "You're the one…" Who brought the Liege's army here. Not something I wanted to say, at just this moment. "You're the one whose idea this is. And you're a better negotiator than I am."

"But you've got the right accent," Fisk said. "It should keep them from cutting you down on the spot. They might even recognize your name."

He put only a slight emphasis on those words, but 'twas clear he'd told them about me when he sent the evidence to bring them. Still…

"You could take one of our prisoners out with you," the officer in charge put in. "To prove our good faith. And offer them the other one if they accept our terms."

"Make it Wiederman," Fisk said. "He's not smart enough to start screaming that your offer to surrender is a trap. Markham is."

This unpleasant possibility stopped all of us in our tracks, including me.

"Suppose he does?" Mustache asked. "Suppose they don't believe Sevenson here."

"Then they'll attack the house," said Fisk impatiently. "Which they're going to do in a few minutes, anyway, so we haven't much to lose by trying. This is our best chance to get out of this un-hung. And they shouldn't want to fight any more than we do."

That was enough for the officers, most of whom went off to get Wiederman and tell their men about the new plan. They left two men behind, to make sure I didn't flee. I cast them an exasperated glance, and pulled Fisk into a corner.

"What is this? You're the one who sent for them. They'll recognize your name, not mine."

"I told them all about you," he said. "And I wasn't kidding about the accent. But mostly, you're the one who can offer them the thing they really want, which is Atherton Roseman's body."

"He might..." He *might* still be alive. The orphans had given me their word. And the fastest way to get there, to remove the temptation to break it, was to take the Liege Guard to arrest the Rose.

"You want everyone out of this house, alive," Fisk went on. "They want Roseman. You might even be able to get these men out of the noose, if you play it right."

I heard a muffled thud from the hallway below, and Wiederman's voice raised in blistering fury.

"You're right," I said. "I'll do it."

Since Fisk had warned them, they gagged Wiederman and set two husky troopers to drag him along, despite the fact that he was bound and hobbled. He wrested himself out their grip twice, anyway.

There then came considerable shouting back and forth, as we told the Liege's men that we wanted to negotiate, that we'd send someone out, unarmed, and to please not use me as a crossbow target.

I knew this was necessary, but 'twas taking too much time. If Fisk was wrong, if the orphans were still holding to their promise… I had to get back there as soon as I could. Not to save the Rose, but to save them, to preserve their clean young honor.

On the other hand, if I was shot down the moment I left the house it wouldn't do anyone much good. So I waited, shifting from foot to foot till the terms were set, and I was free to walk out the front door.

I carried no weapons, but as I crossed the long front yard, I held my empty hands away from my body and tried to mimic Fisk's "I'm harmless" expression.

I could hear Wiederman struggling behind me, the sudden patter of steps as he threw his guards off balance, but I didn't look back.

Beyond the gate stood a young sergeant, also unarmed, who asked if I'd be pleased to go with him. Upon my agreement, he led me down the street to an alley that lay between the homes of two of Roseman's neighbors. 'Twas full of men, armed and ready for assault, and I expected to be seized myself. But instead, one of the three officers clad in Liege blue and silver looked me over and said, "I was right, sir. This is Sevenson."

Lianna had reached her husband in time. Captain Dalton had clearly been involved in the first assault; dried blood streaked his face from a cut near his ear, one hand was bruised and swollen, and sweat and dust stained his uniform. His eyes were bright with determination, and the joy of honor redeemed. In this, at least, I had done right.

"Ah." The speaker was an older man, with the silver braid of a garrison commander on his tunic. "It seems we have you to thank for this, Master Sevenson. You and Master Fisk. He's a friend of yours I take it?"

"Fisk is my…" This was not the time to claim knight errantry, even though I'd never earned it more. And 'twas not the part of a knight errant to abandon the men in the house behind me to the noose. They owed the people of this town a considerable debt, in coin or labor, but most of them probably didn't deserve to die.

"Yes, Fisk is my friend. And I can't express how glad I am to see you, sir. Roseman's men are mercenaries, and I don't think they knew that he planned treason when he hired them. They're willing to surrender, if you'll promise them their lives."

"I can't promise to spare anyone who knowingly plotted treason against the Liege," the commander said. "In fact, I can't *promise* anything. The fate of those who survive the battle will be in the judicar's hands."

"But you can tell the judicars that they surrendered themselves to the Liege's mercy as soon as Roseman couldn't touch them, can't you? That they gave up their treasonous plans the moment they—"

"Why can't Roseman touch them?" the commander asked. "I have to admit, I was surprised he let you out to negotiate with us. He has to know that, whatever happens to his men, there can be no mercy for him or his chief subordinates."

His cold gaze flicked to the man behind me, but returned almost at once. He wanted the boss, not the staff.

"Roseman's not in there," I said. "I...ah... He's being held prisoner by people I... Well, I can't say I trust them, but they'd never let Roseman out of their hands alive. And if we hurry, I might be able to persuade them to turn him over to you—if you can assure them he'll hang for his crimes."

Wiederman made a muffled sound of despair and sagged in the trooper's arms. The Liege's men stared.

"You took the Rose?" Dalton whispered. "You're holding Atherton Roseman, *prisoner?*"

"If they haven't killed him," I said. "I'd like to get back in time to prevent that."

"If the information Master Fisk sent us proves true, I can promise that he'll hang," the commander said. "Where is he?"

Fisk was right. They wanted the Rose enough to bargain for him. "I'll be happy to show you…if you'll agree to plead for leniency for those who signed with Roseman before they learned that he planned to commit treason."

Given how closely Roseman had kept that secret, I thought this would include most of the mercenaries and mayhap even Jack. Though Jack and Wiederman were in the plot so deep, I doubted anything could save them from the noose.

"For lesser crimes," I went on, "you can try and convict them as they deserve."

"All right," the commander said. "I'll plead for any who didn't know of the treason when they signed on. And I'll make it clear that they surrendered voluntarily as soon as they could. But after that 'tis up to the judicars what becomes of them."

'Twas an honest answer, and the best terms I was likely to get.

"Done. Let me tell the others, quickly, and I'll take you to Roseman."

It turned out to be impossible to tell the others quickly, and more shouted conversation ensued as the desperate mercenaries tried to obtain a guarantee of leniency. The garrison commander pointed out that he didn't have authority over the judicars, but he said their surrender might be taken as proof of good faith. If they truly hadn't known…

It soon became clear that this would take a while. Unless the mercenary commanders were more stupid than I thought they were, 'twould end in the deal Fisk had described. But I knew my orphans, and Roseman didn't have time to waste.

"Give me some men," I told the commander. "I'll trust you to keep your word, and take them to Roseman now."

I expected him to abandon the negotiations and go with me, for capturing the Rose himself was what an ambitious officer would do. Instead he sent a full troop, with a captain in charge of it, and remained to oversee the surrender—which was what a commander who cares about his men's lives should do. I thought he would keep his promise, to try to get them off... and now, 'twas time to see if the orphans had kept theirs.

I led the Liege's men to the stockyards. Walking through the maze of pens felt even more eerie accompanied by well-armed allies than it had surrounded by enemies...mayhap because my dread of what I'd find was greater.

We reached the sick-barn, and I stood for a moment with my hand on the latch, breath held in a last moment of hope that for once Fisk might be wrong.

It took only a glance at the bloodied mound of cloth and flesh, half buried in a heap of stones, to see my fears fulfilled.

The soldiers pushed past me, rushing into the barn, but I turned aside to lean against the wall, staring into the yard with eyes that watered in the brilliant light.

And the worst thing, as I listened to them exclaim over the savagery that had been done here, was that I wasn't surprised. I had known, all along I had known, that if I left the Rose in the orphans' power they would almost certainly kill him.

But if he'd been alive and free when the Liege's men arrived, Fisk would have died. I had sacrificed those children's souls to my friend's survival...and even now, I didn't see what else I could have done.

The guard captain emerged from the darkness, taking deep breaths to clear the stench of death. "You're certain that's Roseman?"

" 'Twas Roseman I left chained to the post. If the dead man is chained to the post, then 'tis him."

"Who did you leave guarding him?" His voice was cold— the Liege reserved the right to mete out justice to himself and his judicars. And at the moment, I cared no more for that than the orphans had.

"I left him with people who had such cause for hatred, that even if they knew they'd hang for it they'd have killed him anyway." And I'd still left him there. "Do you really want to know who they are?"

"Not really. And 'twould be far too messy to charge the hero who captured the Rose with refusing to assist the law. Ridiculous, in fact. Assuming Captain Dalton confirms your identification of the body, I think the commander will be willing to accept that after his capture Master Roseman encountered some enemies, who took advantage of his helplessness to wreak revenge. That's more or less the truth, anyway."

"More or less."

But the truth, the real truth, was that I'd left children to kill for me. I didn't know what else I could have done…but this was not the act of a knight errant.

CHAPTER 22

Fisk

I stood at a study window, watching Michael and the two men who held Wiederman's bound and struggling form walk through Roseman's garden to the front gate.

"Will they agree?" Mustache murmured. Like several other officers, who'd come back to watch, his gaze was fixed on an empty street—beyond which lay the army that would decide all our fates.

"Why wouldn't they? The people they want are Roseman and his chief subordinates. Everybody else is small fry. Or at least, you can claim to be. 'I was following orders' is an excuse that will resonate with military men. And they don't want to get their men killed any more than you do."

"Um."

The gates swung open as Michael reached them, proving that there were soldiers sheltering behind...probably not just that wall, but all the walls around the house.

Wiederman was struggling violently now—though what he thought he could do if he broke free, surrounded by armed men, I had no idea. Maybe he wanted to die by the sword too.

But with all eyes fixed on the discussion—on which our lives really did hang—it was easy to turn and walk quietly away from the window. If Michael had been there I probably couldn't have done it...which was why I'd made sure Michael wasn't there. None of the guardsmen gave me more than a passing glance as I made my way to the kitchen, and down the basement stairs.

Jack left off trying to hook the key ring with his belt buckle.

"So you didn't hide any picks down here," I said. "You always were an optimist."

"Fisk! I knew I could count on you to be sensible."

"I hope you were sensible enough to plan an escape route," I said. "Or you're going to have to hide till the search has passed and everyone's asleep. Even then the house will be guarded."

"No need for that. Roseman had an escape tunnel dug when he bought this house. It runs from this room to a garden shed in the next block, and the shed's roof is tall enough to get you over their wall. Wiederman and I were the only others who knew about it."

I wondered if Tony Rose had silenced the diggers, or if Jack simply didn't count them.

"Wiederman won't be going."

I took the time to look at the keys, and found the right one on the second try.

"Like old times, isn't it, lad?" His bright, wild grin brought old memories flooding back. Not all of them were bad.

In truth, enough of them were good that my heart cracked, just a little.

I had long known that Michael would never forgive me for this. But while there was a world of difference between Jack and Michael, when it came to me, how much difference was there between being Michael's squire and being Jack's lad?

It was time to become my own man. Whatever the consequences.

Jack went straight to the back wall, where several large kegs lay in cradles. He pushed aside the block behind one of the levers that tipped them and dragged the lever back, much father than I'd have thought it could go. With a soft click, a section of what looked like solid stone wall swung open about two inches. As neat a mechanism as any I'd seen.

"You'll have to slip out of town with me." Jack pulled the panel wider. "The Liege's men will be all over the place. Your friend with the tattoos will have a hard time getting past them."

"Michael doesn't have to hide from the Liege's men," I told him.

"This is no time to go soft on me. The judicars take treason *very* seriously."

"They probably will," I said. "You're going to have to lay low for a long time. They'll circulate your description, and every bounty hunter in the Realm will be after you."

"Then we'd better get moving." But he stopped, a faint frown gathering as I made no move to follow him.

"I don't have to run," I said. "Michael and I have nothing to fear from the Liege's men. I brought them here."

In the old days, I used to try to startle Jack. He was smart enough, and knew me well enough, that it was curst hard. Now, seeing his eyes widen and his jaw drop, I couldn't help but feel some satisfaction.

"*You* brought them? You... You took down *Tony Rose?*"

"And all his men," I said. "And his empire. And you. You know, Jack, you might want to consider that just because a man doesn't like scattering corpses in his wake, that doesn't make him *soft.*"

The lamplight caught his face. For just a moment, before he swung the panel shut, I saw fear in Jack's eyes.

It wasn't because I'd beaten him, either. I'd become unpredictable. No longer his lad. I would never see Jack again—not if he saw me first.

I found I was glad of that.

I put the block back under the lever, which pretty much guaranteed Jack would be long gone before anyone found his escape route. Then I went back up to the kitchen.

The room was in chaos. The Liege's troops were in the garden now, the Rose's men exiting without weapons, their hands held out, empty, where the troops could see them.

I went into the hallway, where the Liege's troops had already entered the house. Evidently, the kitchen had been the last area to surrender. They were still taking men in the Rose's livery down the stairs and outside. I wasn't in the Rose's livery and carried no weapons, which put me lower on their priority list, but it wouldn't let me leave the house unaccosted—and I wanted to get out before Michael came back. I'd have to talk to Michael, or he'd assume I'd been kidnapped or something and come after me. He'd done it once before. But we couldn't have that kind of fight here, in public...where someone might overhear, and decide to hold Jack's escape against me.

The door to Roseman's office was open, and the crowd of those seeking to get in flowed out into the hall. Going nearer, I could see that the door to the inner office had been smashed, probably with an axe. A clerk came out through the jagged hole, carrying a padlocked document box.

"Lot eight, H through L," he told another clerk, who jotted it down. As he made his way past me, I saw that the box had a tag tied to the lock, marked with the number.

I went on up to my room and packed my things. It took a few minutes to contrive a tag that looked like the one I'd seen, but I had pen and paper, and I managed. I marked my pack as lot fourteen, and carried it down the stairs and out of the house, walking briskly, like all the other clerks who swarmed about the place.

I made it out of the front doors, and it wasn't the Liege's troops that stopped me, but a familiar voice, pleading.

"Let the rats go back to their holes, good sir, the light hurts their eyes, tender, beady, their little feet running over sheets and corpses as they feed. The rats won't like this, won't like it if you cut off their tails. I have to feed them, back in the attic, so you must let me go. They eat blood they do, and flowers and seeds and needles. Let me feed them."

The mad jeweler, surrounded and held by four Liege guardsmen. I couldn't tell if the tears on his face came from crying or the bright light—though they'd let him turn away from the sun.

I went up to the man who appeared to be in charge of him.

"You do understand that his madness is real? He's not faking."

"Well, it can't be a fake, not if he can work real magic," the man said. "But I understand. We'll watch out for him."

That was a phrase that could be interpreted several different ways.

"He's been tormented before, by people studying his magic," I told them. "They got nothing from him. Roseman treated him almost decently, and this man served him well."

Curiosity dawned in the soldier's face. "The Liege wants to understand his magic too, but no one's going to torment anyone. There's a project at Pendarian University, that's where he's headed. Those professors, they teach kids. They aren't monsters."

Looking closer, I saw that the men who held him were gripping his arms quite gently, so it might be true.

"Excuse me, but who are you?"

I turned and walked away, ignoring him. He might have gone after me, if not for the evidence tag on my pack. And the fact that one of Roseman's men, trying to escape, would never have stopped to chat with him.

Carrying "evidence" got me all the way out the gate. I walked to the cart where evidence was being logged in...and right on past it. One yank removed my makeshift tag, and I became just another man in the crowd. It had gathered rapidly, now that the battle was over.

In fact, as rumors that the Liege's troops were sacking Roseman's townhouse spread, it seemed like the whole city was turning out to watch. Making my way through the throng felt like swimming against a stiff current, and it took some time before I got far enough from the house that walking was no longer a struggle.

Those who hadn't gone to see for themselves stood in the street, speculating wildly. Some said they'd got the Rose in chains, to haul off to the Liege to be hanged. Some said they'd hanged him already, from the balcony in the entry hall, or a tree in the yard. Or that he'd had his head cut off in the fight, clean off. Or no, it was his arm cut off, and he bled out before they could stop it, or... Everyone sounded nervous, but no one seemed particularly upset at the thought of Roseman's death. Though I heard a few say the Rose was too smart to be taken, that he'd escaped through a secret tunnel and was long gone by now.

I noted that Jack's so-secret tunnel was no secret from the friends and neighbors of the men who'd done the digging. For such a successful scammer, Jack wasn't very perceptive about people.

I reached the inn where Michael had been staying and told the clerk I'd come to collect his things, since he'd probably be a guest of the High Liege for a while.

"You mean a prisoner?" The clerk was in his early teens. The older staff had probably gone to find out what was happening. "Did he get arrested, along with the Rose?"

"No, I mean a guest," I said. "An honored one, because he helped bring about Roseman's downfall."

"How do you... Were you there? What's going on? Is Tony Rose really dead? How...?"

I gave him a brief description of the battle, and he was so fascinated and distracted that he gave me the key to Michael's room without proof or protest.

The room was bleak and somewhat shabby, like so many rooms we'd shared these last... More than two years, now. I would keep my temper, even if he lost his. I'd known what I was doing. No need to get mad about it.

I was always the one who packed both Michael's and my bags, because I was neater. I'd gotten accustomed to sorting things by weight and fit, rather than what belonged to whom, so it took longer than usual.

I would miss Kathy's letters.

I was finishing up when the door slammed open, and Michael strode in.

"You let Jack go. That's why you sent me out to negotiate the surrender. So you could sneak down to the basement and let him go."

"They'd have hanged him."

"He deserved to hang! He was willingly complicit in starting a war that would have killed hundreds, maybe thousands, and who knows how many other crimes—and you let him go! I left *children* to *kill*, because that was the only way I could think of to save you. How could you do this?"

"I told you from the start that I wouldn't go after Jack," I pointed out. "You just didn't listen."

"But he ran off and left you to take the blame for some scam. He told us about that, Fisk. He bragged about it."

"Yes. He did that. But he also taught me. I owed him."

"*I* saved your life. But I notice that debt doesn't weigh with you."

"If you're going to bring that up, I'd have to say that Jack's probably saved my life more often than you have. That's not what this is about."

Michael clutched at his hair, a gesture I'd never seen him make. "This isn't about loyalty. It's about justice. It's about right and wrong, and all the things that matter."

And here we came to it. As I'd known we would.

"Those things don't matter to me."

"Yes, they do." He'd deluded himself about that from the day we met. "I know they do, for I know you. Mayhap better than you know yourself! We can track him down, make this right. You know how he got out of the house. He may still be in the city. We can find him."

"You couldn't," I said.

"But you could. You're the only one who can. Who can make what I did, what the children did, mean something. Accomplish something."

"Killing the Rose wasn't enough? Your tender little children know what matters. They're probably dancing on the man's grave. And I betrayed Jack to Roseman to save *your* life, though you don't seem to have noticed that."

Despite my resolutions, I was shaking with anger. Michael might be right about some of it. I knew he was right about some of it, but I no longer cared. "You're not the only one who's had to compromise."

"Is that how you see justice? As a *compromise?*"

"I see justice as a scam," I said. "But that's not what matters, really, even to you. The thing that's making you so mad, is that for once it didn't all end up the way *you* wanted it. You couldn't create your perfect, knight-errant ending this time, no matter how hard you tried. Because this time, Michael, it wasn't your call."

"But you're my...my..."

"No. I'm not your poxy squire, I'm not your employee. My debt to you was paid off long ago."

"I acknowledged that! I freed you to go then. And I certainly free you to go now. Go, and make your own lousy, crooked choices. And no doubt get yourself hanged, if that's how little justice means to you. Here's your share of the blood money!"

Michael pulled a fat purse from his pocket and dumped roughly half of it onto the bed. Despite my emotional turmoil, the sight distracted me—the coins that clinked onto the blankets were gold roundels. And there were a lot of them.

"Where did you get this?" Just half of that purse was enough to keep me for over a year, if I was reasonably frugal with it.

"They paid me off as soon as Dalton identified Roseman's body. A *reward*."

He made it sound like a pile of rotting offal, instead of a well-deserved payment for saving the whole United Realm from a bloody war—but then, Michael was always a little bit crazy. I gathered up the cool coins and tucked them into a corner of my pack. I could feel the contempt in his gaze.

"If you're so cursed upset about it, how come you're keeping yours?"

"I'm going to buy the chandlery, for any of the orphans who don't have someone to take them in. They'll never have to kill again."

"They didn't *have* to kill this time," I pointed out. "They chose to."

"Because I gave them the chance!"

"Well, that's more than you gave me." I fastened the last buckle on my pack.

"What do you mean?" He was honestly confused, curse him. "Who did you want to kill?"

"I didn't want to kill anyone. That's the point."

"I didn't *want* to kill," said Michael, still missing it. "I wanted justice."

"Which would have left Jack no less dead. And for once, just this once, I got what *I* wanted—even if I had to go behind your back, and risk getting us both killed to do it."

He frowned, still puzzled, still too furious to care. I picked up my pack.

"I separated our goods. I'm taking Tipple, too. I've earned her."

He was so angry I thought he might object to that. But his curst, knight-errant generosity got in his way.

"Fine. She's yours. Just leave me Chant and True."

"Oh, the dog's all yours. With my blessing."

I threw the pack over my shoulder and walked out. I half-expected him to call after me. On the rare occasions when Michael loses his temper, his anger never lasts long.

If I waited a few days, probably even a few hours, he would apologize and have me back—and spend the next two years trying to convince me to worship justice and principle, as he did. So I kept walking, feeling sad and empty...and strangely light. It was time I moved on.

Michael had some right on his side, for he'd betrayed his precious principles to save me. Just as I'd betrayed Jack to save him...and then betrayed him to save Jack.

If he'd been able to see this, Jack would have laughed his head off. He had been right about something, too. Living with Michael was making me...not soft, but dependant. Too willing to compromise, to obey, to abandon my choices, my way of looking at the world, in exchange for friendship.

I had actually become his squire.

Oh, yes. It was time to move on.

The End

ABOUT THE AUTHOR

Hilari Bell

HILARI BELL writes SF and fantasy for kids and teens. She's an ex-librarian, a job she took to feed her life-long addiction to books, and she lives in Denver with a family that changes shape periodically—currently it's her mother, her adult niece and their dog, Ginger. Her hobbies are board games and camping—particularly camping, because that's the only time she can get in enough reading. Though when it comes to reading, she says, there's no such thing as "enough."